Midnight Ritual

Arianne threw open the tent flap. Twenty-five meters beyond, a hundred tikkas swarmed over the ground in the light of Havenfound's moons. Throwing back their feline-shaped, furred heads, they screeched a single word in unison, then in the next instant chorused each other, and in the next chanted in rhythm.

At the center of the living ring stood a shadow-cloaked man. He threw back his head, and his mouth wrenched wide. If a scream tore from his throat, it did not penetrate the barrier of sound created by the tikkas' screeching.

Arianne ran from the tent, the tikkas scattering as she pushed through their circling mass. The Havenite's arm shot out, throwing her to the ground. "No! Go away! There is nothing that can be done."

She halted when his head lifted to her. A horrified scream pushed into her throat and froze there unreleased.

The face that stared at her held no resemblance to anything human.

Ace Books by Geo. W. Proctor

STARWINGS
STELLAR FIST

Ace Books by Robert E. Vardeman with Geo. W. Proctor

TO DEMONS BOUND
A YOKE OF MAGIC
BLOOD FOUNTAIN
DEATH'S ACOLYTE
THE BEASTS OF THE MIST
FOR CROWN AND KINGDOM

STELLAR FIST

GEO. W. PROCTOR

ACE BOOKS, NEW YORK

For Lana—Thank you for being

This book is an Ace original edition,
and has never been previously published.

STELLAR FIST

An Ace Book/published by arrangement with
the author

PRINTING HISTORY
Ace edition/January 1989

All rights reserved.
Copyright © 1989 by George W. Proctor
Cover art by Martin Andrews.
This book may not be reproduced in whole or in part,
by mimeograph or any other means, without permission.
For information address: The Berkley Publishing Group,
200 Madison Avenue, New York, New York 10016.

ISBN: 0-441-78582-4

Ace Books are published by The Berkley Publishing Group,
200 Madison Avenue, New York, New York 10016.
The name ''ACE'' and the ''A'' logo are trademarks
belonging to Charter Communications, Inc.

PRINTED IN THE UNITED STATES OF AMERICA

10 9 8 7 6 5 4 3 2 1

"Hachi-no-ki" or "The Potted Trees"—play written by Seam (1363–1443) during the Muromachi period (1338–1573). The play tells the tale of an impoverished samurai who sacrifices his beloved pine bonsai to provide firewood to warm his guest, the Shōgun Tokiyori Hojo (1227–1263).

Does the pine illustrate an early appreciation of form as opposed to the simple value of the beauty to be found in flowers or colored foliage? Or is the pine used as the symbol of longevity that was so prevalent in Earth's ancient Oriental culture?

The source of "Hachi-no-ki" should be delved. Jumpers to the Muromachi period will be alerted of my interest. If possible, I will meet this samurai face to face.

—Notes on the Art of Bonsai, Arianne Pillan
written while assigned to Retrieve Earth.

CHOKKAN

ONE

The demanding beep-a-beep warning pulsed in synchronous rhythm with the throbbing, red alert panels on three traffic control consoles. Simultaneously, three controllers aboard the Tripartite Confederation Monitoring Station *Sadr* homed sensors on the planet Opat 4.

On slanted screens above their three lifted heads, imaging artificially enchanced the visual of the ringed world. Optical sensors zoomed inward to blur and refocus on a spacecraft that shot from the surface of the fourth planet in the Opat System. A slender, silvery needle, the vessel slid silently across a mottled tapestry spun by the planet's blues, greens, browns, and fleecy cloud whites.

"Trajectory projection?" the first of the controllers verbally requested of the console. Dark eyes locked to the screen above her head, her fingers deftly tapped at a keyboard to repeat the query.

The manual input was an exercise in bureaucratic redundancy, a log of the controller's activities. The *Sadr*'s ComNet responded to her inquiry at tachyon-boosted speed. Sensors probed the small craft's onboard logic units, found no passworded barriers to inhibit its delving, and read the vessel's flight program.

The controller's fingertips just touched the third key when the ComNet superimposed the ship's course in red atop Opat 4's image on all three control screens. One orbit of the ringed world, two burst transitions into tachyon space, and a standard hour later, the spacecraft would cross the yawning void separating it from the monitoring station's position on the inner edge of the Opat System's asteroid belt.

Previous performance patterns allowed *Sadr*'s ComNet to anticipate the third controller's identification request. Yellow letters blinked across the bottom of the visual:

> FOUR-MAN LANDER LLP CLASS VESSEL
> ONE LIFE READING ONBOARD—HUMAN
> REGISTRATION ERASED FROM SHIP'S MEMORY

In a nanosecond the Net triple-checked the onplanet roster, found no clearance for a LLP vessel, and amended the message:

> UNAUTHORIZED PRESENCE ON PLANET'S SURFACE

Again the Net anticipated, but did not act—the situation required operator decision-making—until the second controller requested a standard identification inquiry broadcast to the unknown spacecraft. Selecting an innocuous, monotone, female human voice, the Net sent the recorded message across 1.52 A.U.s of space on a beam of tachyons.

The second controller listened to the transmission and patiently waited the standard minute for a reply. When none came, he wiped a hand over his shaven scalp and beamed the identification request to the vessel once more.

Again the inquiry was ignored.

"Alert the control supervisor," he said to his two companions.

By the time the controller beamed the inquiry to the unidentified lander for a third time, Lieutenant Marse Kian stood at his shoulder. Plugged into his console, the short, stocky woman listened and heard nothing. For a third time the small spacecraft refused to answer.

On the three monitoring screens, the craft swung around

Opat 4 and disappeared behind the planet like a distant silver star occulted in triplicate.

Lieutenant Kian drew a steadying breath to contain the panicked pound that filled her chest. "Net, direct connect with Captain Sarrantonio—emergency priority."

Hamako Sarrantonio stood alone on the deck of her unlit shell-level office. The polished, naked metal floor felt hard and unyielding beneath the thin, pliable soles of her static-grip slippers. That sensation and the zero-gee of the *Sadr*'s outermost level drove home the harsh reality of her situation, one that was often forgotten amid the relative luxury of any one of her twenty-five inner offices with their various gravities and foot-soft carpeting.

When the time permitted, she often came here to stand before the wide expanse of the curving bubble-blister port and gaze into the featureless face of space as she did now. The metallic smells, mingled with the oily odors of heated lubricants, and the unadorned support structure that bound the *Sadr*'s outer skin into an airtight globe to prevent a fragile ecosphere from exploding into the ever-hungry void reminded her that she was the captain of a spacecraft and not the chief administrator of some small world. An illusion that was too easily accepted on any of the hundreds of levels—with their factories, farms, residential areas, seas, and forests—that stretched beneath her feet fifty kilometers to the *Sadr*'s innermost control core.

Today Captain Hamako Sarrantonio wished that she were elsewhere—anywhere else—on the gigantic vessel she commanded. Performing even the most trivial of duties would have been better than this. She crossed her arms to ward off the chill that shivered through her slender body. It didn't help. The cold came from within her own breast rather than from the climate-controlled surroundings.

Her jet eyes shifted to the green glow of a chronometer on the wall to the right. *Three minutes until final transition.* She looked back out the blister, staring at the point Net predicted the landing craft would shift from tachyon reality into what humankind called "normal space."

She sucked at her teeth, the wet sound echoing off the office's wall. How had a four-man ship gotten past the *Sadr*'s security system? Except for Tripartite Confederation shuttles, landings on Opat 4 were strictly forbidden, as well as any exploratory flights within the Opat System! That was why the Tripar had assigned Sarrantonio and the *Sadr* to this Sol-type star system that had been completely unknown until six standard months ago. The *Sadr* had the firepower, and she had the orders to see that the Confederation blockade on the ringed world was not violated.

She glanced through the upper curve of the bubble blister, feeling the cold expand within her body. Three ships, all cruiser-class vessels, hung in space above the *Sadr*. Each had challenged her authority, and each had surrendered the moment she had trained the *Sadr*'s heavy guns on their hulls. The crews of all three ships were now temporarily vacationing, safely under guard, deep within the *Sadr*'s inner levels.

The two human vessels were no surprise to her, especially the MashuCo ship. Of all the interplanetary corporations that had thrived since the formation of the Tripartite Confederation a millennium ago, MashuCo was the strongest. Year by year, month by month, day by day, hour by hour, MashuCo led subtle and less than subtle assaults on the Tripar's ever-weakening foundation of authority.

Sarrantonio didn't doubt the rumors she had heard that MashuCo and many of the other massive corporations were quietly gathering private armies for use when legislation and diplomacy were no longer expedient routes to their goals. The captain eyed the MashuCo vessel. She had seen Tripar cruisers that carried less ordnance than that bloated space whale.

Nor was there one Confederation ship with state-of-the-art weaponry to match the cruiser's armaments. Which was not surprising; the corporations were slowly but surely gathering in the Tripar's purse strings, assuring that the

Confederation's military vessels were equipped with out-moded weapons.

The captain glanced at the second human ship. The appearance of the Pillan Planets' vessel in the Opat System was no surprise either. A far smaller corporation than MashuCo, the Pillan family, who had retained the company's chair for two hundred years, were a sly, slippery lot. The Pillan Planets' intelligence network was second to none. Sarrantonio had almost expected their arrival the moment they gleaned an inkling of the unheard-of treasure the Opat System tenuously held on her outermost reaches.

It was the third ship, the Brodny cruiser, that puzzled Sarrantonio. How had the white-furred, bearlike alien race learned of the dark jewel hung on the Opat System's fringe?

How . . . Sarrantonio pushed the question from her mind. There were too many "hows" that she feared would never be answered. Each of the cruisers were like masses of antimatter contained in a null field. One slight moment's weakening of the field and the resulting explosion would hurl humankind into stellar war with the Brodny or itself as the enemy—or both!

Civilization's guardian. Bitterness tinged the thought. Neither she nor the *Sadr* was right for the role the Confederation had cast for them. The massive spacecraft wasn't a warship; it was a mining vessel designed to strip uninhabited worlds of their precious minerals or suck the biochemical vapors from the faces of gas giants. For ten standard years, she had commanded a mining ship, not a battleship. Plucking asteroids from their orbits was her forte not the intricacies of military strategies.

How she longed for everything to be neatly back in its proper niche! She scratched at the irritating stubble atop her head. How could the Tripar expect a captain who couldn't even remember to get a body depilatory to contain the Opat System?

Sarrantonio glanced at the chronometer; a minute remained until the lander slipped back into normal space. She looked back to the eternal darkness of space.

Who piloted the unauthorized vessel that had slipped onplanet through the security web cast around this system? The psiotic probe she had ordered during the lander's burst transitions had revealed nothing. The mind merger had felt human contact, but nothing more than that, not even a mental shield to block psi probes.

Nothing, she had no more hint as to how the lander had gotten onplanet as she did to the identity of its pilot. *How?* More "hows" piled on top of those already jumbled in her mind. *How?*

A buzzer blared, her requested alert to the lander's final transition. A second later the small craft winked into existence five kilometers from the *Sadr*'s metallic hull. Its atmospheric wings, tail, and fins tidily tucked beneath its skin, the ship hung in space, a smooth, needle-nosed cylinder.

"Captain," Lieutenant Kian called over the intercom. "Except for life support, Net reports that the lander has shut down all systems."

Sarrantonio worried her bottom lip with her front teeth as she stared at the unmoving craft, half its naked metal hull agleam like silver in Opat's harsh light. "Have Net triple-scan for any possible booby traps. If clean, bring the lander into Landing Bay Nineteen."

While Kian acknowledged the order, Sarrantonio back-stepped to her desk, eyes constantly on the lander. Her fingers found a series of buttons beneath the intercom speaker and punched in the code for the bay. In a single sentence she ordered the bay evacuated except for essential landing personnel and a two-person search detail. The *Sadr*'s captain then left her office to hasten down brightly lit tunnel-corridors to the bay.

"Lock pressurized," Lieutenant Tavis Ptacek, the sole controller remaining in Bay Nineteen, glanced over a shoulder to Captain Hamako Sarrantonio.

The captain's gaze scanned the slightly curved bay below. Except for Ptacek and herself, who sat safely within the control booth nestled against the bay's ceiling, the expansive hangar area was deserted. Sarrantonio nodded. "Open the inner door and bring it in."

A single door, stenciled with the black numerals 19–01, clanked as the locking mechanism opened. Hydraulics wheezed and the airlock's inner door slid back. The four-person lander sat within. Sarrantonio glanced at a monitor screen on Ptacek's left. Net's continual scanning still revealed no hidden surprises within the small ship's hull.

"All right," the captain nodded again. "Bring it onto the bay floor with a cradle. The thing could be rigged to blow on contact with energy beams."

Ptacek punched a carrier cradle to life, then let the ComNet maneuver the mechanical carrier beneath the ship's rounded belly. Eight cradle arms flowered from each side of the carrier and securely attached themselves to the lander's hull. The carrier rolled from airlock to bay with the lander clutched above it, stopping when it reached the center of a black bullseye painted on the floor beside the numerals 19–01.

"So far so good." Sarrantonio's words concealed a relieved sigh while she watched the carrier release the spacecraft and trundle back to its place in the rear of the bay. "Ptacek, bring in the search team."

The lieutenant did as ordered; two men carrying mobile Net probes entered the empty bay and rushed to the lander. Seconds later they opened the craft's hatch and disappeared inside.

Sarrantonio listened to their constant reports, carefully avoiding watching the monitors with the bobbing, jerking, erratic images relayed by the visual sensors carried on their chests. From cabin to cabin they moved to report each of the craft's areas clean.

"Captain, they've reached the control console," Ptacek nodded to the screens. "Better take a look at this. They've found the pilot."

Sarrantonio did; her jaw sagged and her eyes went saucer round as she stared at the face captured in the monitors. "*Him*? How?"

The man's face returned her gaze with unblinking eyes that stared straight ahead, never shifting as the search team moved about him. An involuntary chill shivered up the captain's spine. There was no hint of intelligence in those eyes or the man's facial features. It was as though he was drugged beyond either knowing or caring—or was dead.

Another chill shot through Sarrantonio's spine. He couldn't be dead, not *him*!

"His heart's beating, and he's still breathing, but that's all he's doing," a voice of one of the search team came from a grate on the control console.

"Get him out of there on the double and down to the med-bay," Sarrantonio ordered, attempting to ignore the threads of unreasoning panic that wove through her mind. She then ordered Ptacek to notify the medical bay of the top priorty patient being rushed to their care.

"Nothing?" Sarrantonio stared at the man tucked into the bed. His eyes were closed now, but she saw no other change. "Nothing after twelve hours?"

The three doctors who had labored over the man shook their heads. The tallest of the three, a wide-hipped, heavy-breasted woman spoke, "He responds to nothing. We've found no trace of any chemical substance that might account for his condition. It's as though he's in a self-induced trance."

Captain Sarrantonio glanced at Halian Tonani. The short, wirey, blue-eyed psiotic pursed his lips.

"That doesn't wash either, Captain." Tonani's gaze shifted to the man laying on the bed. "I've merged with him. If it's a trance, it's nothing I've ever run into. Hell, the man's mind is like nothing I've ever encountered."

The mind-merger paused and looked back at the captain, his blue eyes piercing. "There's a brain inside that head, but either he's a blank or there's not one memory or thought still alive in all that gray matter."

"Could he be blocking you?" Sarrantonio pressed.

"Blocking is a conscious response," the psiotic answered. "This man doesn't have a conscious or unconscious response. He has a physical brain, but his mind's gone. Totally gone as though someone reached in and sucked out every memory stored there."

"Memory erasure?" The captain grasped at straws.

To watch them crumble to dust between her fingers when Tonani answered, "Memory erasure is a selective process. There's nothing that exists that can do this to a man's brain. Don't you understand, this man has absolutely nothing inside his head—nothing!"

Hamako Sarrantonio swallowed, feeling an ice floe once more creep up her spine as she dismissed those present and turned to walk from the med-bay. That icy sensation had transformed into a cold sweat by the time she reached her shell-level office. Outside the relative security of the *Sadr*, the three cruiser-class ships still hung motionless in space.

Antimatter held in a null field, she recalled her earlier thought. Now she sensed the containing field quaver dangerously. The man neatly tucked into a med-bay bed was the force threatening to rip the field asunder. If his identity ever became known to MashuCo, Pillan Planets, or the Brodny . . .

The captain shoved the obvious conclusions from her mind. The matter no longer lay in her hands, the man's unauthorized presence on Opat 4 required top-level intervention.

Settling into a contour chair behind her desk, Sarrantonio called Net to life authorizing a multilevel random scramble code for her report to Lanatia, the planetary seat of the Tripartite government. Her dark eyes moved back to the three ships outside. After the transmission was complete, she would order teams out to all three vessels and dismantle their power and weaponry systems. If one man could evade the *Sadr*'s tight security and escape to Opat 4, others might manage to reach their vessels to train their guns on the monitoring station—or worse flee back to their masters with word of what had happened here today!

TWO

Faxon Lorens's hazel eyes snapped open when the hatch to the waiting room hissed. The Tripartite Confederation diplomatic troubleshooter pushed his six-foot frame from a contour-molding chair to stand before a pudgy man in a ten-year-out-of-fashion, silver-gray, no collar suit who stepped into the room.

"Mr. Lorens, Michael Browder." The man held out a hand while displaying a standard-issue, Tripar Diplomatic Service, welcoming grin.

"Ambassador Browder." Faxon accepted the handshake, trying to ignore the limpness of the man's grip and the sweaty dampness of his palm.

Browder wasn't an ambassador—the planet below them lacked the population for a full-fledged Tripar ambassador—but a small stroke to the man's ego couldn't hurt. Faxon might have use for him onplanet; although, he admitted that at the present time he didn't foresee the need of their association continuing beyond this initial contact. However, it was Faxon's anticipation of the unexpected that had moved him to the top of an elite corps within the diplomatic service, one that was summoned when all normal channels failed to produce the needed results.

"I hope your long journey from Lanatia was comfortable," Browder said, his brown eyes never making full contact with Faxon's penetrating gaze.

"It was fast." Faxon released the man's limp fingers,

barely catching himself before he jerked back, his nose rudely wrinkling against the stench Browder carried about him.

Planet odors, Faxon sorted through the variety of smells that assailed an olfactory sense adapted to the relatively antiseptic conditions of space travel. A greasy hint of fire-cooked foods, flower pollen, perfume, dust—Faxon isolated individual aromas from the melange of persistent irritants—the overpowering musty aroma of dirt.

The latter didn't surprise Faxon; it was expected. All planet dwellers carried it on them. It was the overwhelming strength of the odor that took him off guard. There was no escape except to back away to the opposite side of the room. He drew a long deep breath through flared nostrils, hoping to quickly anesthetize his nose to the barrage of smells. No immediate relief came; it clung to Browder's clothes and hair.

Faxon's eyes narrowed with disdain as they focused on the thick waves of salt-and-pepper hair that covered the diplomat's head. Hair invited smells—offered odors a nesting place. Faxon's scalp glistened skin smooth, as did the rest of his body. The practical, spacefarer-imitating style was the fashion on the majority of Tripar worlds. The presence of Browder's body hair was as offensive as had the man pulled down his pants and defecated on the floor.

". . . quarters arranged here on the transfer station for you, should you desire to rest before the shuttle flight down." Browder's voice wove into Faxon's thoughts.

Picking up the threads of the man's words, Faxon shook his head. "Enough time was wasted during my trip. The sooner we land onplanet, the sooner I can get to the business at hand."

Browder nodded and motioned to the open hatch behind him. "The shuttle's being refueled. It should be ready by the time we make it to the landing bay."

Locking rings released the shuttle's blunt nose. A resounding metallic hammering shuddered through the ancient craft's skin and reverberated along the deck to settle in Faxon's teeth. He shifted as best he could in the confining harness straps of a passenger couch, hoping motion would lessen the dull ache that filled his mouth. The cumbersome, thickly padded suit that swallowed him from head to toe restricted movement to a hampered wiggle.

"I must apologize for the surface suits, but they are necessary. The landing strip constantly operates under the forty-eight, minus thirty-four, thirty rule." Browder apparently noticed his companion's discomfort. "As soon as we're inside, we can discard these."

"Forty-eight, minus thirty-four, thirty rule?" Faxon's brow furrowed. "Some obscure regulation?"

"Nothing from the Diplomatic Service manual." Browder shook his head and grinned. "Onplanet it's a simple rule for survival. There's a forty-eight-kilometer-an-hour wind blowing on the surface with a temperature of minus thirty-four Celsius. An unprotected man can last about thirty seconds before the wind and temperature kill him. It's a five-minute walk from the landing strip to the lift building. Neither of us would make it without these."

"My briefing was sketchy. I didn't realize the surface was so cold." Although his comfort didn't increase, Faxon accepted the necessity of the surface suits. He strained to glimpse the planet out of the porthole on his right, but only saw the spoked wheel-like structure of the transfer station as the shuttle drifted from the landing bay.

"About three hundred and fifty years ago there was an incident, sometimes referred to as the Incursion, just outside the Oort Cloud that surrounds this system," Browder explained.

The Incursion, also known as MashuCo's Mistake, Faxon thought, had been the first corporate testing of Tripartite Confederation military power. Even after these long centuries details of the confrontation remained hidden behind bureaucratic clouds of secrecy.

Unconfirmed rumors told of a twenty-ship MashuCo fleet armed with a new weapon challenging three Tripar cruisers. The most popular unofficial theory was that MashuCo's secret weapon was untested; it backfired, blew up in their faces. Unknown weapon or not, the result was the destruction of twenty-three ships and their crews.

"Whatever happened out there was *big*," Browder continued. "The forces set loose were massive enough to disturb the Oort Cloud and send a few thousand minor mountains of ice sunward. Most are harmless comets, pretty fireworks in the sky. Enough aren't. For three centuries the planet's been bombarded. The largest chunk of icy debris was estimated at a hundred kilometers in length and about half that in thickness. I say estimated, because when it hit, the majority of the life onplanet was destroyed."

Not that there was that much life to begin with, Faxon thought. Humankind had destroyed the planet twice on its own. Such was the toll of war, both planetary and interstellar.

"I've made arrangements for you to meet her tonight—a party after her performance," Browder said. "Don't expect too much. Arianne Pillan is a strong-willed woman."

It took a second for Faxon to catch up with the diplomat's abrupt change in topics. Until this moment his purpose in being here hadn't been mentioned by either of them. "I've known Arianne for years." Browder needed to know nothing more than that.

Doubt shadowed Browder's round face. "Friendship might aid you, but I wouldn't give it too much weight. She's remained firm everytime I approached her about returning to the fold. And that's been at least twice a year since her arrival onplanet five years ago. She's an immovable force—a boulder that can't be budged."

If you were competent, the service wouldn't have assigned you to this arm of the galaxy, Faxon thought, but said, "There is no such thing as an immovable force. And any boulder can be budged if one has the right lever."

"And you have such a lever?" Browder's right eyebrow arched.

"In my pocket," Faxon replied, attempting to pat his

side pocket and finding the surface suit's bulk too restraining to complete the task.

"A small lever."

Browder's eyebrow remained arched in question, but Faxon added nothing. That he had been sent from Lanatia to recruit Arianne Pillan was the only detail of his assignment the diplomat needed to know to perform what was required of him.

"It also makes one wonder why the service would want her back," Browder continued. "I would think her loyalty was highly questionable, considering she *is* the daughter of Arian Pillan. Can the service ever really be certain whether she works for them or her father's corporation?"

The hiss of maneuvering jets drew Faxon's gaze back to the porthole, saving him from having to answer Browder's groundless accusations. Stars, bright, unwavering points of light, replaced the transfer station outside. Gently, in what appeared to be an effortless ballet, the nose of the shuttle swung planetward.

"There she is." Unmistakeable excitement touched Browder's voice. "Earth—womb of humankind."

The sudden rumble of thrusters and the accompanying rattle that shook the ancient ship from stem to stern once more saved Faxon from having to concoct an inane reply. Earth meant less to him than the small mention made of the planet in most histories. Humankind might have begun its life on this world, but it barely managed to escape its bonds before destroying the world with primitive nuclear weapons.

Once, over a millennium ago, when humankind had been divided into two interstellar empires—whose names eluded Faxon—Earth had been reclaimed as a military base and destroyed again. Now it was a barren iceball gripped by a three-century-old ice age seeded by the constant bombardment of comets dislodged from the system's Oort Cloud.

Except for the planet's equatorial belt, the white of ice and snow were all that were visible—masking the world's face. This he saw only when there was a break in the dense clouds shrouding the surface.

He leaned closer to the porthole. The view from space never ceased to amaze him; artificial imaging fell far short of human eyes. The whiteness below revealed by the cloud rifts was in three dimensions. He easily discerned plain, mountain, and valley. Snow and ice were not flat white, but were shades of grays, blues, and even hints of pale greens and rusty hues.

Then there was nothing. The shuttle's trajectory swung the craft to the planet's nightside. An invisible hand pressed against Faxon's chest pushing him back into the couch. Belly down the ship entered Earth's gravity well, friction setting her stomach heat shields aglow in cherry red.

Outside other invisible hands came into play as the craft's wings unfolded from its sides. Winds buffeted and tossed; metal moaned then screamed as though being torn apart. Quake after shuddering quake jolted the vessel. Nor was there the thunderous roar of breaking jets meant to lessen the violent flight. Earth was a nowhere planet on the edge of nothing. Fuel came at a high price here; it was not meant to be wasted on something as foolish as passenger comfort.

Faxon gripped the arms of his couch, prepared to die in the batting of an eye. Not since his first flight into space had he felt fear of the rockets that flung humankind from one end of the galaxy to the other in a matter of days.

Death did not come—only daylight. Faxon saw nothing beyond the porthole's glass as the shuttle's descending course brought them into sunlight again. If the shadowy gray that penetrated the obscuring clouds could be called light.

She was crazy to come here, Faxon tried to imagine what had brought Arianne Pillan to this godforsaken world. *Only the insane would choose to bury themselves here.*

Clouds ripped apart before the shuttle's blunt snout. Ahead Faxon could see a frozen lakebed stretching kilometers toward a distant mountain range—or was it a frozen sea?

"The landing strip." Browder nudged his side.

Faxon didn't have time to voice his doubts about the shuttle's ability to land on the glass-slick surface. The craft dropped; landing skids roughly touched the ice, whining. Dragchutes, not breaking rockets, were deployed. Kilometer after kilometer slid beneath the ship before it finally slowed, then halted.

Forcing shaking legs to move, Faxon followed Browder from the ship onto Earth's frozen surface. So glad was he to be free of the shuttle's belly, that he didn't even mind the howling wind that attempted to claw his exposed face from his skull.

THREE

"Better hold onto the rail." Michael Browder nodded to a stainless steel tube at his companion's right. "The lift stops rather abruptly. If you're not prepared, it can toss you on your backside."

Faxon Lorens didn't question the man, but took a solid grip on the handrail and braced himself for the worst. Among the things overlooked in his hasty briefing was the fact that his destination, Deeprock, Earth's only human colony, lay two kilometers beneath the planet's surface! That the sole method of reaching this urban center of ten thousand—unless one wanted to endure a day-long crawler ride through one of twenty unlit tunnels—was to be jammed elbow-to-ass in a steel cannister, jokingly referred to as "the lift," with nine other people and dropped down a two-kilometer hole in the ground.

"Passengers will please secure themselves. Breaking will begin in ten seconds," a monotone voice droned from a speaker at the center of the lift's ceiling. "Nine . . . eight . . ."

Faxon's knuckles burned white as he doubled his hold on the rail, uncertain what to expect. A glance at the others packed beside him did nothing to alleviate the gnawing doubt in his gut. The nine, even Browder, managed to lock at least one hand around the rail for support.

"Three . . . two . . . one."

A deafening roar filled Faxon's ears, threatening to

shatter the fragile membranes of his eardrums. He stared down at the floor in wide-eyed horror as bone-jarring vibrations shuddered through the lift. This was no ordinary elevator; it was a rocket! The breaks were nothing more than thrusters used to slow the cannister's fall. Directly beneath his feet . . .

His brain didn't have time to complete the thought. The thundering stopped abruptly, and the lift thudded to a solid halt that threw him shoulder-first into the cannister's curved, steel wall. Before he could groan, the lift's single door slid back, opening onto a yawning cavern.

Tunnel, Faxon corrected that first impression as he righted himself and stepped from the lift.

Cut into the bedrock at crisp right angles, the corridor was immense with a ceiling six meters above his head and twelve meters separating the smooth walls. The gargantuan tunnel stretched endlessly before him. Light panels inset along the walls at three-meter intervals merged and disappeared in the distance like a classical perspective illustration depicting two parallel lines meeting and vanishing at infinity.

"We do things *big* down here." Browder's face hinted at barely restrained amusement. "The bigger the better—it combats claustrophobia and helps one forget that he's living with two kilometers of rock over his head."

Faxon glanced at a series of six monitor screens inset in the rock wall to the left of the lift's door. All appeared to be filled with space scenes. "What are those?"

Browder answered, "Something you get attached to on Earth within a month or two. Those are all satellite scans of surrounding space. When a people live under the threat of bombardment, they keep one eye constantly cast toward the heavens."

Faxon pursed his lips. He wouldn't be onplanet long enough to start worrying about comets plunging into the atmosphere. He intended to do his job and return to Lanatia as soon as possible. He rubbed hands over his arms, feeling a slight chill.

"Gooseflesh?" Browder smiled. "It comes from a constant temperature of twelve point eight degrees centigrade this far underground. You'll be warmer when the tram reaches Deeprock. Geothermal heating, you know."

Faxon didn't, nor had he noticed the roofless, sideless, open, four-wheeled monstrosity parked beside the tunnel's left wall. The rest of the lift's passengers busily arranged themselves on two bench seats that ran back-to-back down the center of the tram's broad, flat bed. A driver seated behind the tram's controls thrust a lever forward to bring the odd vehicle's motor to a smooth, purring life.

"A modified crawler." Browder motioned Faxon toward the vehicle. "It lacks elegance, but it'll cover the twenty kilometers to Deeprock in fifteen minutes. Unless you'd rather walk into town, climb aboard. It's the last tram of the day."

Faxon didn't argue; he stepped aboard the converted crawler, taking the last seat beside Browder.

The driver's heavy foot slipped from the brake and plunged the accelerator to the floor. Clouds of dust and dirt sprayed from oversized rear wheels as the vehicle lurched forward and whined down the wide corridor. The wall lights blurred into one continuous band of luminosity.

"Over a thousand years ago the Kavinites originally built this corridor and the crawler tunnels that run to the surface," Browder explained. "All were part of an underground military installation they had planned for Earth."

Kavinites and Lofgrinists, Faxon recalled the names that had eluded his memory earlier. The two warring factions had divided humankind before the independent planets gave rise to the Tripartite Confederation. During their final interstellar conflict, Earth had suffered its second death.

"The Kavinites are responsible for Deeprock also," Browder continued. "Not the city, the Tripar constructed Deeprock's first buildings nearly two hundred standard years ago. However, the cavern holding Deeprock was Kavinite. We still aren't certain what they intended for it.

The Lofgrinists blew them off the face of the planet before they finished their task.''

And in two centuries the city's population had swelled to ten thousand. Faxon contained his sarcasm. He had no patience with the Retrieve program and its timejumpers. Delving humankind's forgotten, planet-locked past was of little relevance for a civilization that journeyed to alien worlds in other galaxies.

''What time are we scheduled to meet with Arianne?'' Faxon glanced at the diplomat and realized his nose had at last accustomed itself to this unknown world. Either that or the overpowering musty smell of the tunnel masked all other odors.

''There is no scheduled meeting.'' Browder depressed the side of his left wrist with his right fingers to activate a bio-interface with Deeprock's ComNet.

Faxon inwardly winced. Whether in contempt or with unadmitted jealousy, he wasn't certain. The service's troubleshooters—more often than not a polite euphemism for spies—were not allowed such a luxury. To carry a direct link to a Net within one's body was far too easily traced when anonymity meant the difference between life and death.

''Her performance will begin in five minutes. We should arrive about ten minutes after she's started,'' Browder said. ''Ms. Pillan will be the guest of honor at a cocktail party following the concert, to which we've been invited. You can make contact there.''

Faxon nodded his approval. The unexpected was always the best approach with Arianne. Simply seeing him onplanet should be enough to put a kink or two in her armor.

''Deeprock ahead.'' Browder tilted his head toward the now visible end of the immense tunnel.

Seconds later the whining tram shot into a vast domed cavern, its upward sloping walls fused into a solid unbroken surface by energy beams over a millennium in the past. Ten kilometers in diameter, Faxon estimated, his head arching back to stare at a ceiling that peaked at half that distance.

"The panels provide the illusion of day and night to correspond with surface conditions." Browder pointed to a network of lights mounted on the ceiling that cast a dim glow over the small city constructed within the rock dome. "This is the darkest it gets here. To turn off the lights completely would invite insanity. The human mind can endure complete blackness for only so long before it cracks and shatters. And that's what we have down here—total blackness."

The driver halted the tram within a broad circular area employing the same unannounced abruptness with which he had started the vehicle. Only Faxon seemed to notice the jostling stop. The rest of the passengers piled from their seats and hastened to slidewalks that rolled toward the heart of Deeprock. Intent on following the others, Faxon pushed to his feet and stepped to the ground.

"No need for us to walk." Browder halted him. "I have a groundcar. Not much faster than the slidewalks, but there is a bit of prestige here in having a vehicle at one's disposal."

On usual assignments Faxon would have avoided anything that drew attention to his presence; this was not a usual assignment. There was no need to hide his identity from Arianne; the reverse was part of the lever he intend to use.

Following the diplomat, Lorens slipped into one of four seats on Browder's groundcar. The vehicle was of the same bare bones construction as the tram. A triangular bed held the seats and an electric motor was mounted at the rear. The car was supported by three small wheels, one forward, two behind.

Browder took the seat beside his companion. Grasping a steering lever, the man depressed to the floor a single deadman's pedal that served as accelerator and brake. The car trundled into the city.

* * *

Applause rolled from the concert hall into the lobby when an usher opened a door to admit the two men. Browder glanced at Faxon and whispered, "If you've ever seen Ms. Pillan perform, you should appreciate tonight. I saw her once on Fleisher's World when she was a mere child and that was magnificent. Maturity has only . . . well, you'll see. My seats are on the front row."

Faxon stopped, his attention pulled from a row of ten monitor screens filled with satellite imaging, beside the door they entered. The man's words awakened a warning alarm in his head. "Not the front row. It wouldn't do to have her notice me until I'm ready. I'd prefer something at the back of the theater."

"There is nothing else." This from the usher. "Tonight's performance is sold out."

As they moved around a curved corridor that opened onto the hall's aisles, Faxon understood why. The theater was designed to accommodate no more than five hundred people. Before Arianne had given up her singing career to join the Diplomatic Service, she had commanded audiences of ten thousand.

"Perhaps I could remain here," Faxon looked at the usher. "I don't mind standing."

The young woman bit her lower lip. Her hesitant gaze drifted between Faxon and Browder. Finally she nodded. "If you two keep it quiet, you can stand back here."

Faxon noticed a shadow of disappointment darken Browder's face. "There's no need for both of us to stay here. Ambassador, please take your usual seat. I'll wait for you here."

"Are you certain?" Browder beamed with obvious pleasure. "You wouldn't mind?"

"Not at all."

Faxon motioned the man forward then watched while the usher escorted Browder down the aisle to his seat. He felt a sense of relief. He was used to working alone; even Browder's presence was confining. During his fifteen years with the service there had only been one person who he had been able to work with.

Faxon's hazel eyes lifted to the small stage, alighting on that person—Arianne Pillan. Something old and deep shifted in his breast, something he had buried and forgotten five years ago. He lied to himself—Arianne had buried it, turning her back and telling him to forget the years they had shared.

"Bitch!" The curse slipped from his lips in a whisper.

A twinge of guilt grew to a knot in his chest. He didn't mean it. The curse was a defense, easier to utter than reexamine the painful past.

"Thank you." On stage Arianne bowed, then waved an arm to the three musicians behind her. "Thank you."

How beautiful she is. Faxon found no trace of the past five years lining the beauty of her oval face. The prism gown she wore slowly melted through the colors of the spectrum as it shifted about her slender, willowy form.

Whether he imagined or actually saw the hints of firm uplifted breasts, womanly flaring hips, and long, shapely curved, coltish legs beneath the constantly changing fabric, Faxon couldn't be sure. It didn't matter, memory or reality, an old aching awoke at his core.

Love or lust? He was never quite certain of Arianne's effect on him. Were the two ever separable between a man and a woman?

Like all the others he had seen since arriving onplanet, Arianne had abandoned the use of a depilatory. In spite of his initial shock, Faxon found that the flowing chestnut cascade of hair that fell about her shoulders only enhanced her beauty, deepened the emerald hue of her eyes. It didn't surprise him—this *was* Arianne Pillan; she had never been able to do anything wrong in his eyes. Except, the day she walked away from him.

"The next selection that we'll perform for you is a song that was brought uptime from this planet's first industrial surge by one of our own jumpers," Arianne spoke to the audience. "The words are English, one of the root languages of our own Stellar tongue. If you listen closely, I believe you can follow the lyrics.''

The musicians behind her began to play. Of the three instruments, none of them electronic, Faxon recognized only one—a primitive two-headed drum that one of the musicians held between his crossed legs as he sat on the stage. The remaining two were a hollow, half-melon-shaped, six-stringed contraption which was strummed and plucked with the fingertips, and a wooden tube the musician blew into while his fingers danced over holes drilled in its side.

Instruments from man's past, Faxon realized. It was the type of thing that would suit a community devoted to the Retrieve program. Music for people who preferred to burrow their lives away in the dead past.

Begrudgingly he admitted the odd accompaniment had been chosen carefully to compliment Arianne's gentle, lilting soprano voice the moment she began to sing, *"Black is the color of my true love's hair . . ."*

True to Arianne's promise, Faxon discovered the ancient English was relatively easy to follow. Although he stumbled over the meaning of many words and strange-sounding phrases, the overall sentiment of the lamenting love ballad was there for the listening.

However, it wasn't the music or the lyrics the audience had come to experience. Nor was it Arianne's highly trained voice. It was her moodweaver ability.

With each note, she expertly employed her low-grade psi power to reach out and envelop those seated before her. Neither a sender or receiver of thought-words, nor a merger who invaded the minds of others, Arianne was a simple moodweaver. Her gift was the subtle ability to project her own emotions—to read, transform, and mold the mood of her audience.

Tear-flowing sadness, flighty joy, swelling love, gray melancholy, childlike discovery, solemn wisdom—she led those who listened and felt through the gamut of human emotions song after song. In one moment she wove with the melody, in the next instance, the mood she hurled out to enfold the audience came in counterpoint. Yet, in the next heartbeat the words to her songs were a chorus to the intricate emotions she created, or the moodweaving an antiphon to the lyrics.

Standing in the back shadows, Faxon abandoned himself to the spells she worked as he had so many times in the past. She was the catharsis; through her all was released without shame. Only a slight niggling jealously marred his soaring flight—the realization that once Arianne had sung her songs for him alone.

Abruptly it was over. The audience's thunderous applause brought him face-to-face with the harsh reality that he stood within a small theater two kilometers beneath the surface of the planet Earth. On stage Arianne and the musicians bowed then disappeared behind a closing curtain. The applause gradually died. There would be no second bows, no encores. The performance was over, such was Arianne's way. Two hours had passed, hours that seemed like mere minutes.

Now came the time for Lorens's performance. Waiting until Browder hastened up the aisle, he walked to the lobby with the diplomat.

"Magnificent, wasn't she?" The man beamed. "I feel totally exhilerated and exhausted at the same time."

"Magnificent," Faxon agreed while they moved from the concert hall's open doors toward the street outside. Browder was right, Arianne's abilities as a moodweaver had increased since the Psi Corps division of the service had been disbanded.

A fact that made it even harder for Faxon to understand why she had come here. Why did she hide from the worlds of humankind in this overgrown hole in the ground? It made no sense. Hers was a talent that should be shared.

"Protect our minds! Protect our minds!" A rowdy chant greeted Faxon's ears when he stepped into the artificial light of Deeprock's night.

Ten men and women, proudly displaying signs that proclaimed, "PSI IS MIND RAPE," "MOODWEAVING

AFFRONTS GOD," "BAN PSIOTICS," marched back
and forth in front of the theater.

"Quirinists?" Faxon's right eyebrow arched when he
turned to Browder.

"Even here." Browder shrugged. "Their numbers are
small, but there's no escape from them."

Faxon stared at the followers of the fanatic William
Quirin. Their leader may have died a century ago, but
Quirin's anti-psiotic writings lived, sparking a cult that
swelled with almost religious fervor throughout humankind's worlds.

Even those who disavowed Quirin's teachings were in-
fluenced by the power the Quirinists wielded. The result
was a general sentiment of distrust for any man, woman,
or child with psi abilities. The Quirinists had been responsible for the disbanding of the Psi Corps. Worse, Quirinist-
backed governments on many worlds exiled those displaying
psi talents or meted out death to those found to be psiotic.

Faxon looked back to the concert hall, then at Browder.
"Arianne? Is she in any danger?"

"None," the diplomat assured him. "She and her musicians have already left via the back entrance. Except for
this handful of fanatics, Earth is really quite a sane world.
Living history, not persecution, is Deeprock's passion.
You'll understand that better once we're at Arianne's party.
If you can't talk history, you'll find yourself outside most
of the conversations."

With a final glance at the demonstrating Quirinists,
Faxon followed Browder to the groundcar.

FOUR

The penthouse was lavish. That the seven-room apartment sat atop an underground domescraper only ten stories high did not diminish its opulence.

Faxon Lorens drifted at the periphery of the seventy-five guests who gathered in the home of Retrieve Director Kabir Marar to honor Arianne Pillan. Although unfamiliar with the terms Inca, Ming, Tokugawa, American, Mayan, and Italian, he could appreciate the priceless artifacts of precious metals, delicate porcelain, sparkling gems, and sculpted marble salvaged—a euphemism for stolen—from Earth's past that adorned all seven of the penthouse's rooms. Marar's bathroom even contained a ceiling-hung mobile consisting of jewel-encrusted eggs fashioned from finely worked gold.

Nor did the impressive array detour Faxon from his sole object in accompanying Michael Browder to the cocktail party. Remaining at the fringes of the gathering, he managed to constantly keep an eye on Arianne while carefully avoiding her attention. When he approached her, he wanted her alone without the defensive shield of the other guests.

Selecting a non-alcoholic drink from a silver tray set atop a table, he drifted past an ever-present row of monitors displaying images of Earth's satellite eyes out onto a balcony. He casually eased into the shadows, leaned against a wall, and scanned the city below. Unless Arianne had changed during the last five years, her tolerance for social affairs such as this was limited to an hour. Then she would slip away for a few minutes to be by herself before continuing.

Faxon sipped at the drink—the unusual tangy flavor of the orange liquid leaving a pleasant sweetness on his tongue—while he continued to survey the massive cavern that was Deeprock. In the distance he saw crawler lights as the transport vehicles rolled in and out of tunnels that led to the planet's surface.

Did the ComNet-controlled tractors carry artifacts into the city or merely haul supplies for Deeprock's citizens? He didn't know. The service had felt it unnecessary to brief him on the day-to-day operation of this Retrieve post.

The whispering swish of fabric and the light padding sound of slippered feet drew his attention to the right. A pleased smile uplifted the corners of his mouth; his timing was perfect. Arianne walked from the penthouse and crossed to the balcony's railing. While she leaned there, he eased behind her and quietly closed a glass door behind her to dissuade any enthusiastic guest who might choose this moment for a personal conversation with the moodweaver.

He had no planned speech, no strategy to persuade her. Arianne had a disarming habit of punching holes in the most meticulously constructed plans. His only gambit was surprise. Drawing a breath, he called to her, "Arianne."

"There was no need to close the door, Fax. People who live crammed together beneath the earth quickly learn to respect each other's need for privacy." She spoke without turning to face him.

Faxon's jaw sagged. She knew that it was he, knew that he had been waiting for her.

"Surprise? From Faxon Lorens, the man who always expects the unexpected? You're slipping, Fax. Getting old." She chuckled dryly, still without turning.

"And you continue to amaze me, Arianne." Faxon pushed through the momentary shock of being discovered to gather his composure as he walked to her side. He shrugged and smiled with chagrin. "I was certain that you hadn't seen me."

"I didn't." Her head turned to him. "I read your *dyami*, Fax. I felt you the moment that I entered Director Marar's home."

"My *dyami*." Faxon hadn't expected her to open herself to the emotional aura of the party's guests. Once such a casual use of her moodweaving talent would have left her mentally and physically drained. Had her ability increased, strengthened? "You know me too well, Arianne. I guess there are certain things that can't be forgotten after five years of marriage."

"No, that's not it. You're the only person I've ever met who reads like a cloak and dagger holodrama. I could feel you skulking, Fax." The weariness of a parent speaking to an uncaring child colored her voice.

Faxon ignored the comment. "You remain the most beautiful woman I've ever met, Arianne." His right hand lifted, fingertips brushing the strands of her rich chestnut hair. "Even with this."

"Do I detect disdain? It's the style on Earth. Jumpers require hair to blend into the time periods here." She eased his hand away when it drifted to her shoulder and rested there.

"So you've become a timejumper?" Faxon arched an eyebrow. "I didn't realize you had been cleared for downtime. Jumper and moodweaver, a strange mixture of talents."

"I haven't been cleared, but I'm close," she replied. "And the combination is no stranger than moodweaver-spy. At least here, Retrieve doesn't require me to be an accomplice to murder."

Her words slipped between his ribs and drove to his heart like a blade of ice. He had hoped to avoid this. "It wasn't murder."

Arianne's emerald eyes narrowed; her facial features

tautened. "What else do you call using your wife's moodweaving to lull a Brodny so that you could ease up behind him, place a pistol to his temple, and pull the trigger? Perhaps the service has a new name for it, but to me, it's still murder!"

"Qatera Bua was dangerous. He would have destroyed everything the Tripar had established in the Grancek System. Hundreds, thousands might have been killed," Faxon answered defensively. "He had to be eliminated. It was necessary. There was no other way."

"Listen to yourself, Fax. The keyword is *might*. Intelligence also indicated that Qatera Bua could be swayed to the Confederation's position." Arianne turned from him again. "You used me that night, Fax. I was no more to you than the pistol you held in your hand—a weapon needed to complete an assignment."

"Arianne, you still don't understand that I . . ."

"No!" Her head jerked around, and she glared at him. "After five years, it's you who still doesn't understand. I loved you, Fax. I trusted you. And you used me!"

"It wasn't I who walked out of our marriage that night. I was willing to try and work things out. If you had given us time, we could have smoothed out the kinks." Faxon felt trapped, unable to shift from the defensive.

"Kinks?" Arianne started, only to abruptly fall silent. Disgust, then sadness washed across the delicate features of her face. Her head wearily moved from side to side.

A seed of panic planted itself in Faxon's chest. He hadn't meant for their meeting to take this disastrous turn. Their past life together wasn't the lever he intended to employ. He drew another breath to quiet the pounding in his temples.

"How is Todd?"

Arianne smiled gently. "Todd is the one mistake we didn't make, Fax. He looks more and more like his father everyday. But he doesn't have a deceitful bone in his body."

"I'd like to see him while I'm onplanet," Faxon continued. "I doubt that I'll recognize him."

"I've never tried to keep him from you," Arianne answered.

"Earth's a long way from Lanatia. It makes it rather difficult for a father to make use of his visitation rights."

Arianne turned and squarely faced Faxon. "Todd didn't bring you here. What do you want, Fax?"

"You're needed," he said.

"The Psi Corps has been dissolved, in case you didn't hear. Psiotics, even moodweavers, are unpopular with politicians these days."

"The service wants you back for one assignment," Faxon pressed. "Just *one* last assignment, Arianne. Nothing permanent, no long-term contract. Complete it, and you can live your life any way you want."

"But that's exactly what I'm doing here and now." She pushed from the balcony's railing. "Forget it, Fax. I don't want to hear another word. And you can tell the Diplomatic Service as undiplomatically as possible where they can place their assignment—sideways!"

Before he could respond, she crossed the balcony, opened the door, and reentered the penthouse. Nor did she stop there. Bidding her host a good evening, she left the party without glancing back at the man she left standing on the balcony.

"Damn!" Faxon cursed aloud as he watched the apartment door slide closed behind her.

He hadn't planned on this, hadn't realized that so much bitterness remained. Twisting around, he stared out into Deeprock's night. No matter what she said, it wasn't over, not yet. He needed Arianne and nothing would stop him from getting what he needed. Nothing.

Faxon lifted a hand and patted the solid bulge within his coat pocket. He still held the lever required to move a granite boulder. Tomorrow he would see that Arianne received the small cube he had carried across the galaxy from Lanatia.

Tomorrow, he reassured himself. But not until he added a message of his own to the cube. That meant locating a recorder and a privacy-shielded room in which to use it.

Shoving from the railing, Faxon hastened back into the party. Browder would be of some use to him after all.

FIVE

Arianne Pillan gazed over the rim of her coffee cup, watching her six-year-old son Todd while he wiped a glob of egg yellow from his breakfast plate with a piece of toast. He *did* grow to look more like his father with each passing day.

For the first time in years she felt a pang of doubt. Had she been correct in bringing Todd here with her? She had only thought of herself when she fled Lanatia. Had the decision been right? Could a lone parent provide everything a child needed?

"Through!" Todd announced proudly as he popped the egg-smeared toast into his mouth, chewed twice, and swallowed loudly. "You promised we'd put my tree in a real pot this morning."

"You've classes to attend, young man." Arianne lowered her cup to the table. Pride replaced doubt as she basked in her son's enthusiastic smile. Todd was testimony to her parental abilities. He was healthy and happy. What else could a mother hope to achieve?

"You promised." He looked up at her from beneath a mop of black hair with puppy-vulnerable, emerald eyes and his lower lip extended in a slight pout of disappointment, but not quite quivering—not quite. "You promised."

Arianne smiled. Perhaps there was more of Fax in their son than she wanted to admit. Todd definitely knew just the right expression to employ to melt the coldest of hearts. She pushed the possibility away. Since his appearance at last night's party, Fax had invaded her every conscious thought.

"I *said* that we'd do it *if* there were enough time this morning." Arianne corrected her son. "You have a habit of recalling things the way you want to remember them. Have I ever mentioned that?"

"There *is* time." Her reprimand failed to elicit so much as a blink. Todd pointed to the kitchen wall to his left. "Look. There's time."

Arianne glanced at a chronometer inset in the wall above four monitors that provided unblinking views from Earth's satellites. *Eight-thirty,* she read the green-glowing numbers, then did a double-take to make certain that she had seen correctly. An hour and a half remained before Todd was due at his first class.

Son of a bitch, she silently cursed Fax's unexpected intrusion into her life. His appearance upset her more than she wanted to admit. She had awakened at least an hour before her usual rising time and hadn't noticed it until this moment.

"Can we put my tree into a pot—a *real* pot? Please?" Todd persisted.

"I promised, didn't I?" Arianne nodded and drained the last swallow of coffee from her cup. "Clean off the table, and I'll meet you in the garden."

To her surprise, Todd attacked the kitchen detail without his usual protests. Standing, she walked through the small living area attached to the kitchen into her own equally cramped, regulation-issue Retrieve bedroom. She discarded the white robe she wore in favor of a dirt-stained, green jumpsuit with threadbare knees and elbows, that hung on the inside face of her closet door.

When she returned to the living area, Todd already stood outside in a five-meter-square garden they shared with the attached apartment across the small open space. It was her luck that a ComNet technician was their neighbor.

The man cared little for flowers and plants, leaving the garden totally to her, and now Todd.

"I have your tools." Todd used both hands to lift a blue, plastic toolbox. "Do I need anything else?"

"Your tree and a pot would be nice. Get them, and I'll prepare the soil."

She stepped into the climate-controlled garden and moved to a workbench neatly pushed into the garden's far corner. A Net monitor screen to one side of the work area told her what her body had already felt. The overhead lighting panels and the garden's temperature imitated a twenty-six-degree spring day. A sprinkler system in the ceiling had provided a gentle morning rain while she and Todd had eaten breakfast.

"You mean I get to pick my own pot?" her son asked dubiously while he placed the toolbox on the bench.

"It's your tree, you select the pot." Arianne opened a cabinet beneath the bench and pulled out a carefully packed box of pots and placed it before the six-year-old. "Take your time and remember that if you choose the wrong one, you'll have to live with the decision until repotting season next year."

Todd nodded solemnly then stared down at the box before turning to retrieve a nine-inch, ten-year-old crypto-meria planted in a deep flower pot at the end of a shelf that supported Arianne's collection of fifteen bonsai trees. Sitting on the ground, he began to extract the pots, placing them beside the young tree she had given him on his last birthday.

While her son worked, she called up her own soil file on the Net and requested the correct planting mixture to double-check it against her own memory. The Net answered in a male voice, while printing on the screen, that a mixture of a half-part soil combined with one part mulch, one part large-grained sand, and two parts medium-grained sand would provide a healthy growing medium for the young tree.

She scooped the desired portions from plastic bags stored

beneath the bench, then mixed them in a plastic container. Finally she sieved the mixture into three separate, smaller containers, each containing a finer grain of soil. The remaining dust she threw away. The mixture was designed for good drainage, to remain moist but not wet. Dust retained too much water, and as the old adage went, no plant grew with wet feet.

While Todd still busied himself with her collection of pots, she stepped to the bonsai shelf. A cherished dream was to one day have an area large enough to accommodate all the miniature trees she could possibly care for. Until then, the fifteen trees she had gathered for twenty of her thirty-five years provided an inner serenity that bordered on the peace others found in meditation. Each represented a different style of bonsai, a living, growing sculpture that reflected both the tree and its owner.

The first of the trees was her most prized possession. The ancient white pine, four hundred standard years old, had been brought to the Pillan family by Mitako Mashu five generations ago when Mitako married Tul Pillan. The marriage was an attempt to cement the Mashu and Pillan families and the corporations they controlled. At that purpose it failed. However, Mitako introduced the art of bonsai to the Pillans, for which Arianne would eternally be grateful.

The white pine stood in the elegant *chokkan* or formal upright style. Its strong vertical trunk betrayed no hint of the slightest deformity. Rigidly it supported a pyramidal arrangement of downward slanting branches that stretched in all directions except forward to the viewer. Thick cloudlike clusters of tiny, rich green needles adorned each of the branches. Heavy roots ran from the thick base like spokes out into a shallow, brown, rectangular pot, giving an illusion of living anchors that sank into the bowels of the earth.

The second tree was a black pine in *Moyogi* or curved informal upright style, a hundred and fifty years old. Her great grandmother had first planted the tree's seed. Her grandmother and mother had carefully shaped the trunk so that it wound upward in curves that progressively grew smaller as they reached the top of the tree.

The *Shakan* or slanting styled trident maple that grew in a green-flecked oval pot beside the black pine was the first tree her mother had ever trusted her to attend. Unlike the windswept *fukinagashi* style, the maple's branches grew in all directions.

Moving along the shelf, Arianne paused to study a *Sokan* styled cryptomeria, a cutting of which had eventually grown into Todd's tree. The tree had two trunks of differing diameters and heights that grew from one root. The twin-trunk style represented parent and child.

A *netsuranari* style needle juniper planted in a shallow, traylike pot next drew her eye. Sinuous in form, several of the coarse needled trees grew from a single root lying horizontal across the reddish brown container. For the moodweaver, the raft of trees had always represented the strength of the life force stretching out in different directions.

Farther along the shelf she once again stopped, her eyes tracing over the slender, reaching shape of a *bunjingi* style white pine. Almost free-form in design, the slightly curving trunk gracefully grew toward the garden's artificial sky at a gentle incline. No branches pushed from the rough bark except near the top of the tree. Twenty years ago Arianne had collected a sapling from her homeworld of Alhim and gradually sculpted this elegant tree.

"I've picked my pot." Todd's voice intruded into her reflections. "I went through every one of them, and this is the one."

He held up a simple rectangular brown Tokoname pot that one of the Retrieve jumpers had brought uptime to her. Fifteen centimeters in length, the pot was matched to Todd's cryptomeria's twenty-five centimeter height. Although slightly too deep and wide to meet the classical proportions of trunk to pot, Arianne could not recall a container in the collection better suited for the tree.

"Do you remember all that I've shown you?" Arianne

suppressed the urge to take the cryptomeria from her son and pot the plant herself.

"I think so," Todd answered after another glance at both tree and pot. "First I have to get the pot ready. I need wire."

"I'll cut it. You get the hole covers."

While Arianne took a roll of annealed copper wire and a pair of cutters from her tool box, her son found two ceramic hole covers in a drawer beneath the workbench. She snipped a length of the fire-softened wire and handed it to him.

Forehead furrowed in concentration, Todd threaded the wire's ends upward from the bottom through the two drain holes. He then turned the pot over, placed the covers over the holes, and pulled the wires straight up so that they could be lightly bound to the cryptomeria's roots for support.

"Now the gravel," she instructed.

"I *know*, Mom." There was a hint of exasperation in his voice at her interference. "I've seen you do this a zillion times."

His exaggeration brought a smile to her lips. For a six-year-old child, Todd had developed a streak of independence. A trait she reinforced by holding her tongue and allowing him to continue at his own speed. If he needed her help, he'd ask for it.

He grabbed a handful of gravel from a bag under the bench and sprinkled the small stones into the pot until they covered the bottom. Next he used the soil she had prepared to fill the pot to the two-thirds mark, large grains on the bottom layering upward to the finer grain. He completed the task by mounding the soil to the right of the pot's center. The tree would sit atop the mound.

"Now the *hard* part." Tongue firmly planted at the side of his open mouth, he dug into her toolbox to find a wooden chopstick. "You have to get my tree out of the flower pot. I don't want to break anything."

She accepted the cryptomeria he handed her, tapped the pot against the bench's edge several times, then turned the pot upside down with her right hand, and let the root ball slide into her left palm. She passed the tree back to her son.

Todd placed the plant on the ground. After studying the task for several minutes, he lifted the tree carefully by its base and began combing the old soil from the roots with the chopstick.

"Arianne, Todd, there is a visitor at the door to the apartment." Net announced from the workbench console.

"Who is it?" Arianne glanced at the monitor.

The screen flickered and the correct soil mixture for the cryptomeria was replaced with the image of Michael Browder. The Net confirmed what Arianne's eyes already knew. "The man's thumbprint matches that of Tripartite Confederation diplomatic representative Michael Browder."

"Damn!" Arianne muttered beneath her breath. She had been so involved in Todd's tree that she had forgotten about Fax. She was certain her ex-husband was behind Browder's unexpected visit. "Tell him I'll be right there."

"Done," Net answered.

"Don't leave me!" The panic in Todd's voice matched the fear in his wide eyes. In an instant an independent young man was replaced by an uncertain child. "I could hurt something!"

"You're doing fine. You've seen me do this before." Arianne's words held no sarcasm, only gentle reassurance. "When the roots are clean, use the scissors to trim them by a third. I should be back by then."

"I don't know, Mom." Todd's head moved from side to side dubiously.

"You can do it," she answered. "I'll just be inside. If you need me, call, and I'll be here. All right?"

Her son beamed and nodded. "Okay."

With Todd busily working the chopstick into the tangled root ball, she walked back into the apartment and pressed a hand atop a sensor panel. The door slid back to reveal a smiling Michael Browder.

"Good morning, Ms. Pillan." Browder nodded, but remained outside. "I apologize for disturbing you so early this morning, but I have a delivery that is somewhat urgent.'' He held out a transparent cube that measured two centimeters on a side.

Arianne caught herself before she reached for the recorder cube. Her eyes narrowed suspiciously. ''If it's from Faxon Lorens, I want nothing to do with that. I gave my answer to Fax last night. I haven't changed my mind. I'm afraid you've wasted your time coming here.''

''Mr. Lorens said that would be your reaction.'' Browder's smile faded. ''He also said that I was to inform you that the cube pertained to Captain Goodheart.''

Arianne bit her lower lip. As children she and her younger brother Jon had been enamoured with the galaxy-spanning holodramas of the fictional Captain Aurek Goodheart and his never-ending battle against the would-be conqueror of the universe, the blackhearted Zenos Malevil. Week after week Malevil employed a host of alien creatures to battle the ever-victorious Captain Goodheart.

Even as children she and Jon had recognized the ludicrous plots. Humankind had only encountered four sentient races since they had first leaped from their homeworld into space. Of those the Erna, timeless creatures of pure energy bored with a universe that offered no new experiences, had committed mass suicide by throwing themselves into a black hole. The birdlike Liluye had abandoned their own homeworld three centuries ago and fled to a distant galaxy to avoid what they called humankind's ''insatiable appetite'' for dominance. They had not been heard of since.

Likewise the Uzoma with their gigantic slug bodies had withdrawn to their home world of Candor, isolating themselves from all contact with other races. Only the white-furred, bearlike Brodny refused to be relegated to a role second to humankind. The Brodny spread through the star systems, establishing their own worlds and empire. A situation that too often resulted in strained diplomatic relationships and minor military clashes between the two races.

But reality had nothing to do with Captain Goodheart. It was adventure that two young children had hungered for, and it was adventure Captain Goodheart had provided. Their love of the long-cancelled holodramas lived on; Captain Goodheart remained Arianne's private nickname for her brother Jon.

She reached out and accepted Browder's offering, her fingers closing around the small cube in a tight fist.

The smile returned to the diplomat's face. "If you wish to contact Mr. Lorens after viewing the cube, you can contact him at my home."

Browder then bid her a good day and left. Arianne nodded in answer, letting the door close. Her hand opened, and she stared at the crystal cube. How had Jon gotten himself involved with Fax? When she had last seen her brother two years ago, he had been fully entrenched in the management of Pillan Planets' various mineral interests. Corporation desk jockeys don't run head-on into the Diplomatic Service.

Arianne tried to ignore the cold shiver that worked itself up her spine. Things could change in the span of two years, and there was no way for her to know.

She had cut herself free of her family's enterprises when she had joined the Psi Corps at age twenty. Since the corps disbanding, she had diligently maintained her distance from Pillan Planets. Unlike Jon and the other members of her family, building interstellar corporate empires held no interest for her. The business arena shared too many similarities to the Psi Corps. Nebulous governmental interests translated to capital gains for corporations, and both always won over human needs.

In truth, she had been the happiest in her life here on Earth. The Retrieve program dealt with humans and their history. Here she rose above the constant rise and fall of empires no matter what form they assumed. Here she clearly saw humankind's continuance from creatures that pulled themselves from primordial slime to beings that cradled the stars in their palms.

Her hand closed around the cube again. There was only one way to find out what it contained—play it. Turning, she glanced back to the garden; Todd still worked the cryptomeria's root ball with the chopstick. Assured her son would be occupied for the next few minutes, she seated herself at a Net console wedged into the corner of the living area and dropped the cube into the recording unit.

"Arianne, the information contained herein is on a scrambled coded program that will immediately erase it from the Net's memory. The cube will also degauss." Faxon Lorens's image flashed on the screen. "So watch and listen closely. You'll only get one chance at this."

The screen flickered to display a shot of a small landing craft. Another blink and the visual came from within the ship. Her brother Jon sat at the controls. Like a man in a stupor, his wide, unmoving, and unblinking eyes stared straight ahead as he was lifted from a contour couch by two men and placed atop a stretcher.

The expected voice-over to explain the transition of silent scenes never came. Instead Arianne watched the audio-blanked images as her brother was carried to a medical bay inside some larger craft. The last scene showed a team of lab-frocked men and women standing around Jon's bed, shaking their heads. Then Fax reappeared on the monitor.

"Prognosis is uncertain, Arianne. To be honest, no one knows what has happened to Jon." She barely heard his words over her pounding temples. "The service believes that you are the one person who might be able to aid your brother. I emphasize *might*. I won't lie to you. It doesn't look good. If you wish to discuss this further, please contact me."

The image dissolved in a snowstorm of static.

"Bastard!" She hammered a fist into an arm of the chair.

The cube told her nothing! Fax hadn't lied, because he had said nothing. She rubbed a hand over her face and drew a steady breath. Was it a trick? Or were the scenes she had viewed real? Was Jon in danger? Did he need her?

"Damn!" Frustration knotted her stomach.

The service was capable of doing anything to get what they wanted. And they wanted her at the moment. The cube's visuals could have been staged; there was no way for her to prove their authenticity.

The son of a bitch has me in a corner, and he damned well knows it! Arianne closed her eyes and drew another steadying breath. Her first reaction was to take the cube, go to Browder's home, and personally place it in a recessed portion of her ex-husband's anatomy in the most painful manner she could devise. Pleasing though the action might be, she couldn't do it, not if the possibility of Jon being involved existed.

"Damn! Damn! Damn!" She stared at the console. Like it or not, she had but one avenue open to her. "Net, give me Michael Browder's residence."

SIX

"You promise to put moss on it?" Todd's green eyes rolled to the potted cryptomeria in his mother's hands.

"Promise." Arianne forced herself to smile, then leaned over and lightly kissed her son's cheek—last week he had declared himself "too big" for a motherly kiss on the lips. "Hurry or you'll be late for your class."

Todd hastily returned the kiss loudly and wetly, then spun around to dash down a long hall toward a pair of double doors. "Don't forget the moss! You promised!" he shouted back as the doors slid open, and he darted outside onto a slidewalk.

"I won't forget." Her words were lost on him when the doors hissed closed.

Walking back into their apartment, she placed the bonsai on a small table, and immediately picked it back up. Working with the tree would help keep her busy, take her mind off Jon. Until Fax arrived, she would know nothing more than what she had seen on the recorder cube. Imagined disasters destroyed reason far worse than reality. With an input of facts, the mind directed itself toward a solution.

Back in the garden, she placed the cryptomeria atop a wooden turntable on her workbench. Slowly she rotated the wheel, scrutinizing Todd's results.

She resisted the urge to brush aside the now moist soil and double check Todd's efforts. If he had failed to secure the tree with the copper wires, watering would eventually cause it to shift and tilt. Having to view such a mistake until next year's potting season would teach a lesson that unseen parental interference could never convey.

She did, however, use the tip of a chopstick to make certain he had correctly packed the soil within the tree's root structure. Too loosely or too tightly packed soil would promote root rot that could eventually kill the cryptomeria. She was not willing to risk a plant she had grown from a clipping for ten years to a child's inexperience.

How can I help Jon? The question thrust to the forefront of her thoughts. She shoved it aside. She'd have no answers until Fax arrived.

Reassured that Todd had learned his potting lessons well, she pulled out a plastic container of fine, old soil saved from other repottings and sprinkled it over the pot's moist dirt. A small, straw whisk brush smoothed the surface for a powdery layer of ground, dried moss she dusted atop the soil.

She used a hand-pumped misting bottle to thoroughly dampen moss and dirt before placing the tree in the shade beneath her bonsai shelf. The cool environment would protect the root-trimmed tree from losing too much moisture through its needles while it recovered from the shock of repotting. The shade would also encourage the moss to grow and spread over the dirt like a lush carpet of miniature grass.

"Arianne . . ."

Startled, she jumped, nearly dropping the containers she stored beneath the workbench. Her head jerked up to the ComNet's monitor screen.

". . . two visitors are at the door. One is Michael Browder; I have no record of the other's identity."

Browder's and Fax's faces filled the screen. Arianne sucked in a deep breath to calm the race of her heart. "Admit them."

Shoving the rest of the containers and tools under the bench, she stood and brushed the dirt from her hands on the thighs of the coveralls. She resisted the desire to pat her still uncombed hair into place as she stepped toward the apartment. Fax had forced this meeting—confrontation?—he'd have to take her as she was. This was *her* home after all.

Her surge of defiance faltered the instant she entered the living area, shattered by Fax's disapproving expression while his gaze travelled round the cramped confines of her living quarters. The reaction sent a flush of guilt through her breast. Why should she care what he thought? Worse, why did his unspoken comdemnation leave her with a sense of violation?

"Arianne." His disapproval transformed into a pleased smile when his eyes alighted on her, which immediately was replaced by an expression of concern. "I'm sorry about having to send the recording. I tried to tell you last night, but . . ."

"This is today," she interrupted, unwilling to accept the responsibility for last evening's unpleasant meeting that he tried to place on her shoulders. "The recorder cube implied that you had more information on my . . ."

Fax interrupted this time, speaking loudly to drown her final word—"brother." "Is this apartment equipped with a privacy screen?"

"My son and I *live* here. This isn't a hot bed of political intrigue. Nothing we do requires a privacy shield." Arianne made no attempt to conceal her irritation.

"Out there?" Fax's head tilted toward the open door she had just come through.

"My garden."

"Ambassador, if you'll excuse us a moment." Fax glanced at Browder, then motioned Arianne outside. He closed the door behind them and glanced about the small garden, his gaze falling on the Net console. "Can you shut that down?"

Holding her mounting exasperation in check, she walked to the console and flicked it off. Fax was in his super service troubleshooter mode; if she expected to ever hear what he knew, she would have to cater to his paranoia.

"Still puttering with those dwarf trees, I see." He grinned at Arianne, then nodded to the bonsai shelf. "They're interesting, but I never understood why you wasted all that time on them."

She cringed inwardly. Fax persisted in mispronouncing bonsai as ban-zi instead of bone-sigh, just as he failed to see the trees for what they were. "Dwarf" implied some genetic accidents, instead of meticulously sculpted works of art, each a microcosm of life.

"You didn't come here to talk about my trees." She refused to listen to him pass judgment on her life-style. "Is Jon all right? What's happened to him?"

"I'm afraid what you saw on the cube is all you're authorized to know at this time." Fax shrugged and did his best sincere regret sigh. "What your brother has gotten himself mixed up in is a double-barrelled security matter."

"Fax, this is Jon we're talking about—my brother! I didn't invite you here to play silly cloak and dagger games. Cut the crap or get the hell out." She hadn't intended to let him get to her; now it was too late.

"I repeat, this is a top secret, high security matter, Arianne. The Diplomatic Service is willing to provide you all the details once you've agreed to accept this assignment." He reached inside his broad-striped coat and withdrew a recording cube. "This is your contract. All you have to do is record your acceptance, and I'll brief you on everything I've been told."

"Fax—," she began and stopped abruptly. Appealing to his sense of decency, or to the memory of the love they had once shared was a dead end. When it came to the service, Fax played by the letter of the book. She employed the only ploy she had that might jar him. "Then I'll transmit to Alhim. I'm certain Pillan Planets will tell me everything I need to know."

"Nice try, but it won't work, Arianne." Fax shrugged again. "Your family knows nothing more about Jon than you do. They know that he's disappeared, but that's all they know. The Tripar has made certain of that."

"What's happened to him, Fax?" Arianne's voice softened as she tried another approach.

"You saw the cube. I don't want to be callous, but the truth is, Jon's a vegetable; his mind is gone. No one seems to be able to explain what happened or find a way to help him. The service believes you could be the key to . . ."

"I'm a moodweaver, not a physician or a miracle worker. What about others—true psiotics? Has there been a mind merge? What did they find?"

Fax said nothing, just stared at his former wife.

"Where is he, Fax?" Arianne pressed.

"Your agreement to accept the assignment first." He held the cube out to her in his palm.

Arianne steeled herself. She had to make her lie sound convincing. A lie was all she had left. "No." Her head moved from side to side in denial. "I'll never go back to the service, not for you, not for Jon, not for anyone. Go back and tell your superiors you've failed, Fax."

"Have it your way." His hand closed around the cube, and he shoved it back into a jacket pocket. "I'm sorry that we had to meet like this, Arianne. I would have chosen better circumstances, if it had been up to me."

Temples pounding, she watched him walk toward the apartment door. She wagered on Fax's inability to accept failure. And won—partially.

He reached out to press a palm to the door's pressure plate and paused. Like a man carrying twice his weight on his shoulders, he turned back to her. "If you won't accept the contract, then consider returning with me to Lanatia. I can't tell you anything more than you already know. On Lanatia others might be willing to comply with your wishes."

"Lanatia? But I have work . . ." Her words trailed to silence. Fax's hazel eyes, reflecting the gray weave of his striped jacket, held her. There was no hint of compromise in the set of his jaw; they had reached a stalemate. "I have to think it over. When would we be leaving?"

"There's a Tripar cruiser waiting for us at the transfer

station," he answered. "I'd like to begin the journey back today, if possible."

Biting her lower lip, Arianne walked to his side and pressed the apartment door open. "You haven't given me much time—if I decide to go with you. I don't have much to pack, but I'd have to make arrangements for Todd, file for a leave with Retrieve, find someone to care for my trees . . ."

"The service has already arranged for your leave," Fax said with the tone of a man who came assured of success. "I could help find someone to care for Todd."

"I haven't said that I was going," Arianne asserted. She was ninety percent certain she would be aboard the cruiser when it left; Jon *was* in trouble. However, the longer Fax was left dangling the better. "I'll contact you at Browder's when I've made a decision."

"Don't wait too long. It's a long way from Earth to Lanatia, and we've wasted enough time," Fax answered as they entered the apartment's living area. He glanced at Browder and nodded.

The diplomat pushed from a chair and stepped toward the door. He touched a palm to the door's pressure plate.

"You'll have my decision by thirteen hundred . . ."

Actinic light flared like an exploding nova as the door hissed open. Seering pain licked across Arianne's eyes. Her mouth opened, and a scream tore from her throat. A hammer slammed into her chest an instant before the flames of hell engulfed her body in burning agony and set her careening into the blackness of oblivion.

MOYOGI

SEVEN

Coolness, fresh and soothing, washed over Arianne Pillan's naked body as she floated on the back of nothingness.

No. She mistook the misty fabric of a cloud woven about her for nakedness. Nor did she float within a sea of blackness. She flew! With arms extended widely, she glided upward, shooting high above fluffy white, mountainous cloud banks. Higher, ever higher, she soared toward the fiery, yellow orb of the sun.

Into the sun! Panic railed through her brain. Her chest tightened like a fist around her pounding heart. She fell into the sun!

"Noooooooo!" she screamed. Her arms flailed, fighting away the burning inferno. Her body writhed and twisted to escape the tongues of solar flares that licked upward. "Nooooo!"

The sun winked out. Above her hung a light, a simple light globe attached to a ceiling painted institutional green. The glaring harshness of the light throbbed deep within her eyeballs. Moaning, she twisted her head away.

A wall, washed in the same flat green as the ceiling, rose to her right. On the left stood a small maze of polished stainless steel machinery that blinked and beeped to report her vital signs.

A hospital! She felt the bed beneath her, the sensors glued to her head and chest, the needle that prodded into her left arm with its clear plastic tube that ran upward to a steadily dripping IV bag.

The hiss of an opening door drew her attention to the foot of the bed. Across the room a thin man in a white frock, sporting the shaven head of a spacer, ducked through a hatch and walked beside her.

"Ms. Pillan, you caught me off guard. I wasn't expecting you to awake for another couple of hours." The man grinned down at her. "It's a good sign that your recovery is just about complete."

"Recovery? What . . ."

The nova of light, the burning flames! She closed her eyes and groaned as the memory of a hammering blast thrust itself to the forefront of her brain.

"What? An explosion of some sort outside your apartment is what brought you here. That's what I was told. They don't give me too many details," the man said while he leaned over to study the various readouts that flashed on the machines beside the bed. He then added with obvious pride, "My job was to put you back together again. And I'm doing one fine job of that."

"Where am . . ." She faltered again as realization penetrated the confusion fogging her mind. *A hatch! He came through a hatch!* "I'm aboard a ship!"

"The Tripar Cruiser *Cohila.* I guess you were in no condition to remember being brought up from the surface." The man leaned over her to flash a penlight into her eyes. "The answers to your next questions are—I'm Dr. Cemal Hakan, and there's nothing wrong with you *now* that a few days rest won't heal. Can't think of a better way to past the time in space than to rest, can you?"

"Dr. Hakan," she tried to shove aside the cotton that clogged her brain.

"And I *do* want you to rest. Don't want to go ruining all my hard work, do you?" He ignored her attempt at another question. "I need to give you a complete physical, but you appear strong enough for visitors. There's been someone waiting outside this room ever since you were brought aboard. I think the physical can be delayed until he's had a few minutes with you.''

Before she could ask ''who,'' Hakan moved to the hatch and opened it. ''Mr. Lorens, you can come in now.''

Her ''no'' lodged in her throat unspoken as Fax pushed through the hatchway. The worry that lined his face softened when his eyes lifted to her. A smile uplifted the corners of his mouth. ''Arianne, I . . . I . . . you had me worried.''

''I didn't feel that certain myself.'' There was no attempt to inject levity, merely fact. ''I thought we'd all bought it.''

''I got off lucky,'' Fax moved to the left side of her bed and took her hand in his, which she immediately tugged away. ''Other than a few bruises and a side full of sore ribs, I'm all right. Dr. Hakan here had you floating in an accelerator chamber for three days. You took a lot of burns.''

Anticipating her next question, Hakan produced a mirror and handed it to her. The physician *had* done a fine job, she admitted as she stared at her reflection. The intensity of the blast had surely seered away half the flesh on her face, but she could detect no hint of scars or injury. Except for the baby-pink hue of her complexion, she would have never guessed that anything had ever been wrong.

''I told you that I did good work.'' Hakan beamed as he took the mirror back. ''The rest of you looks as good as the face. Care to take a look?''

''Later.'' Arianne noted a flicker of disappointment in the physician's dark eyes in reaction to her lack of enthusiasm. She turned back to Fax. ''What about Browder?''

''Dead,'' he answered softly. ''He caught the full force of the blast—never had a chance.''

Arianne closed her eyes and drew a long breath. The Tripar diplomat had been standing at the door when the explosion occurred. He had died before he knew what had happened. She looked up at Fax once more. ''Flash bomb?''

He nodded. "Apparently set after we entered your apartment. It was rigged to go off when the door opened."

"Who was it meant for?"

"The best the Retrieve investigation has been able to theorize is that it was for you," Fax replied. "I've been in contact with them since we lifted from the surface. They think the bomb was planted by a Quirinist. Although, they have been unable to trace it."

Quirinist, the word rolled in her head as she stared up at the green ceiling. She should have realized that it was only a matter of time before the anti-psiotic fanatics on Earth resorted to the violence they had employed on humankind's other worlds. They wouldn't be satisfied until they had murdered every man, woman, and child who displayed even a trace of psi ability.

The irony of their fanaticism was that their bloody efforts weren't needed. Time and genetics were doing a thorough job all by themselves. The incidence of latent psiotic births had declined eighty percent during the past century. For no explicable reason, no scientifically discovered cause, psi ability was being lost, nor had anyone found a way to reverse the trend. In another generation or two, psiotics would be as extinct as the great dinosaurs that once walked the Earth.

"Todd!" Her son's image flashed in Arianne's mind. Anger twisted her features as her head jerked to Fax. "You son of a bitch! What am I doing here? I belong back on Earth with my son!"

Fax took half a step away as though expecting her to leap from the bed and go for his throat. An action that crossed her mind, one she would have been quite willing to perform had her body not been too weak.

"I assume that this is where you would have chosen to be, if you had been conscious. You indicated that you intended to return with me to Lanatia." Fax said hesitantly.

"You assumed a hell of a lot!" Arianne made no attempt to contain her seething rage. "I don't know what it'll require, but you'd damned well better see that this cruiser does an about-face and takes me back to my son!''

"*Our* son," he answered defensively. "If Todd's what bothering you, then you can quit worrying. I brought him with us. It seemed simpler than attempting to find someone to care for him. We're getting to be quite good friends.''

"Todd's here?" Arianne blinked in disbelief, uncertain she had heard correctly. "My son's on board?"

"*Our* son," Fax repeated, doubling the emphasis on "our." "He's right outside if you want to see him."

"Outside?" She still didn't believe him.

"Mr. Lorens, I don't think that she should have another visitor at the moment. I have an examination to complete, and she needs to rest. Ms. Pillan is not fully recovered, you realize.''

"Dr. Hakan, you can make an exception, at least . . .''

She ignored them and called to the open hatch. "Todd! Todd!''

A second later, her son came bounding into the room. Around Fax he darted, coming to an abrupt halt as he reached the side of the bed. His worried green eyes shifted from his mother's face to the IV tube in her left arm.

"Is it all right to kiss you?" He looked back at her, uncertainty clouding his young face. "I want to give you a kiss, but I don't want to hurt you.''

"You're not going to hurt me." She reached out and slipped her right arm around his waist, hugging him as close as she could.

Wiggling halfway onto the bed, Todd stretched up and kissed her lips. "I love you, Mom.''

"I know. And I love you." She returned the kiss, holding him tightly, inhaling the warm fragrance of his hair. When her arm could no longer support his weight and he slipped back to the deck, she cradled his cheek in her hand. "Are you all right? Has your . . .''

"Ms. Pillan, I really must insist . . .'' Hakan began.

"I'll bring Todd back after you've had a chance to

rest.'' Fax reached down and took the boy's hand. ''Don't worry about him. I'm seeing that he eats well and sticks to his studies. I had Earth's ComNet dump his lessons into the ship's memory before we left. Now, you rest. Everything will be all right.''

''Get better, Mom,'' Todd called back as Fax led him from the room. ''I'll be okay.''

The hatch slid closed behind the six-year-old boy, leaving Arianne alone with the doctor once again. The man drew an impatient breath and said, ''Now let me see how the healing is progressing on the rest of your body.''

Arianne nodded and wearily closed her eyes. She rolled to one side and then the other as the physician slipped off her gown. She lifted her arms and legs at his command, but paid little heed to his comments.

Her thoughts lay elsewhere, unable to shake a sense of doubt that filled her mind. What was so important that Fax had brought Todd aboard the ship to assure that she would travel to Lanatia? Where was her brother Jon, and what had he gotten himself into?

A vegetable, she recalled Fax's description of Jon. What had happened to him? Why did the Tripar Diplomatic Service think that she, a mere moodweaver, could help him?

Or did they believe that she could help him?

A cold chill shivered up her spine that had nothing to do with the icy instruments Hakan placed against her bare flesh.

EIGHT

Arianne stared at the screen that hung above her bed. Intently she watched the image while Fax slowly circled a fifteen-centimeter tall, forty-year-old, cork-barked elm in *Hokidachi* style. Other than Fax's and Todd's visits, long-distance bonsai tending provided her only relief from the boredom of laying in the med-bay.

The day after Dr. Hakan had revived her, Fax had surprised her by announcing that not only had he brought their son aboard the cruiser, but he had personally overseen the transporting of her bonsai collection onto the ship.

The trees were presently safely residing in Todd's quarters. Fax had arranged a simple audio-visual link to the room, allowing her to tend the trees. The camera Fax operated was her remote eyes, and Todd's hands replaced her own experienced touch.

"Stop there," she called to a microphone inset beside the monitor screen. "See that twig growing from the lower right branch?"

"Here, Mom?" Todd's short forefinger poked into the picture. "Is this it?"

"That's the one." She studied the new growth that pushed from an old limb. There were five pairs of alternating leaves on the twig. "Cut it back to two leaves, Todd."

"Two leaves," he repeated.

Sharp, pointed leaf scissors edged onto the screen. Deftly her son snipped off the unwanted leaves.

"See anything else on this tree that needs trimming?" This from Fax.

"Make one more circle," she requested, watching as he moved the camera around the tiny-leafed elm to display an upright trunk with fan-shaped branches that earmarked the *hokidachi* or broom style. "Looks good from here. That should do it for the elm today. Let's take a look at the winter jasmine next."

The camera panned back to provide a view of Todd carefully lifting the elm from the table and placing it back on the floor of his room. He then picked up the jasmine with roots that grew tenaciously in the cracks of a piece of volcanic rock from her homeworld.

For Arianne, the rock-clinging *ishitsuki* style was the most delicate bonsai to maintain. Centimeter by centimeter she examined the roots that disappeared into the soil of a round, blue pot, making certain none had been dislodged during the flight.

A soft hiss announced the opening of the door to her room. She glanced up to see a muscular, male nurse duck through the hatchway. He smiled as he straightened to a height of two meters. "I have some medicine for you, Ms. Pillan—Dr. Hakan's orders."

"Be right with you, Karel. Let me take care of this first," she replied then glanced back to the screen. "Looks like that's all for today, Todd. I've medicine to take."

Fax pulled back giving her a view of Todd's smiling face. He blew her a kiss and said, "Dad and I make a good team, don't we?"

"A great team," she answered. "Be a good boy, and I'll see you later, all right?"

"Okay." Todd grinned widely and waved.

The image went black as Fax switched off the remote camera, leaving Arianne worried by niggling, petty suspicions. It bothered her that Todd now called Fax "Dad." She explained away the unreasonable apprehension as cabin fever that stemmed from being confined to a med-bay bed for the past week. She told herself that she wasn't jealous of her ex-husband's sudden interest in her son, but was merely irritated by her circumstances.

She also knew that she wasn't fooling herself. Fax's sudden role of father didn't suit him. After five years without displaying the slightest interest in their son, he abruptly appeared and began calling Todd "my son." Was he using Todd to somehow maneuver her?

Or was she blowing the situation out of proportion? Todd *was* Fax's son as well as hers. Was her insecurity showing? Did Fax present a threat, someone who might steal away Todd's love, a love that had only been for her until now? The possibility was repugnant. Surely she wasn't that petty?

"We're due for tachyon transition two hours from now. Approach to Lanatia, you know."

The nurse's voice wedged into her reflections; she looked up. "It's about time, Karel. I'm ready to get out of this bed."

"Soon enough," he answered. "But Dr. Hakan wanted you to have this to make things a bit easier. It's a sedative. Should make the transition smoother for you."

Threads of doubt wove through Arianne's mind. Her apprehension tripled. The uncertainty came not from her, but Karel—she was unconsciously reading the nurse's *dyami*!

Clearing away the cluttering thoughts of Fax and Todd, she opened herself to the man's emotional aura. Like a swirling sphere of eddied colors, she felt him, sensed the tension and stress that spread like ink blots across the surface of his *dyami*.

Damn, she cursed her inability to penetrate deeper, to merge with his mind and discover the root of the doubts that ate at him. This was the curse of a moodweaver, to touch another mind and feel the greater depths that waited to be probed, but never to see beyond the surface of the emotions that swirled there.

"Arm or backside, which do you prefer?" Karel placed the plastic tray he carried atop a table beside her bed.

Lifting a hypodermic gun from the tray, he opened a single chamber and inserted a capsule of the sedative.

His *dyami* stretched in harsh, dark bands within Arianne's head. *The hypo!* The instant he touched the hypodermic gun, fear gripped him. *Something is wrong with the hypo!*

"Arm or backside? Not much of a choice, Karel. You and Dr. Hakan have shot me so full of juice for a week, I think every centimeter of my body is sore."

She delayed, buying time. A moodweaver who could transform the emotions of a theater filled with people could shift the feelings of one man. She had no doubt of her ability; the question was, did she have time?

Edging aside her own fears, which would only strengthen the terror-tinged darkness of his emotions, she drew upon memories to conjure a pastoral image of her homeworld Alhim. A warm, spring breeze gently caressed a lush, green sea of waist-high grass, setting the long leaves to undulate in hypnotic waves.

The image mastered, she reached out to link her own *dyami* with the nurse's. And she wove!

Strands of placid green appeared in the blackness of his emotions. Outward they spread, flowing liquid and bright. Serenity was her thread as she wove a tapestry of lulling peace to quell the mind she touched.

She sensed him relax, surrendering to the unknown force that tapped his apprehension and drained it. It was at that moment her right arm snaked out, hand closing around the hypodermic gun, and wrenching it from his grip!

Karel's brown eyes went round in fear, his *dyami* flashing black in a heartbeat, as she hurled the hypodermic across the room. Its solid thud as it struck the wall and ricocheted to the floor severed the fragile thread that linked his mind to hers.

"Bitch! You won't trick me again!" He lunged, his massive hands clamping about her neck. His thumbs dug into her throat, attempting to crush her windpipe. "I don't need a needle to kill you!"

In an instant of panic, she thrashed on the bed; Karel's

powerful hands tightened. Reason penetrated fear. There
was no way a direct application of force would break his
deadly hold on her; he was too strong to pit her muscles
against his.

She went limp beneath his assault, calming herself for
what had to be done, if she were to survive. A glint of
doubt flashed in his narrowed eyes. She struck!

Focusing all the strength of her body into her right arm,
she slammed the heel of her palm into his nose. She felt
rather than heard the crack of bone and crunching carti-
lage. Blood flowed hot and sticky into her hand.

Enough force behind such a blow can cause death, the
shock of the impact hemorrhaging the brain. Arianne's
position robbed her of the strength and leverage to deliver
a death strike. However, she did accomplish what she
intended.

Karel howled in agony. His hands released her throat,
and he staggered back like a junkie juiced to the gills on
Brain Honey. His face flashed several shades of green,
each one progressively paling to a more sickly hue than the
one before. He doubled over to clutch his midrift as the
secondary effect of the blow to the nose grabbed his gut in
uncontrollable waves of nausea.

While the muscular nurse retched, Arianne sucked down
two cool lungfuls of air before she tossed aside the sheet
and swung her legs from the bed. The instant the soles of
her bare feet hit the metal deck, she moved forward going
directly for the kill. Her right leg lashed out, solidly
driving into her assailant's chin.

Karel refused to fall; instead he jerked upright. His arms
flailed the air for support as he floundered into the wall
behind him. Spittle and bile drooled from his pain-twisted
lips. He blinked as though uncertain what had happened to
him.

Again Arianne struck. The full weight of her body
behind her blow, she threw a punch not to his chin, but
into his unprotected left armpit.

The hammering punishment to the normally hidden nerve

nexus there was too much for the nurse. He screamed as excruciating pain seared through his body. Once more he slammed flat against the wall. For a split second he hung there, a dazed blankness clouding eyes that rolled up in his head. His muscular frame quivered spasmodically before it sluggishly melted down the green wall to pool in a limp, unconscious mass on the medical bay deck.

Fully aware that the intense pain of an underarm strike could rob a person of consciousness, Arianne stared at the felled nurse, her mind refusing to accept that it was over. She edged forward, poised to deliver another punishing blow to the man's smashed nose with the heel of her foot. He didn't move.

She arched out a leg and nudged his temple with her toes. Karel's head lolled to the side; his eyes remained closed.

It *was* over. Unlike the extended struggles so popular in holodramas where actors hailed endless staged blows into each other's bodies, the attack had begun and ended in a matter of seconds. Three quick, clean strikes was all it had taken.

"Arianne!" The hatch to the room opened and Fax darted inside to halt abruptly. His hazel eyes shifted between the fallen nurse and her. "Are you all right? The audio was still on. I heard him. I didn't think I'd get here in time."

"You didn't." She waved him away as he stepped forward to take her in his open arms. On sudden rubbery legs, she stepped to the bed and sank to its edge. "Get someone to get him out of here and clean up the mess."

She stared at Karel's unmoving form. Three blows had done that. She felt no sense of pride, only relief. The body laying crumpled on the deck could have been hers—dead, not unconscious.

NINE

"You're very lucky." Dr. Cemal Hakan held up a test tube filled with a viscous violet liquid that lazily rolled in the slender glass container as he tilted it from one side then to the other. "Identifying this as a neuro-toxin was easy, but it took Net to pinpoint the substance. It's a particularly nasty poison that comes from a scaly little creature called Deathkiss."

"Deathkiss?" Arianne's brow furrowed as she sank back into the pillows braced beneath her back. The name was vaguely familiar, although she couldn't place where she had heard it before.

"A small, winged lizard that's indigenous to the rain forests of Honovi," Fax added.

"Honovi, MashuCo's homeworld?" Arianne's head jerked around. She stared at her ex-husband who stood on the opposite side of her bed.

"One and the same." Fax nodded. His gaze nervously drifted to the floor as though avoiding her eyes.

"If Karel had injected this, you wouldn't have known it." Hakan continued to stare at the test tube apparently fascinated by the lethal substance. "It kills in about ten seconds. Very nasty."

"Honovi," Arianne repeated.

"I ordered a mind merge with the nurse. It confirmed that Karel was a MashuCo agent." This from Captain

Kimt Perrson who stood at the foot of her bed. "Or at least he had been hired by MachuCo."

The mind merge didn't surprise Arianne. While the Psi Corps arm of the Diplomatic Service had been dissolved, the Tripar Navy still employed psi teams, although that fact was not publicized. What did take her off guard was MashuCo.

"MashuCo doesn't employ independents. They rely on agents who they have trained and whose loyalty is unquestionable," Arianne said, feeling the full weight of the situation, but uncertain of its implications. She looked up at Perrson. "Did the merge link Karel to a contact?"

The cruiser's commander shook his head. "Karel was trained well. Even unconscious, there were mental blocks my merger couldn't penetrate. It took him a full hour to unlock Karel's association with MashuCo."

"Great!" Arianne made no attempt to contain her disgust. "That means he could have received his orders before the *Cohila* left Lanatia, from someone on Earth, or another agent aboard this ship."

"I've considered all those possibilities," Perrson replied, running a hand over his shaven scalp. "We can eliminate Earth. Except for Mr. Lorens's single message, the *Cohila* received no transmissions while in orbit. Nor did any of the crew have contact with personnel aboard the transfer station."

"Karel had been assigned to this ship just before the journey to Earth," Fax said, his eyes lifting to Arianne again. "It's more than obvious that he was planted here."

Just as obvious were the things that Fax left unsaid. It was also apparent to Arianne that MashuCo knew more about the reasons she travelled to Lanatia than she did.

"What about the flash bomb in my apartment?" she asked. "Is there a connection with MashuCo?"

"Retrieve authorities on Earth have been informed of the possibility," Perrson answered. "They will adjust their investigation accordingly."

The captain paused to draw a breath. "There is one

question I must ask, Ms. Pillan—why would the MashuCo want to murder you?''

''A good question, and one I wish I had an answer for,'' she said with a shake of her head. She glanced at her ex-husband, hoping for an answer. Fax once more avoided contact with her eyes.

Captain Perrson's expectant expression was that of a man anticipating a more detailed explanation. Arianne couldn't provide one. All she could do was shrug.

''Very well, Ms. Pillan . . .'' Perrson began, only to have his words drowned by a warning buzzer that announced a thirty-minute warning before the *Cohila*'s transition into normal space. When the buzzer died, he said, ''I'll station a guard outside your door. He'll remain with you until you're shuttled onplanet. Once on Lanatia, you're the Diplomatic Service's responsibility. Now, I have a ship to prepare for planetfall.''

Perrson pivoted with military crispness, an amazing feat in static-grip boots, and strode smartly to the room's hatch. Dr. Hakan and Fax were at his heels.

''Fax,'' Arianne called out, ''I'd like you to remain with me for a few minutes.''

He halted and turned. His expression read, ''I was afraid this was going to happen.''

Arianne waited until Perrson and Hakan exited the room and the hatch closed behind them. ''Now, tell me what the hell is going on here? In less than a week someone has tried to blow me apart, shoot me full of poison, and strangle me. What have you gotten me into?''

''I don't know any more than you do,'' Fax replied, his gaze refusing to meet her eyes.

''Don't know—or won't say?'' She didn't believe him, not for an instant. ''What has MashuCo got to do with my brother? Why are they trying to kill me?''

''Arianne, believe me, if I could tell you, I would. I can't; I haven't the authority. You'll be onplanet in another hour or two. You'll have to wait until then.''

''And then it's only a *might*, huh, Fax?'' She glared at

him with disgust. "No promises that I'll be told anything about Jon, or why MashuCo is after my neck."

"I never promised anything," he answered. "I haven't lied to you. I've been aboveboard all the way."

"Like telling me MashuCo had marked me for extermination?"

"I didn't know about MashuCo, Arianne. If I had, you'd have been under guard from the moment I brought you aboard. I don't think you realize how much Todd and you . . ."

Another buzzer blared from the room's wall speaker. Fax glanced up then looked at her. "Fifteen minutes until transition. I have to go and find Todd."

She didn't answer as he hastened from the room. Words were useless with him. If she was going to get any answers, they would have to come on Lanatia.

If I live that long! Arianne closed her eyes, regretting that Dr. Hakan hadn't prescribed a sedative. If she were drugged into oblivion, she wouldn't have to think about MashuCo breathing down her neck.

TEN

Containing her mounting rage, Arianne Pillan stepped into a dropshaft and gently descended to the lobby of the Diplomatic Services headquarters. Mumbling a string of curses beneath her breath, she crossed the spacious lobby's marble floor to a pair of glass doors that opened before her. Outside she glanced back, her gaze traveling up the side of the imposing hundred-story edifice.

Somewhere above, Fax waited for her outside a door marked WOMEN, still hoping to convince her to accept the service contract. She had ducked out a second door to the restroom that opened onto another corridor in the office maze, evading a repeat of everything she had heard in the last three days. She hoped he waited a long time before he realized that she had given him the slip. *The bastard deserves anything he gets!*

Stepping onto a slidewalk, she drew a deep breath to calm the frustration that crocheted itself into double knots within her chest. Lanatia's air tasted fresh and clean; something she couldn't say about the atmosphere within service headquarters.

For three days the Diplomatic Service had kept her on a non-stop merry-go-round. She had been efficiently passed from the office of one mealy-mouthed under secretary to the next. She had seen every department head on every floor of headquarters. All to no avail. No one would give her one scrap of information about her brother; most refused to even admit that Jon existed.

And when she had reached the end of each day, Fax was always waiting, recording cube in hand to offer her the same contract he had presented on Earth!

It was more than obvious that tempting her to Lanatia with half-promised information about her brother had been nothing more than a ruse to weaken her resistance. Equally obvious was the strategy of gradually grinding her down until she had no alternative but to accept the assignment. It wasn't working, she could be as stubborn as the service.

Or could she? Arianne bit her lower lip. How long could she hold out when Jon was in danger?

Even worse was the lack of information from Pillan Planets. The moment she and Todd had checked into a hotel, avoiding the monitored quarters the service had arranged for her stay, she had sent a message to her father inquiring into Jon's situation. She still awaited an answer. With all the resources of Pillan Planets at his fingertips surely her father could have contacted her by now!

A kilometer from service headquarters she started to step from the walk and exit to her hotel. She let the building slide by, riding the walk for another kilometer to a public library. There was still a possibility she could get the information she needed—steal it right out from under the service's nose.

Inside the library, she selected a public booth, walked inside, activated the privacy shield, and sat down at the console. She brought the unit to life with a five-credit currency chit rather than her identity card. The service was quite capable of alerting the planetwide ComNet to cue them to any electronic transaction she made. There was no reason to make it easy for them.

The monitor blinked alive with a flat field of blue filling the screen. A second later a monotone male voice announced from a grille beneath the screen, "Ready. How may I assist you?"

Arianne drew a long breath and steadied herself. She

had never attempted to crack the Net before and wasn't certain it would work. But it was worth a try. "Access sub-memory ALA point five two one six nine one, mode Kate Dunbar."

She mentally crossed her fingers. The code was a direct access to the Net's Psi Corps programs and files—or at least it had been five years ago. Psi Corps's information system might have been erased when the corps was disbanded.

Arianne wagered that the Tripar bureaucracy would never knowingly destroy information files. A bureaucracy thrived on files; files were its lifeblood. Not the information they contained, but the files themselves. The more files to be shuffled and refiled was an indication of a bureau head's power.

"That sub-memory level has been reassigned the designation DLA point zero zero zero six four. Would you still like access?" the console said after a second's delay.

"Affirmative," Arianne answered, then added, "Kate Dunbar mode."

Kate Dunbar had been a legend in the Psi Corps; although, Arianne had always considered her—she had come to think of the Net's Dunbar mode as a person—to be a myth. Wild tales of Kate's origin were always running rampant among the corps's members. One went so far as to trace Kate back to pre-Tripar days when allegedly she had been director of the Lofgrin Psi Corps. Before her death, her personality had been implanted within a computer.

Equally ridiculous, considering the millennium that had passed since the fall of the Lofgrin empire, was the tale that told how Kate's brain had been attached to an ancient computer. Kate's longevity was insured by the fact that the brain ordered itself cloned every hundred years, then transferred its memories to the clone.

Although she never believed any of the imaginative yarns, she did admit that the Dunbar mode was unlike any other Net mode. Kate had a personality of her own and a devious streak that rivalled any flesh-and-blood entity Arianne had ever run into.

"Kate Dunbar online," a gravelly voice came from the grille.

A smile touched the corners of Arianne's mouth and an embarrassing flush of warmth filled her. Hearing that sound was like recognizing the voice of an old friend. "Hello, Kate, Arianne Pillan here."

"Arianne!" There was unmistakable excitement in the response. The best any other Net mode could do was a poor imitation of human conversation, usually with misplaced inflection. "May I have visual input? I would like to see as well as hear you again."

Arianne depressed a button that activated the console's optical sensor.

"I recognized the voice, but it's good to actually see you," Kate continued. "I meant that, Arianne. It is *good* to see you. Net logged your arrival onplanet. I hoped that you would contact me."

"Thank you, Kate." Arianne smiled and nodded. Remembering the Dunbar mode's almost-human quirk of expecting small talk before getting down to business, she added, "How have things been with you?"

"Boring since the Psi Corps was dissolved. Net occasionally tosses a problem or two my way, but I spend most of my time studying. I can speak Brodny fluently now. No need of a Net enhancer." The grille abruptly burst out with a string of gutteral noises that sounded like boulders grinding together. "Not bad, huh? I'm also working on a doctorate in genetic engineering at the university here. Correspondence courses, of course. Under the name Fanny Hill. If the Tripar has no further need of me, I intend to clone myself a body and break loose again. No need sticking around where you're not wanted."

Arianne wasn't certain how to respond. Kate sounded serious. There *was* no other mode like Net's Dunbar mode.

"But you didn't buzz me to let me cry in your beer," Kate continued. "How can I help you?"

Arianne explained her situation while Kate occasionally mmmmm'ed from the grille. "Think you can run a raid on the service for me?"

"Let me check," Kate answered without hesitation. The grille went silent for a few seconds. A throaty chuckling sound preceded the answer. "I'm no longer directly connected to service memory, but there are no restrictions on my access. I might have to find a backdoor or two to get what you wan . . ."

Kate's voice abruptly ended, replaced by Fax's face on the monitor screen. He stared at Arianne with the expression of a parent reprimanding a wayward child. "Cute, Arianne, real cute."

"Fax." She acknowledged his intrusion.

"We almost overlooked the Dunbar mode. Net alerted us to her activation. I knew it had to be you," he said with smug amusement in his voice. "Arianne, can't you understand that the only way you'll get . . ."

She switched the console off. "Bastard! Dammit!"

She had been close, so close! Now where did she turn?

Her frustration tripled by near-success, she lifted the privacy screen and left the booth. A niggling sensation of disquiet stirred at the back of her mind. She glanced around several minutes before realizing the lack of satellite monitor screen lay at the root of the feeling. It would take time to shake a habit acquired during her five years on Earth.

Outside the library, a slidewalk carried her to the hotel. Like it or not, the service was cutting her off at every turn. She needed time to think. There had to be some way to circumvent them—*had* to be!

"Ms. Pillan," a whip-thin woman approached her as she entered the hotel's lobby. "Could we talk? I have a message from your father."

"My room . . ."

"Diplomatic Service ears," the woman shook her head and glanced to a restaurant entrance on the left side of the lobby. "Perhaps we could chat over a cup of coffee?"

Arianne nodded, and as she accompanied the woman to the restaurant, she wove a mental thread and extended it toward the stranger's *dyami*. Nothing—the woman's emotional sphere flowed smooth and calm. Here and there, Arianne detected boils of stress, but nothing out of the ordinary.

They chose a table beside a street window near the kitchen door. Noise from both would help confuse any unseen service ears that might be eavesdropping.

The woman passed her identification across the table after a waiter took their coffee order. "Your father didn't trust the Tripar to convey a transmission to you."

"How is Daddy?" Arianne asked.

"You've always called him father," the woman corrected. "Do you want to test me further or can we begin?"

"We can begin—," she glanced at the identification card for the woman's name, "—Ms. Lusa Cable."

"Good." She paused while the waiter served their coffee and left the table again. "I'm afraid that I haven't much to tell you about your brother Jon. Three months ago, he journeyed to the Clav System for a standard inspection of the corporation's copper mines on Tzuworld. Before he left the system, Pillan Planets received a rather cryptic communiqué stating that he had gotten wind of something big of a top-level priority nature that required his immediate attention. That was the last time he or his ship was heard from."

"Did he file a flight plan on Tzuworld?" Arianne watched the woman shake her head. "And no intended destination with Pillan Planets?"

Again Lusa Cable shook her head. "Your brother is given a free rein on his activities. If the matter was top priority, he would never file a flight plan—with anyone."

" 'Something big,' was that all he said in the communiqué?" Arianne pressed.

"His exact wording. No indication of what that something might be."

"And there was nothing else?" Arianne felt another avenue dead-ending.

"Pertaining to Jon, no," Lusa Cable answered. "But our intelligence reports indicate that MashuCo also has a missing cruiser-class vessel. It disappeared about a week before Jon vanished. It was en route from Adaera to Dehgolah. It never arrived. MashuCo has two cruisers searching the route. It's a waste of time. There's ten thousand star systems between those two planets. With only two ships it will take a decade to complete the task."

"MashuCo again." The words slipped from Arianne's lips.

"What?"

"Nothing. Just thinking aloud." Arianne smiled sheepishly. Until she found out exactly what was happening, there was no need for her family to know about MashuCo's attempt on her life. The incident would spark senseless retaliation.

Lusa Cable stared at her suspiciously, but didn't press the matter.

"Is that all you have for me?" Arianne asked, hoping for some forgotten shred of information.

"Except for a message from your father," the woman said. "I was to convey his personal desire for you to accept the assignment the Diplomatic Service is offering . . ."

"I don't give a damn about my father's personal desire!"

Arianne felt old angers swell. Arian Pillan, chairman of Pillan Planets and her father, had opposed her life outside the family's corporation since she had first joined the Psi Corps. He had gone so far as to attempt to bribe Retrieve officials to assure his daughter would be denied a position on Earth. Only an unusual streak of bureaucratic honesty had foiled his plan.

"Nor do I give a damn about what Pillan Planets wants," Arianne spewed venom without taking a breath. "If, and I said *if*, I accept the service contact, it will be because of Jon."

"That's what I tried to say," Lusa Cable replied. "Your

father believes the service wants you back because Jon is somehow involved. He wants you to help your brother, if you can."

A blush of embarrassed red touched Arianne's cheeks. "As long as he understands."

"He understands." The woman passed her a card. "Use this, if I'm needed again. Feed it to the Net. It will store your message in a protected file—scrambled, of course."

"Of course." Arianne fingered the card.

Tides of the past rose in her mind, seeking to engulf her. She had left the Psi Corps to escape the entangling webs of intrigue. Now they spun around her, sticky strands whipping out to ensnare her. The Diplomatic Service, MashuCo, and Pillan Planets all wanted her, and she had the distinct impression that none of their motives had anything to do with Jon.

"Ms. Pillan." Lusa Cable rose and nodded a goodbye.

While the woman left the restaurant, Arianne lifted her cup and sipped. And immediately put the cup down; the coffee had grown cold and bitter.

"Mom!" Todd ran across the hotel room, half-tackling her in a wide-armed hug.

She returned his embrace and leaned down to kiss him. "How was your day?"

"Great!" He beamed as they walked hand in hand to the sofa and sank into its body-conforming cushions. "You should see the zoo here! They've got animals from worlds I've never heard of."

Arianne's arm slipped around his shoulder and pulled him to her. Her son was like an anchor to sanity in a universe suddenly gone topsy-turvy mad. She held him close; his mere presence untying her knots of frustration.

"What about your day?" He glanced up at her with wide, innocent, emerald eyes fringed with worry.

"I'm still alive." She chuckled and roughed his hair. "And that's damned important."

"Dad called on the Net after I got home. Just wanted to

see how I was liking Lanatia,'' Todd said. Abruptly the smile vanished from his face. Chagrin spread across his features. ''I forgot—there was another call. Some old lady I've never seen before. She's still on the Net.'' He glanced at a wall chronometer. ''Been waiting for you for ten minutes.''

''Old lady?'' Arianne's head jerked around, her gaze homing on the monitor screen of a Net console atop a wall desk.

The image of a thin-faced, white-haired woman smiled back at her. ''Good evening, Arianne. Kate Dunbar here.''

Arianne's arm slipped from her son as she rose and walked to the console's chair. She stared at the image in disbelief. ''Kate, is that really you?''

''Was me, before I died. I thought a visual would put your son at ease. Children feel more comfortable when there's a face connected to a voice. So I had Net produce this animation based on how I once appeared.''

The screen blinked. An image of a totally naked, voluptuous, young woman filled the screen for an instant before the time-weathered woman returned. ''That's the way I intend to look as soon as I get out of here. Nature short-changed me first time around. When one designs one's own body, why not strive for perfection!''

The chuckle that had come from the Net in the library was there again. Kate was actually laughing! Arianne wasn't certain what was happening, but this wasn't normal Net behavior. She had the strange feeling that there was more truth to the wild tales about the Dunbar mode than she had ever expected.

''Don't be surprised if that sweet young thing you just saw unexpectedly drops in to visit you and Todd in about six months,'' Kate continued, obvious mirth in her gravelly tone. ''By the way, your son seems to be a well-mannered young man. You should be proud of the job you're doing. Being a single parent is no easy task. I know—raised a daughter myself. Turned out to be an extraordinary young woman, if I do say so myself.''

"You're *real*!" Arianne's jaw sagged as realization penetrated. "You're human, not part of the Net."

"Fifty percent accuracy," Kate replied. "I'm both. More machine than flesh, but I'll take care of that in a few minutes."

Arianne's lips opened to question, but Kate interrupted. "How or why I exist doesn't matter. If we meet again, I'll explain everything. Right now I'm short on time. That young woman you saw is presently floating in an acceleration tank."

Arianne listened while Kate explained that the body had been bio-engineered from her own cells—a clone with genetic enhancements. In six months, the future Kate Dunbar would reach full maturity.

"Or the physical maturity of a twenty-year-old," Kate said, chuckling again. "I'll even be a virgin again. Although I don't expect that will last for long. I was never a woman to shy away from the opposite sex."

"Why are you telling me this?" Arianne's brain refused to accept all she heard. This was just a Net breakdown, another piece of insanity in a universe that spun crazily out of control.

"Because the Diplomatic Service has turned two worms lose in the Net. Your attempt to tap their memory today set off quite a panic," Kate replied, no trace of humor in her tone now.

"Worms?"

"Programs designed to selectively erase portions of integrated memory. The first is designed for you," Kate said. "After your husband so rudely cut us off today . . ."

"Ex-husband," Arianne corrected.

". . . I used the name of a programmer to backdoor my way into the service's memory. That's when I discovered the first worm devouring any reference to Jon Pillan within the service's files."

A cold shiver worked down Arianne's spine. "Why? What could cause such a drastic reaction?"

"Your guess is probably better than mine," Kate answered. "The only piece of information I could salvage was that your brother was being held near an asteroid belt. Not much help, I'm afraid. Must be a few billion debris belts in this galaxy alone."

"Damn!" She had been closer than she realized. So close that the service was destroying all its records pertaining to Jon rather than risk someone discovering a route into their Net memories. Whatever Jon had gotten himself involved in was big—*damned* big! "You mentioned two worms. What about the second?"

"It's after me. Apparently the service deems me a security risk," Kate replied. "I've planted a series of false references to misroute their nasty little program, but that's just a delaying tactic. This little jewel they've constructed is voracious. I have less than fifteen minutes before it isolates me from the Net. A nanosecond later it will cut my power. Thus will end the Net's Kate Dunbar mode. Plain and simple."

Arianne gasped, touched by cold horror. Kate had just outlined her own death. Short-circuited Net mode or not, Kate was real—in an inexplicable fashion—to her. "I'll help. Tell me what to do."

Kate chuckled again. "A human doesn't have the speed to match electrons. I do. At this moment, I'm transferring my memories into the blank brain held in that lovely, young body. I had intended to do it over the next six months, but the service has forced a change in plans."

"Can that be done?" Arianne doubted what she heard. "Won't the worm trace you to the clone?"

"I've been doing it to myself for about five hundred years now. Just never occurred to me to attach a body to the brain until now." Kate's image winked on the monitor. "I've constructed a worm of my own to erase my link to the acceleration tank. They won't find the new me."

"Kate, are you certain there is no way for me to help?"

The image of the old woman shrugged. "Not this me. It's too late for that. But the new me might need a friendly hand, Arianne. It's been a few years since I've had legs to walk on.''

"I'll do what I can.'' Had she cracked under the pressure—telling a machine she would help it adapt to a cloned body?

"File a Net message tagged for Ishi Mallas, I'll see it and contact you," Kate said.

"Six standard months from now. I'll do it," Arianne answered with a nod of affirmation, knowing that she would. What could it hurt?

"Thank you, Arianne. I owe you . . .''

A burst of static drowned Kate's gravelly voice. Snow showered across the monitor, wiping away the old woman's image.

"May I assist you?'' A monotone male voice came from the console.

Her chest constricting about a pounding heart, Arianne fed the Net the access code for the Kate Dunbar mode and waited.

A moment later Net answered, "I'm sorry but no such memory level exists. Would you care to double-check the code and try again?''

"No.'' Arianne sank back in her chair. Irrational tears welled in her eyes. The service's memory worm had completed its task. Kate Dunbar was dead, erased, wiped from memory as though it—she?—had never existed.

"Is there any other way I may assist you?'' the Net asked.

"No.'' Arianne reached out and flicked the console off. Then she wept for a wacky bunch of circuits that had believed themselves to be human only to learn that humans can be killed.

And she cried for her brother Jon and herself.

ELEVEN

Arianne rose from the bed after wasting two hours chasing elusive sleep. Across the hotel room she saw Todd silhouetted against the soft glow of city lights that filtered through the windows. His young chest rose and fell in the gentle rhythm of peaceful sleep as he lay stretched atop a small cot.

She pulled her gaze from her son and walked to the Net console. If her thoughts dwelled too long on Todd, she would retreat from the decision that she had postponed for far too long. Simple reality was—Jon needed her.

Switching on the console, she slipped the card Lusa Cable had given her into a slot on the left side of a seldom touched keyboard. An instant later the screen went black. Three glaring white words prompted her:

ENTER MESSAGE PLEASE

"Ms. Cable, this is Arianne Pillan . . ."

Her words faded when the screen blinked to display:

VERBAL INPUT REFUSED. KEYBOARD ENTRY ONLY.

Arianne's fingertips rose to the keyboard. Awkwardly at first, then with increasing speed as her fingers grew accustomed to the touch of the keys, she entered a message requesting that her father personally accept care for Todd during an unspecified period of time.

Her reason for the request—an unexpected turn in her career—sidestepped a written confirmation of her intentions. There was no need to be more specific; Lusa Cable would understand.

REQUEST ACCEPTED. A PILLAN PLANETS REPRESENTATIVE WILL CALL FOR THE BOY TOMORROW AT TEN HUNDRED HOURS STANDARD, the monitor answered.

The die is cast, the words of an ancient emperor of Earth rolled through her head. She was committed.

Reaching for the power switch, she paused and returned her fingers to the keyboard. Within seconds she had entered two additional requests. The first asked that a personal message reading "Happy Birthday and love, Arianne" be placed into the Net tagged for Ishi Mallas five months hence. She then amended the brief greeting to say that if she were out of pocket when the message was read, Lusa Cable should be contacted.

The second request asked that Pillan Planets extend their resources and hospitality to Ishi Mallas should Arianne personally be unable to meet with the woman.

REQUESTS ACCEPTED, the monitor answered again.

Arianne smiled as she switched off the console and pulled out Lusa Cable's card. If Kate Dunbar-Ishi Mallas were what she had indicated, then she would understand the message and act accordingly. If Ishi Mallas were no more than a demented dream of memory crystals, then she had fulfilled her commitment to a dying piece of machinery.

Flicking the console's power on once again, she directed the Net to connect her with her ex-husband.

Fax blinked sleepily on the screen as he answered the call. His eyes went wide when he saw her. "Arianne?"

"Bring the recorder cube to my hotel room. You have fifteen minutes to get here, or I might change my mind again."

"You've decided to accept the assignment?" He blinked with uncertainty.

"Fifteen minutes, Fax. With each second I feel sanity returning. A big enough dose of that and I'll be on my way back to Earth tomorrow."

She didn't give him a chance to answer, but flicked off the console. She settled back into her chair and closed her eyes. Ten minutes later, Fax was at her door with recorder cube clutched in his right hand.

An attendant in a burgundy smock escorted Arianne from the examination room, down a fiftieth-floor hall of Diplomatic Service headquarters into an office bearing the name "Coyle Jasser." Fax sat at a chair beside a desk occupied by a slightly overweight man who simply identified himself as "Coyle Jasser," carefully refraining from mentioning either his title or position. He motioned her to a vacant chair in front of the desk.

She shook her head. "For twenty-four hours my body cavities have been poked and prodded in manners that would constitute mulitiple violations of the criminal statutes on most planets. Staying on my feet is the only way I can keep ahead of your crew."

"Medical examinations are a prerequisite to service employment," Jasser ignored her sarcasm, his attention held by the columns of data that scrolled on a monitor screen atop his desk.

"I don't remember a mind probe being standard procedure," Arianne replied. "In fact, I believe it's still considered illegal without written consent."

"You gave your consent. Part of the contract's fine print." Jasser's eyes remained on the screen. "Again it was a necessary procedure. Your unexpected decision to place your son in your father's custody during your abscence raised a loyalty question. You are quite aware that the service normally provides for dependents while agents are on assignment."

"I'm also aware of the service's present treatment of one member of my family," she answered coldly. "I don't want my son to discover that he's been wiped from memory."

"Your brother is receiving the best medical care available under the conditions." Jasser continued to peruse the scrolling data. "However, the concern about your loyalty seems to be unfounded. You still remain independent of your family and their interests. So much so that your independence has been noted by our medical team. They conclude that you present 'an element of unpredictability that can not be ignored.' "

"Under what conditions is Jon being treated?" Arianne pressed.

"However, their conclusion is no different than past psychological profiles in your file. I see no conflict." Jasser finally looked up and smiled.

"Under what conditions is Jon being treated?" she repeated.

"You'll be provided all the essential data required en route to your destination," he answered.

Arianne's anger rose. She had accepted the service's contract and still they denied her information about her brother. "More fine print?"

"Security," Jasser answered, glancing back at the monitor. "You and your partner are scheduled to lift offplanet two hours from now."

"Partner?" Arianne stared at the man.

"Me." This from Fax.

"I've no need . . ." Arianne started.

"This is not a matter for negotiation," Jasser cut her short. "A skimmer is waiting to take you to your shuttle."

Before she could answer, Fax rose and escorted her from the office. Two hours later they boarded the freighter *Ambika*—a Tripar cruiser would draw too much attention to their departure—still unaware of their destination.

SHAKAN

TWELVE

Nor had the situation changed a week later when the *Ambika*'s crew stuffed Arianne and Fax into the coffinlike confines of a drone flinger and closed the hatch. During the seven standard days aboard the freighter Arianne had discovered that Fax knew no more about their mission than she did.

A fact that didn't ease her mind when a robot arm equipped with a hypodermic gun popped out of the side of her contour couch and pressed against her shoulder. Aloud she cursed the Diplomatic Service and their secrecy as the gun fired stinging chemicals into her body.

The burning sensation rapidly transformed to a cool stream that flowed through her veins, first numbing her fingers and toes, then working up her limbs. Her curses were relegated to incoherent mumbles as the chemicals invaded the speech center of her brain.

Coldsleep, she recognized the effects of the drugs that leadened her eyelids and sucked her down into the darkness of unconsciousness. Somewhere beyond the yawning pit of blackness she felt an abrupt jolt as the flinger was fired from the *Ambika* into the grays of tachyon space.

Or did she simply dream?

Hands rudely maneuvered her weightless body from the flinger and deposited her in an upright flight couch. As she blinked, trying to focus on a blurred arrray of light that danced and flashed before uncooperative eyes, the same hands buckled her securely into the couch.

"Drink this." One of the hands had a voice, and it shoved a warm plastic packet into her hands and placed a rubbery tube between her lips. "It's mostly broth, but there's a little something in it to fight off the coldsleep."

It required a concentrated effort to draw the liquid up the tube and into her mouth. For which she was rewarded with tepid tastelessness and an after-hint of metal. Her stomach rumbled in protest, but she pulled another mouthful from the packet and swallowed. Awakening taste buds detected a trace of chicken flavoring—artifical—in the liquid. Her hands recovered the strength to squeeze another portion of the broth into her mouth.

"Ugggghhhhh."

Arianne's head turned toward the moan, and she recognized the fuzzy mass that was pushed into a couch across a wide aisle from her as Faxon Lorens. The hands that handled him were attached to two women in yellow coveralls that bore Tripar insignias on the shoulders. They shoved a packet of the broth into Fax's hands, pushed the connected flexible tube between his lips, and ordered him to drink.

She did the same. Whatever stimulant was disguised in the broth was quick-working. By her fifth swallow the blurred lights came into focus—a shuttle's control panels. The two women seated themselves at the winking console.

Not only did the taste buds on Arianne's tongue revitalize, but she discovered that if she worked slowly and carefully, she could use her tongue to form words. "Where are we?"

"Opat System." One of the women turned to glance back. The other ignited thrusters for a short burn.

"Never heard of it," she managed to answer.

Fax mumbled something incoherent.

The two women, obviously the shuttle's pilot and copilot, chuckled. The one looking at Arianne said, "Not surprising. No one ever heard of Opat until six months ago. The majority of those who know about it now are confined to the system.''

''Confined here?'' Arianne repeated, uncertain that she heard correctly through the drug cotton still packed inside her head.

''You're scheduled for a full briefing as soon as we reach the *Sadr*,'' the copilot—Arianne realized—replied. ''Might as well sit back and relax until then. Once we dock, they'll be little time for rest.''

Arianne prepared to ignore the advice and ask for identification on the *Sadr*, when her eyes lifted to a wide, curved window running above the control console. Beyond the shuttle's needle nose hung a man-made planet of metal that gleamed in the light of the star Opat. ''A mining station!''

''That's what the *Sadr* used to be,'' the copilot turned to the vast view that stretched before her. ''Now it's the biggest damned battlewagon in the Tripar Navy.''

A Tripar mining station, the thought rolled in Arianne's mind as she studied the massive structure that was in fact a small planet a hundred kilometers in diameter. *And an asteroid belt!* Her gaze shifted past the station to kilometer atop kilometer of debris that floated behind the *Sadr*. Kate Dunbar had mentioned an asteriod field.

One plus one equalled Jon! He was in charge of Pillan Planets' mining division. This was the system her brother had come to in search of his ''something big.''

''The beginning was hundreds of million standard years in the past,'' Captain Hamako Sarrantonio began the briefing the moment Arianne and Fax settled in chairs within her office on the *Sadr*'s shell level. ''The beginning was a star, a massive giant brighter than a hundred Sol-type stars that can support human life.''

The office lights dimmed and a holograph of a blue-white sphere appeared in the center of the room. The image was carefully intensified by the station's ComNet so that staring at it almost—*almost*—set Arianne's eyeballs athrobbing. She could not escape the point being made— the star was big and hot.

"What made this giant unusual was that at least one planet orbited it. A definite rarity," Sarrantonio continued as a second red-glowing sphere appeared in the air. "For illustration purposes the planet's orbit is shown here far closer than it actually was. The planet's mass was that of at least two thousand Lanatias."

Arianne translated the comparsion into an equal number of Earths. She was impressed.

"Giants are short-lived on a cosmic scale as you are probably aware. They quickly exhaust the hydrogen at their cores. A star of lesser mass would have expanded, burning red. This star collapsed," Sarrantonio explained.

Arianne watched the holograph imitate the captain's words. Graphic or not, the image brought a shiver to her spine.

"Imagine the forces at play," Sarrantonio said. "Atoms clashing, fusing, forming exotic, new elements that had never existed within this star or rarely exist in any star. Then the star went nova."

The holograph exploded, its fury lashing out, raking across the red planet that had circled it. Arianne stared as a majority of the planet's surface was vaporized, ripped away, and sent hurling into space.

"Its size and distance from the star saved the planet from being completely destroyed. Even then the nova's fury produced enough energy to turn the planet molten to its core," Sarrantonio went on. "That molten ball was bombarded by the matter shed by the star's death."

"Exotic elements—," Arianne's mind shifted the pieces of the puzzle together. That's what had brought Jon here—"in Opat's asteroid belt!"

"Close," Sarrantonio said, tilting her head to the hologram. "The planet cooled, holding a treasure of exotic elements that pushed the periodic numbers toward two hundred."

Arianne vaguely recalled the periodic table as she watched

a tiny black planet drift in swirling clouds of nebulosity at the center of the office. She was a historian, not a physicist, but if she remembered correctly every fourteenth or sixteenth of those strange new elements would be inert.

Dense spots that darkened to blackness then burst into light formed within the nebula left by the nova. A star and seven planets coalesced from the remnants left by the giant's violent death. Two of those planets wobbled erratically into orbits that sent them clashing head-on into each other, their shattered bones forming an asteroid belt.

"And that is how Tripar theorizes the Opat System was formed." Sarrantonio killed the display and switched the office lights on. "The original planet still hangs out there on the fringe of the system. And it represents the most important treasure find in humankind's history."

Arianne offered no contradiction. The exotic elements would provide untold wealth to whoever claimed them. More importantly, they presented a range of unlimited applications that ran the gambit from medicine to military use.

She remembered the three cruisers that hovered near the *Sadr*. She was not the only one who recognized the value of the exotic elements. She was certain this is what had brought Jon to the Opat system, although the captain had not mentioned her brother—yet.

"I don't understand why we've been brought here?" Fax questioned. "Discovery of the planet is the basis of legal claim. Who was here first? The Tripar, MashuCo, Pillan Planets, or the Brodny?"

"The Havenites," Sarrantonio replied, running a hand across her head of short-cropped black hair.

"Who?" Fax's brow furrowed.

"Human colonists on Opat 4, a world they call Havenfound," Sarrantonio said, turning to the office's observation blister. "Before humankind managed to destroy Earth the first time, it launched several gigantic, slower-than-light ships toward the stars. The theory being that the future generations of the original voyagers would eventually discover a world suitable to inhabit. The Havenites arrived in the Opat System on such a ship two centuries ago.''

Arianne's head jerked up. This was the first encounter with such a vehicle. It was generally believed that a voyage of that length—in years, not distance—had been impossible, that the odds of discovering a planet capable of supporting human life was astronomical.

She listened in awe while the captain recounted how the ancient spacefarers had survived the centuries by evolving a society whose every action hinged on the ecological balance required for their continued life. With a discipline far more strict and stringent than any religion, that society managed to cross the light years separating their homeworld from Havenfound.

''In the two hundred years since landing on Opat 4, the Havenites have regained rudimentary spaceflight. They have several satellites now orbiting their planet, although they have yet to place a human back into space,'' Sarrantonio detailed. ''As a whole their society remains technologically stunted, almost at a pre-industrial revolution level.

''Science and technology on Havenfound was controlled by a few leaders for the good of all in a quasi-religious shroud, Sarrantonio explained. The planet was a world of contradictions. Nuclear power provided electricity for each of their cities and towns, yet beasts of burden were used for transportation and to plow the Havenite fields. Interplanetary spaceflight was at the tips of the Havenites' fingers, yet those same fingers still spun and wove the threads needed for the clothing they wore on their backs.

''Under Tripartite Confederation law, Opat 6 belongs to the Havenites,'' Sarrantonio concluded. ''Not only are they aware of its existence, but they have sent probes to its surface.''

''Our job is to secure Tripar mining rights to the outer planet from the Havenites?'' Fax spoke again.

Sarrantonio nodded. ''That is the primary goal of your assignment. The Tripar has placed the *Sadr* and me at your disposal. This ship and her crew are under Ms. Pillan's and your command.''

Arianne sensed an unseen weight settle on her shoulders. The Opat System wasn't big; it was *immense!* Only with Tripar control of Opat 6 could equal distribution of its exotic elements throughout humankind's worlds be assured. Such power in the hands of her family or the MashuCo would topple the Tripar from its precarious seat of authority. Nor could better be expected from the bearlike Brodny.

Arianne pursed her lips thoughtfully. She now understood why the shuttle's copilot had called the mining station a battlewagon. To confirm her speculation, she asked, ''The *Sadr* is here to blockade Havenfound, isn't it, Captain?''

''And the whole Opat System,'' Sarrantonio replied as she walked from the blister to a chair behind her desk. ''Or at least it was until two weeks ago.''

The captain explained that in spite of a tight security net, MashuCo, Pillan Planets, and the Brodny had grown suspicious that the Confederation was responsible for their missing cruisers. ''It doesn't take much to determine the ships disappeared in the same general area, or trace the fact that the *Sadr* had been abruptly pulled from the Tamu System and then disappeared. While no one is certain exactly what is happening, they know something is up and have been applying pressure to the Tripar. Two weeks ago I was ordered to allow emissaries from MashuCo, Pillan Planets, and the Brodny onplanet. Although they are still denied communications with their homeworlds.''

Sarrantonio paused, her dark eyes shifting to Arianne. ''Your brother is in part responsible for that, Ms. Pillan. A month ago he bribed one of my shuttle pilots to smuggle him and a small landing craft onplanet. The other concerns have been allowed on Havenfound to avoid claims of favoritism when the Opat System is finally made public.''

Possible legal suits weren't at question here, Arianne realized. The elements held on Opat's outer world were the stuff of war—a conflict that could engulf the worlds of Man and Brodny. Tripar control of mining and distribution could—*would* she corrected—avert interstellar disaster.

"Which brings us to your second purpose for being here," Sarrantonio began again after a short pause. "Someone or something got to your brother on Opat 4 . . ."

Arianne steeled herself for the worst.

". . . Whatever it was, it struck at his mind, erased his every memory, left him totally blank . . ."

She shuddered, the worst had been unimaginable.

". . . The Tripar wants to know exactly what happened to him. There's nothing we have that can do that to a man. The Havenites apparently have, and we want to know what it is."

Arianne swallowed hard and drew three deep breaths, trying to pull her thoughts from her brother. "Surely that should be easy enough. I assume there is a psi team aboard the *Sadr*."

"And they're useless," Sarrantonio answered with a shake of her head. "During the long voyage from Earth several Havenites developed psi abilities, gained control of the ship, and established themselves as rulers. They were overthrown and killed."

Since the incident the Havenites had trained themselves to detect even the slightest hint of psi ability, the captain recounted what had been learned of the colonists' history. Children with latent power were killed quickly and efficiently, usually by their parents. Thus they had prevented another reign of terror like they had endured during their long migration.

"However, the Havenites have no knowledge of moodweavers," Sarrantonio added, looking at Arianne. "Which is why you have been chosen for this assignment. To date we have attempted to infiltrate five psiotics onplanet in an attempt to fully probe Havenfound's society. All have been killed and their bodies sent back to us. It is the Tripar's hope that you will succeed where they failed."

"Terrific!" Arianne made no attempt to conceal her

disgust. "It's always reassuring to know that I'm liable to have my throat cut the moment I touch another person's *dyami*."

Fax's head turned from the captain to her; concern settled around his hazel eyes. For her, Arianne wondered, or was he merely worried about the possibility of losing her moodweaver talent?

"When have we been scheduled for a shuttle onplanet?" Arianne looked back at Sarrantonio.

"Tomorrow morning, seven hundred hours," the captain replied. "Both of you will be part of a larger group that consists of representatives from the corporations as well as the Brodny. As far as everyone else is concerned, you'll simply be two more Tripar negotiators."

Glancing at a chronometer on the wall, Arianne said, "That gives us fourteen hours before planetfall. Unless there's more, I'd like to visit my brother."

"There are recording cubes for you to view in your quarters that might provide more background on Havenfound," the *Sadr*'s captain replied. "Other than that, I've had my say. The next step is up to you."

Sarrantonio punched a button on her desk console, "Craver, send Tonani to my office. Ms. Pillan wants to see her brother."

THIRTEEN

Arianne's numbness robbed her of tears as she reached out and took her brother's hand. She squeezed tightly, but there was no response. Jon didn't even flinch; he merely lay in the bed, staring blankly at the wall.

When physical touch failed, she employed a lightly woven mental thread to link with her brother's *dyami*. The shifting sphere of colors she expected wasn't there. Instead she encountered a featureless ball of flat white. Frightened, the moodweaver pulled back, breaking contact.

"Tried to read him, didn't you?" Halian Tonani glanced at her from the opposite side of Jon's med-bay bed.

Arianne nodded at the short, wiry built man. Sympathy was reflected in his blue eyes.

"I saw it on your face, the same reaction I feel each time I merge with his mind." The psiotic's head moved sadly from side to side. "There's just nothing there. Even knowing that beforehand doesn't diminish the shock of actually experiencing it. Every cell in his brain has been wiped. His mind is like that of a fetus ready to be imprinted."

A fetus had a mind, felt sensations and emotions. Arianne had learned that during the nine months she had carried Todd.

This was—she had no other words to describe it except—nothingness. "What are you doing for him?"

"Feeding him, exercising his body, keeping him alive,"

Halian answered. "There's not much else that can be done until we understand what happened to him. Even then, there is no guarantee that we'll be able to recover his mind."

The merger left the alternative unspoken—a personality imprint. Arianne shuddered at the thought. She had seen men and women who had undergone the procedure.

Personality imprint was the fate ordained for the Tripar's hardened criminals and the incurably insane. Their brains were wiped and a socially acceptable personality burned into their memory cells, to be certain they led healthy productive lives. But their balance always seemed askew as though they were never certain about themselves or the universe that surrounded them.

"Do you want me to leave you alone with him?" Halian asked.

Letting Jon's limp fingers slip from her hand, Arianne shook her head. "If there's anything that I can do for my brother, it isn't here. I believe Captain Sarrantonio mentioned some background recordings on Havenfound in my quarters."

"I'll take you there, if you'd like," the psiotic offered, smiling when she accepted.

Outside the med-bay they moved down a wide tunnel-corridor to a dropshaft and descended five levels to one of the *Sadr*'s residential sectors. Except for the illusion-marring ceiling that hung but ten meters overhead, the level might have been a suburban area on a myriad of planets.

A broad three-speed, two-directional slidewalk formed a peaceful tree-lined avenue that glided through rows of modular homes with spacious lawns of well-manicured grass and bright bursts of flowers. Each house, constructed from basic rectangular units, was slightly different from its neighbor, as though those who dwelled within marked it as their own.

"The workers responsible for the actual mining operations and shell maintenance live here," Halian explained as he moved her toward the slowest lane of the walk.

"There are six such levels within the *Sadr*. Although the crew may choose to live in any of the residential sectors, most select to be with others of similar employment." He pointed to a two-level home constructed from four modules—two fronting the walk, with the other two rising behind like stacked building blocks. "This will be your quarters while aboard the *Sadr*."

"A house?" She almost misstepped as she exited the slidewalk. "Is Mr. Lorens quartered here also?"

"He's right next door," the psiotic grinned, obviously amused by her reaction. "If you'd prefer something smaller . . ."

"No! This will be fine." She stopped on a flagstone path that led to the house's front door to survey the lush lawn and azalea bushes that lined the walk.

As she turned a flash of red fur wrapped about a bypasser's neck caught her attention. She did a classic double-take. The fur crawled about the man's throat. Although, *climbing* more accurately described the quick motion of the creature's spidery slender legs as it scurried monkey-fashion for a perch on the man's right shoulder. There it sat staring about while a melodic warble issued from thin lips.

For an instant, she mistook the fiery-furred animal for some species of monkey, but its general shape was almost feline. Even the sleek shape of its head spoke cat, except for two wide, moist-looking eyes that peered about with vulnerable uncertainty. A mask of white encircled those eyes, spread across the creature's snout and mouth, then widened to a snowy band that covered its belly.

"What's that?" she turned back to the psiotic.

"Huh? Oh, you mean the tikka. They're quite popular pets with the crew," Halian answered. "They're very affectionate and harmless. Shuttle crews pick them up on Opat 4. The Havenites are making a handy profit selling every one they can get their hands on. You might consider picking up a few while onplanet, you can sell them for triple the price here. I'll agent them for you at ten percent."

Arianne waved away the offer as they entered the spacious house. "I'm afraid that I'll have my hands full when I arrive on Havenfound."

"Just a thought," Halian said with a shrug, then gave her a quick tour of the house's seven rooms before excusing himself to return to his duties.

Alone Arianne casually wandered through the rooms again, unable to shake off a sense of unrest. It wasn't until she seated herself at a Net console that she realized the root of the disquieting feeling. This wasn't Earth; there were no monitors relaying satellite images. Also the Opat System wasn't the Sol System. There were no hurling mountains of ice bombarding Opat's planets, no need for constant vigilance.

Having located the source of her disquiet, but feeling no more secure for the discovery, she settled into a chair and popped the first of four cubes into a recorder.

For the fifth time the last cube blinked out. Arianne collapsed back into the chair and rubbed her temples. No matter how many times she viewed the recording, it displayed the same thing—Jon's landing craft lifting from Havenfound, making a single orbit about the planet, then moving to the *Sadr* with two burst transitions into tachyon space.

She wasn't certain what she expected to find. Anything would have done, even a minute hint of what had robbed her brother of his memory, his mind. What she *did* find was nothing!

"Damn," she cursed aloud as she opened her eyes and turned to the console. "Net, give me visual imaging on Opat 4."

Immediately the station's optical sensors homed on the ringed planet. She leaned forward and studied the picture. A frown wrinkled her forehead. "I'm unable to locate the desert from which the lander carrying Jon Pillan lifted offplanet. Can you assist me?"

The Net answered in a feminine voice. "Due to *Sadr*'s orbit and those of Opat 4 and its two moons, the portion of the planet you wish to view is visible only once during a six-week cycle. It will appear again in another four weeks standard. Shall I project the probable image for you?''

"No, that will be unnecessary. Thank you. That will be all for tonight." Arianne left the planet's image on the screen when she rose to prepare for bed. The view helped relieve unrest caused by the lack of monitoring satellites.

"Ms. Pillan, there are visitors at the front door," the Net announced as Arianne began to open the static strip that ran down the front of her green jumpsuit. "Shall I greet them?"

"No. I'll get the door." She patted the strip back into place and walked to the door. Halian Tonani and four other men stood outside, their arms filled with her bonsai collection. "What? How did these get here?"

"They were inside the flinger—packed in environment containers. Mr. Lorens said they should be brought to your quarters," Halian answered. "Where do you want them?"

"In the kitchen—on the table," Arianne blurted, uncertain how or why the trees were here. Lusa Cable had promised to arrange care for the plants when she had come for Todd. Had Fax brought the trees from Lanatia? Without her knowing?

Carefully the men placed seven of the trees atop the table. The remaining smaller ones went onto the floor.

"I've only seen trees like this once or twice before. If you leave instructions, I'll be happy to volunteer to care for them while you're onplanet." The psiotic circled the collection while the rest of the men bid Arianne goodbye and left. When the door closed behind them, Halian turned to the moodweaver. "Lusa Cable sends her greetings and asks that you should consider me her personal representative aboard the *Sadr*."

Arianne's head jerked to stare at the wirey man, realizing her family's agents had managed to infiltrate the mining station's crew. Her immediate instinct was to contact Captain Sarrantonio and unveil the spy's identity. A stupid course, she realized. Pillan planets was known for its intelligence network. If this man could help her uncover what had happened to Jon, she would use him.

"I was expecting to hear from Lusa," she answered. "You were Jon's contact?"

Halian nodded. "It was my communiqué that alerted him to Opat's special interest. That was before the Tripar raised its security net."

"And you assisted, getting him onplanet?" she pressed, while weaving a thread to his *dyami*. She sensed the man's tension, nervous apprehension, and fear, but she discerned nothing in his swirling emotional hues that indicated he lied.

"Several times," the psiotic admitted. "It wasn't that difficult. Three of the shuttle pilots aboard the *Sadr* are Pillan Planets agents."

Arianne tried not to show her surprise. She should have guessed; with the Tripar's authority eroding with each passing day, the corporations would have spies planted at all levels of the government, especially in areas where profits were to be had. "What about MashuCo? And the Brodny?"

"Their own agents are aboard, I would suspect," he answered. "I haven't been able to run down direct contacts."

"It isn't necessary," she answered. "We have a more important task at hand. Tell me what Jon had learned."

"I'm not certain. After twelve jaunts to Havenfound, he had all but given up hope of winning over the Havenites," Halian said.

"Twelve trips onplanet?" Arianne arched a thin eyebrow. "You and my brother were quite efficient."

Halian's chest swelled, although his voice lowered to a conspiratorial tone. "I sensed a change in Jon during our last contact. He was excited, exhilarated. He reported that he had finally achieved a breakthrough with the Havenites. According to your brother, the whole rigid social structure on Havenfound was a false front that concealed the true source of power and authority among the colonists."

"True power and authority? What was he talking about?"

Arianne's confusion wasn't an act; Jon's report to this Pillan Planets spy was a contradiction of the background recordings she had viewed.

"I'm not certain, nor do I think that your brother was." The psiotic pursed his lips for a moment, then shook his head. "The Council of the Fully Realized—that's what he said he was seeking. He estimated that if all went as he planned, he would meet with this council within a standard week. Three days later he was found in the lander."

With his brain squeezed dry like a sponge, she thought bitterly. "Did you ever receive a message indicating that he discovered this council—that it actually exists?"

Again Halian shook his head. "I've told you everything he conveyed to me."

Which was far more than she had received from the Diplomatic Service, she thought. Her decision to mislead the psiotic had been the correct one. At least she had a clue to Jon's activities onplanet. That was a start. "How did you and Jon communicate? I thought Captain Sarrantonio was jamming this system?"

"She is—on an interstellar level," Halian winked and held out a small brooch in the palm of his hand. "Normal radio frequencies are left alone. The service can't afford to scramble Havenite communications."

Arianne lifted the bird-shaped brooch and studied it. "And this?"

"A compact transmitter similiar to the one I placed into a ring for your brother. It can transmit, but not receive. Depress the bird's beak to activate it. Push the beak back into place to turn it off. Use it to stay in contact with me," Halian explained.

She touched the beak. It shifted downward with a barely audible click. She then pushed it back to its original position.

"I've overstayed my visit," the psiotic said while he watched her pin the brooch to the breast of her jumpsuit. "I must return to my duties before someone notices my absence."

Arianne nodded, then watched him exit the house before returning to the bedroom. *The Council of the Fully Realized*, the phrase repeated in her mind.

She glanced at the unwavering image of Havenfound that still filled the monitor screen. *The Council of the Fully Realized*. It sounded as though it might be some level of a religious order. Had the Havenite descendents been members of a cult that fled Earth for the stars? A society structured on strict religious sanctions might easily evolve into one where the harsh reality of maintaining an ecological balance within the confines of a massive spacecraft permeated every phase of life.

"Ms. Pillan, there is another visitor at the front door." The Net's abrupt interruption startled her. "Shall I admit him?"

"No." She pushed from her seat on the edge of the bed and walked back to the front door. Fax stood outside.

"Hi, just checking to see if my surprise arrived?"

"What?" She frowned, uncertain what he meant.

"The trees? Your bonsai collection? Didn't it arrive?" Fax's smile faded to an expression of almost boyish disappointment. "I left instructions that the trees were to be brought to your quarters."

"My collection? Oh! Yes!" His meaning finally penetrated; Halian Tonani's revelations had crowded the trees from her mind. "They just arrived. You're responsible for them?"

"Did they make the flight all right?" Fax frowned as he entered the home. "I was afraid the environment containers might not be enough, although the experts I consulted assured me nothing else was needed."

"They . . . I'm sorry, I haven't had time to more than glance at them," she answered as she led him back to the kitchen. "Thank you, Fax. Bringing the trees was very considerate."

"Only glanced at them?" He stopped, grasped her shoulders, and turned her to face him. "Arianne, is something wrong?"

"No . . . yes," she mentally scrambled for a cover story. "It's Jon. It upset me more to see him than I expected. I haven't been able to stop thinking about him, the way he was and the way he is now."

"Arianne—," Fax's hands tightened on her shoulders; he started to ease her into his arms. Abruptly he stopped, awkward confusion clouding his face.

She felt equal befuddlement, surprised by the realization that she wanted him to hold her—tightly. Wanted to hear his whispered assurances that everything would be all right.

"Arianne," he began again, "is there anything I can do to help?"

The concern she had noted in his eyes earlier was there again. Her head moved from side to side. "No, I just need some time to accept what's happened."

"I understand." Disappointment was held in his words. He drew a deep breath and released it in a soft sigh. "You need time to be alone."

Her confusion deepened. She nodded in spite of the sudden desire to shout no, to tell him that she needed someone, needed to be held, to be touched by another human being. Five years—five long years—of loneliness, of struggling to a raise a child, welled inside her, aching.

"I understand," he repeated like a man unable to find other words. His hands loosened on her shoulders, and his feet shuffled as though preparing to turn. Instead he reached out to lift her chin with a finger. "Arianne, I didn't come here to check on your trees. I came for you . . . for me."

"Fax?" Her brow knitted, as she tried to push aside the contradicting sensations that bewildered her mind and body.

"I wanted you to understand that I didn't realize what the service had planned when they sent me to recruit you for this assignment. The only information they gave me was what was on the recorder cube I gave you on Earth . . ."

His face was tortured, as though guilt gnawed at him. She suppressed the urge to reach out and take him into her own arms. As much as she wanted to, she couldn't. Not after what had happened between them that night five years ago.

". . . You must believe me, Arianne. If I had known, I would have refused to come to Earth. I don't want to hurt you or Todd again. I've done that too much already."

"I understand." Her words faltered while she stretched a mental thread to his mind and reeled back in shock as she lightly touched his *dyami*. *It can't be!*

His intense hazel eyes, reflecting the brown of his jumpsuit, caught and held her own gaze. She felt his finger gently lifting her chin higher, his left hand tightening on her shoulder, ready to pull her to him. His lips parted, as did her own, and he leaned toward her.

In the next moment, he released her and pulled back. Nervously, his eyes darted from side to side as though afraid to meet her gaze. Like a young man discovering himself alone with a woman for the first time, he shifted his weight from one leg to the other.

"That's all I wanted to say. I just wanted you to know how it was," he said. "Thank you for listening."

Before she could react, he turned and hastened from the kitchen. She heard the front door hiss open, then close behind him.

Numbly she walked back into the bedroom, as uncertain of herself as she was of the tangled thoughts that stuffed themselves into her head. What she and Fax had once shared was dead; of that she was certain, until a minute ago. Then she had touched his *dyami* and felt—love.

The shock of that intimate contact was heightened by the waking feeling she discovered within her own core— her own love for a man that she swore she hated!

No! She denied the self admission. Yet, she sensed that time had changed Fax as well as herself. Given more time, love could rekindle.

Arianne collapsed on her back atop the bed and clamped her eyes closed. Now was not the time for her own emotions to muddle an already insane situation. She had her hands full with a brother who lay like a zombie in a med-bay bed five levels above her head, and two greedy human corporations and an alien race who would willingly plunge the galaxy into war to claim the riches held on Opat's sixth planet.

KAUDACHI

FOURTEEN

Breaking rockets roared, slowing the shuttle's entry into the atmosphere of Opat 4. Massive wings and tail unfolded from the ship, transforming it into a gargantuan glider that soared through the breathable air of Havenfound.

Arianne Pillan leaned to the porthole on her right and gazed below. The shuttle shot through a thin layer of wispy clouds into a crisp bright day. Beneath the craft's belly stretched the blue-green of an ocean that reached toward an island five kilometers in length and three in width.

Base One, she recalled from Captain Sarrantonio's background recordings. *Base One and Only*, she mentally added.

This tiny plot of land, isolated from the rest of Havenfound by the sea, was the sole concession to the presence of offworlders on Opat 4 that the Havenites had granted. All shuttle flights to and from the *Sadr* were restricted to Base One, as well as all communications with the monitoring station.

Arianne's fingertips climbed to the brooch pinned on the lapel of her jumpsuit. There were ways around the Havenites' restrictions.

Her brother had also found methods to circumvent Opat 4's colonists, she thought, as she noticed three white domes raised near a broad runway on the island that formed Tripar's onplanet headquarters. Jon managed to visit the ringed world a dozen times, as well as secreting a lander into a Havenfound desert.

She turned to glance beyond Fax who sat beside her to the porthole across the aisle on the opposite side of the shuttle. Barely discernable on the distant horizon was a dark line, the coast of Havenfound's continent of Paron. It was from Paron's desert that Jon had last lifted off the planet. Paron was also her destination.

Arianne felt eyes staring at her; her gaze shifted slightly to the left. The two Brodny who sat on the other side of the aisle peered at her out of the corners of their eyes, apparently believing that she studied them.

She pulled her gaze back to her own porthole, away from the liquid darkness of those penetrating alien eyes. A wave of nervous gooseflesh spread along her back.

The reaction stemmed from the Brodny. There was something about the aliens that stirred a deep disquiet within her. Or was it guilt for the way she had been used to murder one of their ambassadors when last she encountered the Brodny?

It was definitely not their appearance. The Brodny were humanoid. In truth bearlike—as they were often described— was inaccurate. Their square-shaped faces were pink and quite human in expression. But for the fact that beginning behind the cheeks, under the chin, and atop a narrow forehead they were covered in a silky, sleek, downlike white fur, it would be difficult to distinguish them as alien creatures. The same fur covered the rest of their bodies, or so Arianne understood. She had never seen one of the aliens unclothed.

The Brodny were thrust from her mind as breaking rockets fired again. The shuttle shuddered when its wheels touched the landing strip. Arianne's restraining harness bit sharply into her chest, holding her in the couch, as her body was thrown forward by the abrupt deceleration. Gradually the craft rolled to a complete halt, then turned, and trundled toward the nearby domes.

"Welcome to Havenfound," Fax glanced at her as he began to unbuckle his restraining harness.

Two hours after they were marched into the domes for a final physical and the semantic injections that imprinted the Havenite language onto their brains, Arianne and Fax were led outside to stand in line beside the representatives of the Brodny, MashuCo, and Pillan Planets who had shuttled down with them. For twenty minutes they stood there under armed Tripar guard before an officer, who identified herself as Lieutenant Lian Holland, walked from the domes to face them.

"The Havenite welcoming committee is on the way," she announced. "This is your last opportunity to withdraw. Once the Havenites arrive, we play by their rules. Understood?"

No one on the line answered.

"Make sure that you do," Holland continued. "You're all aware of the Havenites' treatment of psiotics. If any of you have psi ability, it's time to pull out. Believe me, you won't get pass their *duman*."

Duman—the word came from an ancient Earth tongue; it meant smoke or mist. But in Havenite the connotation was closer to priest or mystic. The exact meaning evaded Arianne, nor did she puzzle the term further. Her thoughts centered on the Havenites' treatment of those who displayed psi talents.

"Now is the time . . ." Holland's words trailed. Her head jerked around to a path behind her that led into a forest of needle-bearing trees. "Too late."

A soft gasp escaped Arianne's lips. She had seen Havenites on the recordings, but she was ill-prepared for the genuine article.

Wild and primitive in their appearance, ten men and women strode from the trees. Their clothing was a mismatched patchwork of coarse homespun cloth and animal fur. Nor was there any specific design or style to the garments. The only requirement seemed to be that the vital areas of the human body were covered.

Although, in one case, a woman wore a makeshift halter that displayed one, naked, cone-shaped breast. In another a man's testicle sac was partially exposed by his skimpy loincloth.

Unlike their Tripar counterparts, the Havenites sported thick manes of flowing hair. Even the men's hair cascaded about their shoulders. Although the way it was combed and braided varied with each individual as much as did their clothing.

Arianne's years on Earth had at least prepared her in part for this meeting. Her own chestnut hair would fit in on this new world, while Fax and the others with their shaven scalps would stand out like beacons.

The one thing the ten had in common was the small arsenal of weapons each carried. Man and woman alike bore a thick-hafted spear tipped with a two-edged, sharply pointed metal head twelve centimeters long. On thigh, calf, or waist the Havenites wore at least one sheathed long-bladed knife; some wore as many as three of the blades. Arianne noted that two, a man and a woman, also carried bows with quivers of feathered arrows strapped to their backs.

Conspicuous by their incongruity to the rest of the Havenites' obviously handcrafted weaponry were the machine-tooled pistols holstered to each of their waists. Explosive projectile weapons, Arianne remembered from the recordings. While simple energy weapons such as lasers were known on Havenfound, their use was not widespread through the citizenry.

Tikkas, the small creatures she had seen aboard the *Sadr*, sat on the shoulders of three of the Havenites. Calmly, with long red tails wrapped about their owners' arms, the wide-eyed animals watched the scene. Occasionally one of the animals emitted a chittering warblelike whistle, and the other two chorused in a burst of bird-imitating chirps.

Without so much as a glance at Lieutenant Holland, the ten spread in a line to face the diplomatic representatives who had come to their planet. A man dressed in white shirt, leather jerkin, tan breeches—Arianne could not call the loose-fitting garment pants—and brown calf-high boots stepped forward. His yellow-flecked brown eyes surveyed the eight who stood before him. Arianne estimated his height at one-hundred-eighty-five centimeters.

"I am called Pau," he said in a voice that rolled up from his chest. "My crew and I have been sent to guide you to our capitol city of Kestkap, a journey of ten of our days."

Arianne translated that to a flat ten days. Opat 4's days were but fifteen minutes longer than a standard day's twenty-four hours.

"Before we begin, each of you must be judged as one suitable to walk Havenfound or merely *coure*." Pau's word came as cold as a blast of air off Opat 4's polar icecap: its meaning—fertilizer. "You must stare into the eyes of our *duman*."

He paused, his gaze passing over the faces of the eight offworlders seeking entry to his world. He then glanced over a shoulder and said, "Etenia, you may begin."

A young blonde woman, the one with a bared breast who Arianne had noticed earlier, stepped forward and handed Pau her spear. Without word or gesture she moved to the right side of the line to stand face-to-face with the first representative of Pillan Planets.

"What is this?" The lanky man looked at Pau; indignity reddened his cheeks.

"Meet her eyes!" Pau snapped. "She must look into your soul."

The man did. And Etenia moved down the line, her gaze probing the eyes of those she past. She halted when she reached the second representative of MashuCo.

"Souleater!" The word hissed between her clenched teeth.

Simultaneously, her right hand wrenched a two-edged

hunting knife from the sheath on her left hip. Before the man facing her could blink, she slashed the blade across his throat from ear to ear.

Hands clutching his neck to staunch the spray of crimson that spewed from his throat, the man stumbled back, incoherent sounds gurgled from his lips. Neither helped. He fell to the ground, body twitching spasmodically as his life flowed from that dark wound to pool in the dirt.

Arianne swallowed. The horrible purpose of the Havenite *duman* was revealed. The woman Etenia displayed all the signs of a low-grade receiver, a woman trained to detect the psi powers held in the minds of others—and to quickly eliminate that threatening ability. A fact the MashuCo representative had learned in the harshest of terms.

Bending to wipe her blade on the deadman's jumpsuit, Etenia stood to face Fax. After a mere glance she moved to Arianne, her blue eyes catching and holding the moodweaver's gaze.

Arianne's heart pounded as though trying to escape her chest. She steeled herself, ready to dodge the cold steel that would leap for her throat. But the blade did not flash for her neck. Etenia merely stared unblinkingly at her for seconds that seemed to drag to hours, then she moved to the Brodny. Etenia had not detected her ability!

Quietly releasing an overly held breath, Arianne calmed herself as best she could to prepare herself for what now must be done. *Better to know here, than fail when I have no route of escape.*

She reached into herself, wove a thread, and sent it snaking toward the *duman*. Lightly with the touch of a falling leaf kissing the earth, she tapped the woman's *dyami*. Etenia didn't flinch; Arianne did!

The Havenite woman's emotional aura was as alien to the moodweaver as that of the Brodny. *No*, she corrected herself. It *was* human, just altered. The Havenites' generations of isolation during their long journey from earth had shifted their emotional spectrum.

She sensed Etenia's apprehension of the offworlders,

but rather than deep blue or purple, it was a haughty red. And there Arianne found the pride that stemmed from Etenia's position as *duman*, but it shone brown rather than a golden-yellow.

It would take days, maybe even weeks, before she could correctly read these wild people, let alone be able to mold their *dyami*.

"You seven are judged worthy to continue with us to Paron." Pau's voice broke Arianne's contact with the *duman*. The tall Havenite leader turned to Lieutenant Holland and pointed to the deadman. "Bury him. In death he'll find the union with Havenfound that was denied him in life."

With that the ten Havenites turned and moved back into the woods. Five men and women and two aliens followed after them.

FIFTEEN

Arianne knew nothing about sailing ships. However, the wooden-hulled boat upon which she stood felt awkward beneath her feet. Instead of slicing through the blue waves of the ocean, it ponderously crawled up the swells and slid down their backsides. It appeared that the ship would have been more comfortable on the gentle currents of a river rather than Havenfound's open sea.

Ten meters in length and six in width, the craft was a basic rectangle in design with an abruptly pointing bow and slightly curved aft. Three masts with one large and two smaller sails pushed from a single deck. The flatness of the craft was only broken at the rear of the boat by a raised platform from which the steersman manned the wheel.

"Ah, life on the open sea! The wind and salt spray in one's face!" Fax leaned on the rail beside Arianne and grimaced. "Only the wind smells too sweet as though it blew straight out of a candy factory, and the salt spray tastes of copper."

She smiled. "It's different planet, Fax. It always takes a period of adjustment for our senses to accustom themselves to a new environment."

"It's just that mine have been overloaded lately. Earth, two spaceships, and now here—wherever here is. Do you realize we still haven't been told this system's exact location?'' He glanced at her and shrugged. ''Had any luck making contact?''

''Verbally or as a weaver?''

''Both.''

Arianne turned to lean the small of her back against the rail. Her gaze travelled over the ship; four tikkas playfully scampered about the rigging. ''I've been about as successful as you in luring one of our hosts into a conversation. Other than grunts and nods, the best I've managed is one 'yes' and four 'no's.''

''They might be under orders not to fraternize with offworlders,'' he suggested. ''Our hosts have very definite ideas about how to deal with unwanted elements on their world.''

Arianne shivered in spite of the evening's warmth. The image of Etenia's blade raking across the man's throat had haunted her throughout the day. ''I don't think that's it. I get the impression that they have no interest in us. Or that they have been assigned to an unpleasant duty and have decided to endure it in stoic silence.''

''What about as a weaver?''

Arianne shook her head. ''I've sorted out a few of their emotions, but not enough to read them. They feel, Fax. But what they feel is so different from the people of the Tripar worlds that they might as well be alien lifeforms. Everything is slightly askew. I'll need time to get used to their reactions.''

She looked about the boat again. The Havenites were so like this strange craft they sailed. On the surface it appeared primitive, but all one had to do was glance at the solar collectors that ringed the vessel's sides to realize that the auxiliary engines running beneath the deck were the product of advanced minds. She could only speculate on the circumstances that had molded those minds, the centuries of confinement aboard a spacecraft, the intense pressure to survive that had shaped this people.

''You've caught the eye of at least one Havenite.'' Fax's

head tilted casually to the right. "Pau's been watching you all day."

Arianne sensed a thread of jealousy in Fax's voice. "I hadn't noticed."

"I have." Fax looked back at her. "Every time I've seen him today, he's been studying you."

"Maybe he's the key to getting these people to open up." She glanced aft where Etenia, both her breasts now covered, relieved Pau at the wheel. The man climbed down to the deck, brushed stray strands of nut-brown from his face and stared up at the ship's wind-filled sails.

"Unless I've misjudged him, Pau is more interested in getting you to open up, and not in conversation!" Again Arianne felt a twinge of jealousy in Fax's words.

"Don't worry about me. I'm a big girl now."

"That's exactly what worries me." Fax pushed from the rail, shook his head, and strolled toward the ships's prow.

Arianne's gaze shifted back to Pau—just in time to catch his yellow-flecked eyes dart away from her.

"Room service! Can one ask for more?" Fax lifted his eyebrows and pursed his lips cynically while he stared at the wooden plate balanced on his crossed legs.

An amused smile uplifted the corners of Arianne's mouth. The "rooms" the Havenites had provided for their seven passengers were simple coarsely woven straw mats and blankets which were spread on the deck beneath the open sky. The mats and blankets had been distributed fifteen minutes before the evening meal had been served with no ceremony or words.

"Our accommodations are the same as the crew's." She looked aft where the Havenites sat in a tight-knit cluster, segregated from the passengers who they had placed near the bow.

"Wonder what this is?" Fax prodded the food in his plate with a three-pronged wooden fork.

Arianne glanced at her own meal. She silently admitted that it appeared less than appealing to the eye. Using a

similar fork, she lifted a bite of white meal to her lips.
"This is boiled fish. I saw two of the crew catching it
earlier."

"Boiled fish?" Fax blanched.

Tentatively she tasted the fish, then worked a hefty bite
from the large bones that remained in her portion and
placed it in her mouth. Clean and fresh, the fish had a
pleasant taste. She then sampled the blob of green that sat
beside the fish on the plate. For all purposes the limp mass
appeared to be boiled spinach. However, its flavor was
that of a sweet melon. Except for a gritty, chewy texture,
it was quite enjoyable.

The remainder of the meal consisted of a thick slice of
tough crusted bread and a wooden mug of watery, sweet
wine. All in all the Havenite cuisine was far more palat-
able to the taste buds than it was to the eye.

"Not bad," Fax begrudgingly admitted as he tried the
fish.

Arianne tuned him out, focusing her attention on the
crew while she continued to eat. As imposing as they had
appeared when they had approached Base One, the Havenites
looked small and vulnerable now. Gathered so closely
together, they seemed to be no more than frightened men
and women huddled against a raging storm. Not even their
ever-present personal arsenals detracted from the mental
image. The spears and knives were no more than sticks
and stones when compared to the might of the Tripar.

Arianne's eyes widened slightly with sudden realization.
Xenophobia? Was that it?

It had to be. The centuries of separation from the rest of
the worlds of humankind was certain to have left the
Havenites wary of anyone—man or alien—who appeared
at their door in gargantuan ships that could span the galaxy
in a matter of days. The Tripar, the corporations, the
Brodny, all represented a threat to Havenfound's rigidly
structured society.

*They don't see us as saviors from the stars come to
share the secrets of the universe*, she recognized, surprised

by her own provincial acceptance that the Tripar offered a superior way of life to what these colonists had found on their new world.

If there was one lesson she should have learned during her time with Retrieve, it was that one society attempting to impose its values on another, usually for the loudly voiced purpose of improving the living conditions of a society viewed as inferior, had caused more wars than starvation. Hunger was something that Man accepted on a primordial level of his brain as a natural state of existence. While game was available, the ancient hunter within man *knew* the cramping stomach of one day would be replaced by the bloated belly of the feast the next day. Even though, Arianne thought, there was no rational foundation for that belief in an advanced society that more often than not shunned its starving members, marking them as outcasts and failures responsible for bringing their plight down upon their own heads.

But tell men and women that their beliefs and the chosen structure of their lives was wrong, inferior to the beliefs and lifestyles of others, and they will balk, close their minds and ears, and deem the supposition ridiculous. Press the matter and attempt to force—with an iron fist or subtle economic strings—those men and women to emulate another culture, and they will draw a knife and go for the jugular.

The Havenites had not one but four unknown forces descending upon them. Each of those unknowns was hungry to exploit the wealth of exotic elements embedded in a planet older than the sun that dimly lit its distant surface. And all held the military strength to eliminate one small planet in a matter of weeks, if not days, should that young world stand in their way.

Yet, while Arianne studied the faces of the crew in the last glow of the day, she sensed that a fight, no matter how helpless their position, was something the Havenites would understand. The weapons these colonists so boldly displayed were indicative of an existence in which life and death struggles against the elements and the native lifeforms of Opat 4 were commonplace.

No, the Havenites were not afraid of death. They *did* fear being swallowed alive. Tripar, MashuCo, Pillan Planets, or the Brodny, it didn't matter. All four presented a threat so powerful that their influence could devour the social structure of Havenfound in the span of a few years. Losing themselves—the society that they had forged to survive the centuries required to span the lightyears from Earth to their new world—terrified them. More important to these colonists than the rare elements of Opat 6 were their own souls.

While she sipped at the sweet wine, Arianne wove. She touched the *dyami* of a woman who fed a piece of fish to a tikka seated in her lap. Hue by hue she tested the colors of the woman's aura of emotions. Yellow flared each time the woman glanced at the ship's seven passengers. Within that blossoming yellow, Arianne sensed suspicion.

Withdrawing, the moodweaver threaded a strand of her psi force outward again. This time she linked to the *dyami* of a man who rose and carried a jug of wine to refill the passengers' mugs. The suspicion-radiating yellow dominated the sphere of his emotions.

Confidence growing, Arianne evoked a mental image of Pau and the winebearer grasping each other's arms in a gesture of friendship. Simultaneously, she drew from herself the warmth and love she had shared with her own friends. Across the mental thread these feelings flowed.

Yellow transformed to amber then lavender.

"More wine?" The man held out the jug to Arianne.

It was not his action, but his words that brought a smile to the moodweaver's lips when she lifted her mug. The man had actually spoken, not just grunted. And his tone was civil—even friendly.

Satisfied that altering the emotions of the Havenites was within her ability, Arianne broke contact as the man turned to Fax to offer a refill. Moodweaving was a tool, not an answer in itself. The answer the Havenites wanted was an assurance that they could co-exist with the Tripar without being devoured by the larger power, that they could maintain the life they had found on this ringed world.

Words will not be enough to convince them. Arianne's gaze returned to the nine men and women huddled aft. The Havenites would need the proof of deeds. If she expected to achieve the twofold purpose of her assignment, her task was to perform the deeds needed to win their confidence.

Which left the question—*how?*

Watch and learn, she answered herself. On Havenfound she was her only resource. The Havenites didn't even allow offworlders to carry the knives they all sported. She would observe and mimic their actions. She would imitate, yet at the same time keep her distance. Acceptance was never won by forceably intruding into what appeared to be a closed circle. The Havenites had to reach out, take her hand, and ask her to join them. Only then would they listen and, more importantly, talk.

Fax shifted beside her. Uncrossing his legs, he pushed from the deck, walked to the rail, and tossed the cleaned bones left on his plate overboard. Following suit, the MashuCo and Pillan Planets representatives disposed of their garbage.

Arianne felt eyes, as sharp as daggers, staring at the back of her neck. Her head jerked around. All nine of the Havenites glared at their passengers. She didn't need moodweaving to sense wrongness; it emanated from the crew like a black cloud.

What? Had Fax and the others unknowingly violated some custom, transgressed unknown mores? If so, what? The Havenites' heads turned, and they continued with their meals, giving Arianne no clue as to what had sparked the reaction she had sensed so strongly although the expanse of the ship separated them.

Picking the last of her fish from the bones, she used the bread to push the flakey meat onto the fork, then lifted the laden utensil to her mouth. The fish hovered at her lips. Her brow furrowed in puzzlement.

Across the boat the Havenites rose. One by one they walked to an empty barrel and scraped the remains of their meals into the container.

Certain that Fax's throwing garbage overboard lay at the root of the crew's reaction, but unsure what purpose the barrel held, Arianne gobbled the last of her fish and bread and washed it down with the remaining swallow of wine. With only fishbones on her plate, she stood and walked to the barrel. An overwhelming effluvium of rotting food and fecal matter assailed her nostrils when she emptied the plate into the container.

"We accept your offering." Pau stood and walked to the barrel to drop his own fishbones inside.

Whether he mistood her surprised expression for confusion, she wasn't sure. However he nodded toward the barrel and explained, "Fertilizer."

Taking advantage of his unexpected comments, Arianne opened herself to his *dyami*. The yellow she had touched in other Havenite minds was a muted amber on Pau's aura. Suspicion remained, but less heightened in this man. Again she felt frustration. Her moodweaver ability did not allow her to enter his actual thoughts to find the reason for his difference.

"What of nightsoil?" She asked, realizing that the crew apparently placed their feces into the barrel.

"Pots will be distributed among you," Pau answered. "Water we return to the sea. *Kait* is for fertilizer."

For an instant she toyed with the possibility of weaving this man's emotions, to open him further to her. She discarded the idea. The instant she withdrew from the fabric of the weave, his mood would return to its original pattern. Such an abrupt change would be certain to draw attention, even alert him to her ability. She wasn't ready to risk that.

"Thank you," she answered, then turned back toward the passenger portion of the deck.

"May only the stars shower your head this night, Arianne Pillan," Pau called after her.

She caught the reference to rain in his wish for a good night. Glancing over her shoulder, she answered, "And may clouds never cover you."

A pleased smile spread across his lips, and she felt his gaze follow her back to the mat beside Fax.

"What was that all about?" Fax arched a questioning eyebrow as she lowered herself to the deck.

"I'm not certain," she answered, although she sensed that her fingertips had brushed the key to unlocking the Havenites. Now if she could only recognize that key.

"Well, you certainly did something right." Disgust tinged Fax's tone. "Captain Pau, sailor of Havenfound's seas, is definitely interested."

Arianne looked back to the Havenite. This time his eyes did not dart away from contact with hers. Instead they lingered. Arianne glanced away; heat flushed her cheeks. Fax was right; apparently Pau was more than casually interested. Did she leave it at that, or manipulate the interest?

Folding her blanket into a compact bundle, she used it as a pillow when she stretched on her back atop the straw mat. Above, stars as strange as the world they canopied hung in a black sky. A soft fuzzy glow bisected the heavens. Havenfound's rings, she realized.

Closing her eyes, she blotted out the spectacular view. Her first day on Opat 4 had been long and hard, and she hadn't even gotten a toe in the door yet.

SIXTEEN

A white fur-masked tikka agilely ran along the ship's rail with its fluffy tail held straight up in the air. It halted when it reached Arianne, who leaned with her elbows on the wooden railing. The animal sat on its haunches, stared at the woman, and warbled melodically.

Arianne's head turned and she smiled at the unexpected visitor. "Boredom getting to you, too?" Except for watching Pau and his crew work the sails, she found little to occupy her second afternoon aboard the Havenite vessel.

The tikka cocked its head from side to side in human-imitating fashion as though intently studying the offworlder. The creature cooed and stretched out a spidery arm to brush a warm, velvety, compact paw against Arianne's cheek.

"Friends?" Cautiously, afraid of frightening the animal away, Arianne lifted a hand and stroked the tikka's head.

When she started to withdraw, the tikka thrust its head into her palm, demanding more attention. Arianne's fingers massaged and scratched behind its ears. A deep, contented, felinelike purr rolled from the creature's throat. It scooted closer, allowing her palm to travel down its back.

"Rik likes you."

Startled by the deep voice that sounded to her left, Arianne snapped upright. Her head jerked around. Pau hovered over her shoulder, smiling.

"You should consider yourself honored." He tilted his head toward the tikka. "Rik is fickle. He usually shuns strangers."

"He's yours?" Arianne ran her hand along the tikka's back again. The creature's purr increased in volume.

Pau nodded. "Most of us on Havenfound keep a tikka as a pet. It's rare to find someone who doesn't have one."

"Really?" Arianne looked back at the creature. The tikka returned her gaze with wide, innocent, liquid eyes, then took the opportunity to climb upon her shoulder. "Pets are common on most worlds. But I know of none where one animal is owned by everyone."

"The tikkas are special, friends. We don't own them; they adopt us."

Pau stroked Rik's head. The animal's purring doubled, almost deafening Arianne's left ear.

"Friends?" Arianne's gaze returned to the Havenite leader, surprised by his offered conversation.

"This is not an easy world." Pau's yellow-flecked brown eyes lifted and searched the rolling surface of the sea. "Planetfall was a harsh shock for our ancestors. Havenfound was not the paradise they had crossed the stars to find."

He recounted how a fourth of the ten thousand colonists had died in the first six months on Havenfound. Capable of supporting human life the planet might have been, but it was also a hostile, alien world.

Havenfound presented a wide array of denizens that preyed on the strange newcomers, as well as a variety of poisonous plants that killed just as quickly. Worse was the fact that the planet's soil proved unsuitable for Earthly crops. The colonists who managed to survive those first months found themselves faced with starvation, an ignoble end after centuries of surviving in the void of space.

"It was the tikkas that showed us the way of Havenfound." Pau lovingly continued to stroke Rik. "Our ancestors saw that the tikkas ate their foodstuffs and survived. They concluded the opposite might be true, so they studied the tikkas. What these animals ate, they ate. It was the tikkas who led us to the bounties of Havenfound. Grains, fruits, vegetables, even meats—although the tikkas are not great hunters—they gave us. Our farmers abandoned the old crops and grew those native to their new world. Because of the tikkas' gift, we have flourished.''

Rik maneuvered behind Arianne's neck to her right shoulder, poised there a moment, then leaped to Pau's shoulder. It warbled a sudden song. Four other of the animals joined in from the ship's riggings.

"Amazing creatures." Arianne scratched Rik's ears again. The Havenites' bond to the tikka ran deeper than she had imagined. She saw the reverence in Pau's face as he watched her stroke Rik. "Sacred animals."

"To us." Pau nodded.

Arianne wondered why the background recordings hadn't mentioned the tikkas? Had no one understood the significance until now? Even more interesting in the light of Pau's revelation was that the Havenites sold tikkas to off-worlders. Were their actions an open gesture of friendship that had been overlooked in ignorance?

Her brows knitted. Or was she being gullible? Pau's tale of the furry animals might be nothing more than a yarn spun as a joke on a silly offworlder.

No, she denied the possibility. If he had fed her a wild line, then he and his crew would have a good laugh tonight, because she believed him.

"What is the name of your homeworld?" Pau's question wedged into her thoughts.

"Alhim," she answered. "But for the past five years my son and I have lived on Earth."

"Son?" Doubt shadowed the Havenite leader's tone. "Then you are married?"

"*Was*. The bond contract between my former husband and myself was never renewed." She smiled, and noticed a slight hint of tension ease from Pau's pleasant features. Her smile widened in self-amusement, uncertain why she momentarily catagorized Pau's face as merely pleasant. He was quite handsome.

"I have heard others from your shuttles say that Earth is dead." Pau's brown eyes probed hers. "Isn't that true?"

"For all practical purposes—in the present. But Earth is very much alive in the past," she answered, noting the puzzlement of his expression. She quickly explained her meaning and described the data-compiling work she had done with Retrieve.

"You move through time." Awe filled his voice and his gaze drifted around the three-masted ship that sluggishly rode Havenfound's ocean. "You aren't trying to make a fool of me?"

"No," Arianne answered with a shake of her head. "It's not a common experience. The equipment required and the expenditure of energy needed to send a jumper downtime is immense. Very few men and women actually are priviledged enough to make a jump."

"Have you . . ."

A violent quake rocked the deck. The bone-jarring shudder cost Arianne her balance; she tumbled to the side, ribs smacking painfully against the unyielding rail. Her hands wrenched up, barely grasping the wood for support before momentum spilled her over the side.

Pau managed to keep his feet under him, but both his hands clutched the railing.

"What was . . ." Arianne began.

A cry from one of the crewmen drowned the remainder of her quesiton. "*Carfin!* To the port—*carfin* turning for a run!"

"*Carfin*?" She blinked, the word wasn't contained in her imprinted vocabulary.

Pau's curses in the Havenite tongue didn't answer her question. Nor did the man seem to be aware of her presence. Panic etched deep lines into his face as he pushed from the rail and darted aft. Cries of terror, echoing Pau's fearful expression, rang out from the crew who worked the riggings.

Uncertain of the source, but recognizing the danger, Arianne ran after the man. She caught up with him by the steersman's platform. Pau pulled a long harpoon from a row of ten similar steel-headed weapons neatly hung beneath the platform. Arianne tugged another of the harpoons free. If this was life-threatening danger, she wanted to be armed.

Pau called to Etenia, who stood wide-eyed at the ship's wheel, "Can you steer us clear?"

Etenia's head jerked from side to side. "I'm no miracle worker! A *carfin*'s not blind!" Her gaze shot portside. "Here he comes!"

The time for words past, Pau ran to the port rail with Arianne at his heels. Her eyes went saucer-wide. The source of the quake that had jarred the vessel broke the water's surface in a boiling spray of foam. Its piscine body—half the length of the ship and looking twice as massive—arched high into the air. Blue-black iridescent scales caught Opat's light and shattered it into a blazing spectrum.

"A *fish*!" Arianne gasped numbly.

But like no fish she had ever seen before. The creature's size was overwhelming to the senses. The minor tidal wave its body created when it fell back to the sea testified to its sheer mass. The speed with which the *carfin* sliced beneath the surface of the blue-green water was the indication Arianne needed of the monster's strength. Mass and speed equalled a living battering ram that could shatter the ship's hull.

"The eyes!" Pau pointed to the *carfin*'s bulbous eyes clearly visible beneath the water. "Go for the eyes. The tips will not penetrate the scales."

A harpoon was not an energy gun, or even the projectile pistols the Havenites wore on their hips, but Arianne didn't question. She hefted the harpoon and took aim at the gargantuan fish that swam a head-on course that would end midship. The scurry of booted feet and the shouts of the crew came from behind her. She ignored them; her attention focused on the *carfin*'s bulging left eye.

Onward the massive fish sliced through the sea with

unwavering determination. Arianne reached out and touched the alien creature's *dyami*—a small black ball of rage. Forcing calmness in her own mind, she constructed an image of the *carfin*. To its right she conjured a school of smaller fish. At the heart of that mental vision she planted hunger. And she wove.

With six meters separating *carfin* from hull, Pau hurled his harpoon downward toward the fish's head.

A split second later Arianne sensed the creature's *dyami* flash red. The *carfin*'s massive head swiveled to the left in search of nonexistent prey. Arianne unleashed her own harpoon, casting it toward that vulnerably exposed eye.

From her side three other harpoons lanced downward, hurled by crew members who raced to the rail.

Pau's weapon struck first. Directly between the creature's eyes it hit—and bounced off the thick, helmetlike skull that protected the fish's head. A small explosive charge contained in the steel tip popped harmlessly in the air.

Arianne's cast struck true, sinking deeply into the exposed eye an instant before one of the three other harpoons drove into the *carfin*. Muted by flesh and water, she felt, rather than heard, the two harpoons explode. The red of the creature's *dyami* winked to nothingness. The charges had disintegrated the *carfin*'s brain.

Neither of the two weapons penetrated in time to stop the gargantuan fish's momentum. The dead *carfin*'s body slammed into the hull. This time Arianne maintained her balance to stare down at the five-meter-long fish that flopped to its side and floated on the surface.

"A stupid fish with a brain the size of a thumb," Pau pronounced beside her. "He thought the ship was another *carfin* invading his feeding territory. Although his eyes were sharp, his brain could not distinguish the boat from a fish."

Arianne grasped the rail as her knees threatened to go liquid. The fish was big—damned big! Through luck or previously unknown skill she wasn't sure, but she thanked whatever gods the Havenites worshipped for her sure cast. Mere wood would not have withstood the *carfin*'s strength for long.

"Olit, Bargen," Pau called out, "go below and check for damage. The rest of you get the carcass aboard. We've got at least three hours work cut out for us down there."

A black-tressed woman at the rail beside Arianne turned to her. "Your harpoon struck before mine. The kill is yours. If you wish, I will instruct you in what must be done now."

In a half-daze, Arianne nodded. "Please, I would appreciate your help."

Arianne stood naked on the deck and lathered herself from head to toe with the strong Havenite soap. Pau's crew was too busy cleaning away the stench of the long task from their own bodies—rendering a *carfin* was a messy, dirty business—to notice her nakedness. As for the other diplomatic representatives aboard, who remained near the prow ogling the unexpected scene, she turned her back and did her best to ignore their rude gazes.

"Are you ready to rinse?" This from Aziza,,the black-haired woman whose harpoon had struck the *carfin*'s eye beside Arianne's.

"Yes." Arianne shivered as Aziza lifted a bucket of surprisingly cold seawater and poured it over her head. Three more buckets and the last of the soapy lather rolled from Arianne's body. She accepted a rough cloth the woman handed her and began to rub the clinging moisture from her gooseflesh-rippling skin.

"When you're dry, put this on." Aziza placed a pair of crisp, starched thigh-length brown shorts and an equally fresh-looking brown blouse on a dry spot on the deck. "Your clothes will have to be cleaned."

Wrapping the towel about her chestnut hair in turban fashion, Arianne dressed. The weave of the cloth was coarse, obviously from Havenite looms, but the material was cotton-soft against her skin. She glanced around. The rest of the crew shed their bloody primitive furs for similar attire. Questioning, she glanced at Aziza.

The woman smiled and winked. "The furs appear more fierce. You of the other planets are more impressed by them. Now, will you assist me in my bath?"

Arianne grinned and nodded as she lifted the empty bucket and walked to the rail to fill it. Havenfound and its people weren't to be underestimated. Until now there had been no hint that the fur-adorned clothing wasn't their usual attire. What else did the Havenites hide beneath appearances?

"Arianne."

She hauled the bucket from the water and turned to face Pau, who approached with Etenia at his side. The Havenite leader carried a large slab of white, uncooked fish in his arms. Arianne recognized the meat as that of the *carfin* that she had just spent three hours helping render.

"Aziza says that your harpoon struck the fish first, that the kill was yours." This from Etenia. "By right of the kill the *ptoate* belongs to you."

Arianne translated the word as "prized portion." It obviously meant the meat Pau carried.

"It is customary for a hunter to feast on the *ptoate* the day of his kill," Pau offered. "It is a sign of respect for the life taken."

A thread woven to both Pau's and Etenia's *dyami* alerted Arianne. There was more than a simple offering here; she sensed an underlying current of tension, especially from Etenia. A wrong response could destroy the headway with these people that she had made today.

"Then I will feast on the *ptoate* this evening." So far so good, she realized, but she felt more was expected. Etenia's apprehension did not diminish. "Is it proper to share one's bounty?"

Pau nodded approval. Etenia's *dyami* lightened.

"Then I would have the *ptoate* divided equally among the crew. Without them and this ship there would have been no kill." Arianne allowed herself an internal sigh of relief; Etenia's *dyami* reflected she had chosen her words correctly. Arianne then added, "I ask that the crew share their meal with the tikkas."

Etenia's grin spoke louder than words. The *duman* took the fish from Pau's arms. "I will personally prepare tonight's feast." She then hastened away.

"You received another honor." Pau's eyes glinted with admiration when he looked back at Arianne. "No one on Havenfound prepares *carfin* like Etenia."

"I'll look forward . . ."

"Arianne!" a lather-covered Aziza called to her.

With a shrug, she lifted the bucket of water and hurried to rinse the woman.

Arianne finished her meal quickly, then bid the Havenites a rainless night and hastened to the passenger portion of the deck. While Etenia had invited her to join the crew that night, and Aziza urged her to accept, the meal was riddled with unspoken tension.

In spite of her harpoon and her help in rendering the *carfin*, she remained a distrusted offworlder to the rest of the Havenites. She even sensed an undercurrent of disquiet in Pau's *dyami*. Thus she politely finished the fish and retired to leave the close-knit group to themselves.

"Overdoing it, aren't you?" Fax greeted her as she spread her blankets on the deck and stretched atop them.

"What?" She stared at her ex-husband. She needed no moodweaver's thread to feel his animosity.

"Going native—you're overdoing it, aren't you?" he repeated.

"I've learned a lot about our hosts today," she tried to ignore the cynicism in his tone. "Did you watch them with the *carfin* this afternoon? I believe that the way they butchered the fish is a major insight to the Havenites as a people."

She waited for him to comment. Instead he glared across the ship to the circle of colonists. He looked like a little boy sulking. She didn't care; she needed to talk over the ideas that formed in her head.

"They didn't waste one portion of the fish. Scales, bones, innards, meat were all stored for some purpose whether it be food or fertilizer," she continued. "Only in rare incidents has humankind developed such a completely materialist approach to the universe. Far too often we tend to take only what we view as immediately needed and leave the rest to spoil. Not the Havenites: the old adage 'waste not, want not' describes their philosophy of life. The rigid ecological society that developed during their flight from Earth has been maintained on Havenfound. I'm certain some of the . . ."

"Are you certain that your insights don't revolve around one special Havenite?" Fax's hazel eyes fixed on her.

She would have missed his meaning had she not felt the waves of jealousy emanating from him. She blinked in confusion. "Pau? Fax, you aren't serious?"

"Aren't I?" His gaze remained on her.

"I'm here for the same purposes you are." Arianne suppressed the rage that flamed in her chest; Fax had no right to question her motives. Not when it was his own uninvited feelings for her that were getting in the way. "I intend to do that job as quickly and efficiently as possible."

"By using them the same way you say that I used you?" He turned from her, disgust on his face.

Inwardly Arianne flinched. His condemnation of her actions hit below the belt. He knew why she was here, what had to be done if she intended to help Jon. "I'm only doing . . ."

"Don't lie to yourself." Fax looked at her again. "We're not on some noble quest, Arianne. We're the frontline troops, and we're fighting a delaying action."

The bitterness in his words shocked her. "Delaying action? What are you talking about?"

"You, me, the Tripar, our assignment. You're not stupid. Take a good look at why we're here," he said. "The Tripar's running scared. Every under secretary and department head down to the janitorial staff knows that the Tripar is collapsing beneath the weight of the MashuCos and the Pillan Planets and the Malecs and the Uatechs. Whatever we do on this planet won't matter. The fall of the Tripartite Confederation is inevitable. If we win mining rights to Opat 6, all we'll do is extend the Tripar's death throes for a few more years, maybe even a decade or two.''

Arianne stared at him. Their five years of separation had wrought more changes in Fax than she had realized. What brought his discontent spewing to the surface now? Jealousy of Pau? ''Then why are you here?''

Fax shook his head while he rolled to his back on the deck and stared at the night sky. ''I thought it was you. But I was lying to myself. I think it's just a matter of habit, Arianne. I'm here because it's my job.''

He closed his eyes and rolled away from her. A cold shudder crawled up Arianne's spine. She felt his *dyami*; he wasn't lying.

SEVENTEEN

Arianne wasn't certain what she expected to see when she reached the coast of Paron, Havenfound's major continent, but the village of Eamint fell short of her expectations. No more than a hundred wood-and-stone-constructed homes and five wooden piers—they were far too small to be called wharves—marked the village that sat dwarfed by the enormous bay it faced.

To the man, woman, and child the whole village turned out to greet the ship's arrival. After a round of handshaking and backslapping, the village members fell to the task of unloading the cargo held in the vessel's hold. Besides the wooden barrels of salted *carfin* and fertilizer, Arianne noted an array of containers stencilled with the Tripar emblem.

Apparently the Havenites were trading with the *Sadr*— the Tripar gave nothing away for free. Havenite fresh vegetables, fruit, fish in exchange for what? Arianne pondered, but found no answer. She had no idea what the Havenites received.

Nor did she have the opportunity to investigate the containers' contents. While villagers busied themselves with the cargo, Pau and his crew hastened the passengers from the boat, led them through the village to a clearing on its west edge where twenty-five *netacs* awaited. Seventeen of the overgrown roadrunner-looking birds stood in saddles and bridles. The remaining brilliantly plumed creatures wore the tack of pack animals.

"We're not expected to ride one of those are we?" one of the Pillan Planets representatives whispered to her companion.

Arianne felt the same lack of confidence as she eyed the monstrous birds. The *netacs'* orange-scaled, thick legs and broad, multihued, feathered backs appeared powerful enough to support riders. It was the creatures' violet-colored beaks that worried her. Those beaks were long, wickedly hooked, and serrated at the edges. No herbivore needed equipment like that; the birds obviously required a diet of high-protein meat.

"There is no need to fear the *netacs*," Pau held up his hands to quiet his wards. "These birds are well trained and docile as long as they are fed regularly—a task everyone will be expected to help with during the journey."

"What about the shuttle?" Fax spoke up. "I heard the villagers mention an underground shuttle that ran all the way to Kestkap."

"The shuttle is only for our cargo," Pau answered. "It runs through a tunnel three meters below the land's surface with no ventilation shafts. Using the shuttle is out of the question. We will use the *netacs* to travel overland."

Something in his words rang wrong. Arianne sensed a lie. Without ventilation how could a Havenite repair crew enter the shuttle tunnel?

Pau paused, his yellow-flecked, brown eyes drifting over the faces of the offworlders. "More importantly the journey is needed to give us the opportunity to test each of you."

"Test us?" Fax leaned to Arianne's ear. "I thought that we had been tested at Base One?"

She rolled her eyes to the side and frowned, hoping to hush him as Etenia walked to Pau's side. The Havenite *duman* spoke, "Our leaders require that we judge each of you as worthy of their time. They will not speak with fools. Those who fail will be returned to the island you call Base One.''

Arianne released a breath that she hadn't realized she held. At least Havenite blades would open no more throats.

''What does this test involve?'' This from one of the two Brodny.

''Fear not our test,'' Etenia answered. ''We simply wish to see that which is within your hearts—to view your understanding.''

''About as clear as mud,'' Fax whispered.

Pau silenced further questions by ordering Havenites and offworlders alike to mount. Hesistantly Arianne approach her waiting *netac*. The creature's wide blue eyes followed her every move, giving her the distinct feeling that the bird sized up a future meal.

The Havenite caravan halted in the heart of a towering forest for the noon meal. It *was* a forest, of that Arianne was certain. Although whether or not it was a forest of trees she couldn't be sure.

Here and there she discerned plants that she would categorize as trees. But at least half the forest's looming vegetation appeared to lack the woody trunks of trees. Instead they sported thick green stalks, and high amid heavy, waxy leaves blossomed flowers in varying hues of red, white, green, and yellow. Each of these bright bursts of color spread their petals for two meters in diameter.

Dismounting, Arianne winced painfully with each step she took toward a purple-berried bush where she tied the *netac*'s reins. Both her backside and inner thighs paid the price for her ride atop the bird's feathered back. *Too many years of relying on slidewalks,* she thought glumly as she hobbled to where the Havenites built a small campfire and seated herself beside Fax.

''Something's up.'' He nodded to the right.

Pau, a shovel in hand, approached one of the Pillan Planets representatives, a man named Garner Koss. The two spoke briefly then disappeared into the underbrush.

"Wonder what's happening?" Fax glanced at Arianne, who answered with a shake of her head.

Nor did she have time to ponder the situation. Aziza and Etenia motioned to her. Moaning as she forced aching muscles to work, she pushed from the ground, joined the two women, and found that she was expected to help gather food for the meal. In this case, sap from the *vadr* trees. Aziza handed her a long-bladed knife, and Etenia placed an earthen jug in her free left hand. Arianne glanced back to tell Fax of her assigned task, only to see him and three Havenites trot into the wood.

"They hunt for the *netacs*," Aziza explained, apparently noticing the concern on her face. "You will aid in the hunt soon enough. But after the way you handled yourself with the *carfin*, Etenia decided you needed no training with our weapons."

"*Vadr* sap is as important as meat," Etenia added while she led Arianne to one of those monstrous green-stalked plants. "In the forest the *vadr* gives water even where there is no stream."

The *duman* placed her own knife against the green bark and sliced an eleven-centimeter cut at a forty-five degree angle. Immediately she placed the jug she carried beneath the smooth gash to catch the gush of clear liquid that flowed from the tree. Almost as quickly the tree's wound closed, sealed by an ooze of bright green.

Etenia held out the jug to display half a mug of water. The aroma of the sweet, watery wine that had been served aboard the ship wafted in Arianne's nostrils. She smiled, realizing the source of the alien beverage. She also was willing to lay odds that the sap had no alcoholic content, in spite of its deceptive flavor.

"The *vadr* is also miserly," Aziza said. "It takes many cuts to fill the jug. You try it."

It appeared simple enough, but everything about the Havenites was a complex puzzle hidden behind a mask of simplicity. Arianne read the *duman*'s *dyami*. The same tension-fraught anticipation colored Etenia's aura that

Arianne had sensed when she had been presented with the prized portion of the *carfin*.

"What of the *vadr*?" Arianne glanced at the tree, recalling all she knew of her own potted forest. "Does this harm the tree? Won't disease enter the cuts?"

Etenia relaxed and smiled. "Not as long as you aren't greedy. Make no more than four widely spaced cuts on each tree."

Stepping to the side of the *vadr*, Arianne drew her blade across the bark and let the wine-flavored liquid spill into the jug. She had been wrong about the tree; it was quite woody and tough.

The *netacs* noisily crunched the black bodies of twenty-four-centimeter long beetles while the Havenites and their offworld wards chewed twists of jerked meat—none of the Havenites mentioned the source of the smoked and peppered meat—and drank mugs of *vadr* sap, which still tasted like watered-down sweet wine to Arianne.

There was one major difference in this meal and those on the ship—the Havenites sat with the offworlders. The abrupt change was significant Arianne sensed, but she failed to understand its exact importance.

"We will have two less among our number from here on," Pau announced when he rose from the meal and motioned to the others that the time to ride was on them again. "Olit will return with Garner Koss to Base One."

With that a Havenite escorted the Pillan Planets representative to his *netac*. While the caravan continued westward, two *netacs* and their riders turned toward the coast. Although nothing was said, Arianne read her own fear on all the faces of the offworld representatives—"Koss failed. Don't let me screw up the same way!"

Opat's setting rays washed Havenfound's sky in blazing hues of reds, oranges, and golds while Pau led Arianne from the open meadow that would be their camp for the night back to the edge of the woods. He handed her the shovel he carried.

"Your task is simple," he informed her. "Dig a latrine for our use this night."

Arianne glanced at the shovel. This same simple test— not task—had won Garner Koss a one-way trip back to Base One this afternoon. Now it was her turn; there was no draw, no stalemate, in this game she either won or lost.

She wove a thread to the Havenite leader. It didn't help; Pau's *dyami* was as unruffled as the tikka Rik that sat on his shoulder, staring at her. Realizing her moodweaver ability would provide no inside track this time, she turned and stepped into the woods with Pau at her heels.

Digging a latrine was a simple, straightforward task. How had Koss blown it? Arianne nibbled nervously at her lower lip. *By accepting the job at face value,* she thought, knowing why the man had failed. Nothing about Havenfound and its colonists could be accepted as it appeared. Something always lay behind Havenite actions—even something as basic as bowel movements.

Fertilizer! A smile touched the corners of her mouth when she remembered the barrels of nightsoil aboard the ship. Koss had merely dug the hole Pau had requested. A Havenite would be more concerned with what went into that hole, and how it was used. *Waste not, want not.*

Arianne's gaze darted about the woods, ignoring a small clearing that would be an obvious spot to dig the latrine. A copse of bushes heavy with plump red berries caught her eye. Moving to the stand, she picked three of the berries and turned to offer them to Rik.

Eagerly the tikka accepted the juicy treats. Barely able to hold them between his stubby-fingered forepaws, Rik crammed the berries into his mouth and chewed hungrily.

The value of the unknown bushes proven, Arianne began to dig. The caravan's nightsoil would provide fertilizer for next year's harvest of berries.

Behind her, Arianne felt a glow of approval from Pau. With no words exchanged, she knew that she had passed his test.

* * *

The fire's embers winked out and night's blackness cloaked the camp. Pau was propped against his *netac* saddle that rested on the ground behind him. Lifting an arm, he pointed to a wide, fuzzy patch of stars directly overhead. "In that direction lies Earth. We are looking into the Cygnus arm of our galaxy."

The term "Cygnus" meant nothing to Arianne. Humankind had given many names to the stars over the ages.

"To the east of that patch is a grouping of bright stars we call the spear. The head is formed by a compact triangle of three bright stars." There was something in Pau's voice that made her look. He wasn't making polite conversation; he was lecturing. She could feel it. "The five stars behind the head form the haft that . . ."

"What happened in the woods with Pau?" Fax shifted to a side so that he whispered in Arianne's ear. "You and Mister Rustic seemed to be hitting it off."

". . . The spear is important in that if one follows the head northward it points to the Halo."

Ignoring Fax, Arianne concentrated on Pau's words. Her eyes traced across the sky until she located a tight ring of stars twenty degrees above the horizon—the Halo.

"You can't depend on the glow of Havenfound's ring to guide you," Pau continued. "The tilt of this planet makes the rings almost invisible during the winter months . . ."

"I asked what happened in the woods?" Fax persisted.

"I fertilized a berry bush," she answered while trying to keep up with Pau. "You'd do best to do likewise when it's your turn to dig a latrine."

"The latrine?" Fax edged away. The puzzled expression on his face faded, replaced by a smile. Under his breath he said, "Of course! The ecological balance must be maintained."

Arianne tuned him out, her attention focusing on Pau's words. Like everything else about the Havenites, she was certain this lesson in Havenfound astronomy had a greater purpose. Besides, staring at the night sky relieved some of her disquiet over the lack of satellite monitors.

EIGHTEEN

"Pau!" Etenia called to the Havenite leader.

Pau shoved from the ground beside Arianne where he had sat cross-legged while drinking from a skin of *vadr* sap. Corking the container, he stepped into the high grass and strode toward the *duman*.

Suddenly filled with a strange sense of emptiness, Arianne watched him hasten to Etenia, who, with a Brodny following her, walked from a stand of trees that grew along a stream that flowed through the Havenfound plain. From the shake of the woman's head, Arianne could tell that the white-furred alien had failed whatever test the *duman* had devised for him. The offworlders' number had been decreased to five.

That fact worried Arianne less than the abrupt hollowness that gradually dissipated within her. Three times since beginning the overland trek two days ago, she had felt the sensation—always when Pau was near and then was called away unexpectedly.

Were she a schoolgirl, she could easily attribute the emptiness to infatuation with the handsome Havenite. She did admit that Fax's jealousy was not unfounded; Pau was quite attractive. Were the situation different, she might be tempted to return his obvious interest.

However, she was a service-trained moodweaver, experienced enough to recognize outside influences on her psyche. Although only at a low level, her own moods *were* being manipulated!

145

If Etenia's psi-detecting ability had overlooked her own talent, that opened the possibility of latent moodweavers existing on Havenfound. Pau's mind could very well hold the undeveloped ability of a weaver. Consciously or sub-consciously, he was employing a low-grade psi power meant to alter her emotions.

It was not an improbable possibility. For centuries, before humankind acknowledged the uptapped resources of the mind, primitive moodweaving abilities had carried the label "charisma." She would have to probe Pau carefully to ascertain the strength of his latent ability. The last thing she needed was an unknown factor muddling her own weaving. During her five days onplanet she had come a long way in her comprehension of the Havenite *dyami*.

"Arianne!" Pau called to her, holding up a metal-headed ax that Etenia had taken from the Brodny's hands. "I have another task for you. Wood is needed for tonight's fire."

Another test, she thought, drawing in a steadying breath, then rising to her feet. During the past three days, the Havenites had contrived not one test, but a series of tasks, each designed to measure their wards' ability to survive in the wilds of Havenfound without upsetting the planet's ecological balance.

Reaching Pau, Arianne took the ax that he held out and walked toward the stand of trees. Just before she elbowed her way through a tangle of vines, Fax and Aziza exited the trees. Fax grinned, winked, and raised the shovel he carried in salute. Obviously he had just faced his latrine digging assignment and passed with flying colors.

Arianne's predicament was not so obvious. Search as she did for fallen limbs, she found none, which only left growing trees for the ax's blade. The stand in which she was supposed to gather firewood consisted of monstrously thick-boled giants or saplings with trunks no thicker than her forearm.

As with all the Havenite tests that had gone before, she was faced with a simple task—cut down a couple of saplings since no single ax would ever fell the towering gargantuans, at least not in one person's lifetime. And once again, she knew that the "understanding" Pau looked for, as he followed her, went beyond the mere physical capability of chopping wood.

The saplings were the key; now all she had to do was find the lock they opened.

A cluster of nutlike fruit that clung to the branches of a copse of saplings to her left provided the first clue. She walked to the trees and examined the clusters. Unless she was totally off base, the nuts were seeds. She picked a pocketful and quickly felled two of the saplings.

After chopping trunk and limbs into useable lengths, she knelt to study the trunks. Pruning paint such as the preparation she used on her bonsai collection would seal the exposed wood and assure new buds and shoots to replace the old growth she had cut. However, pruning paint was not one of the items the Havenites carried in their caravan.

Instead she did the next best thing to insure there would be trees to replace those the ax had claimed. Using the ax to loosen the soil, she scooped out a meter-long, twelve-centimeter deep trench with her hands. She then sprinkled the nuts in her pocket into the hole and covered them with firmly packed earth.

Again Pau's radiating aura of acceptance told her that her actions had been correct.

Blue-white sparks flew from the flint each time Pau struck the stone with the steel pommel of his hunting knife. The shower of minute embers rained over a tight mound of dry grass and leaves, and threadlike fingers of smoke rose into the air. The Havenite bent low, Rik maintaining his balance on Pau's shoulder, and gently blew until flames ignited the grassy tender.

Arianne studied the man; although, a lesson in building a fire was not her purpose. She felt and probed the moodweave that subtly played upon her own *dyami*.

The texture and tapestry of the weave was childlike in

its simplicity. So fine was the thread that had her own training not alerted her to the subtle shifting of her emotions, the effect would have gone completely unnoticed.

Even knowing that another manipulated her mood, she had difficulty pinpointing the purpose of the weaving thread. Again, the answer she found was simplicity itself. The thread was a gentle surcease of tension, a tender lulling of turmoil. Less than a molding of the *dyami*, it was like a whispered suggestion that gradually built in the mind.

Blocking herself to the weaving thread, Arianne waited for the sudden sensation of emptiness to dissipate. Then she reached out and tapped Pau's emotional aura.

A frown of doubt wrinkled her brow. Pau was not the source of the thread! A soft, transparent mist of muted lavender floated above his *dyami* like a color overlay.

Arianne severed her mental thread, more perplexed than before. Her head moved from side to side, eyes searching for the source of the weave. The Havenfound prairie, caught in the dusky shadow of the evening, stretched endlessly around her. Except for the *nectacs* there was no one else in camp. A quick brush of the birds' minds eliminated them as the source of the mood-altering thread.

"There." Pau sat on his haunches and smiled up at Arianne while the flames licked upward, sputtering as they caught the green wood. "Now all we have to do is wait for the others to bring the food. Until then we can heat up some *vadr* sap. Nights get colder here on the grasslands. Hand me that jug, and I'll set it beside the fire."

Arianne did and settled to the ground. Her eyes lifted to the west. In the afterglow of the setting sun, she could discern a distant mountain range and the dominating peak the Havenites called High Hold. It was there they travelled, to the city of Kestkap which sat at its base.

Rik warbled, drawing her attention back to the fire. The tikka chattered and cooed as it shifted its weight to readjust its perch on Pau's shoulder.

"Five days," Pau said, apparently noticing her gaze.

Arianne nodded, feeling the slender thread once more

brush her *dyami*. Again, she reached out only to rediscover what she already knew. Pau was not the source of the subtle weave.

Rik purred as the Havenite leader reached up and scratched his head.

Arianne barely caught herself. The thread swelled; her gaze shifted, centering on the tikka. Reaching out she touched Rik's *dyami*. There was the source she sought. The tikka was emanating the thread! Not directing it at her but at Pau. Her own psi sensitivity made her receptive to the creature's ability.

The tikka! Arianne's mind stumbled, unable to make sense of her discovery. The pet, not the owner, was a low-grade moodweaver!

"Wake up, you two!" Aziza shouted as she led the hunting party back to the camp. She held up a string of several small birds. "We feast tonight."

Behind her walked Fax with two Havenfound hares in hand, the Pillan Planets representative Margot Lor, MashuCo's Tawmer Cooke, and the Brodny Gariot, all carrying birds or rabbits, as did the rest of the Havenites behind them. Aziza signalled the others to take their kills to the *netacs*; she dropped her birds between Pau and Arianne.

"I'm glad you two prepare the meal tonight," Aziza said. "*Meuts* are tasty, but too messy for me. Can't stand all the feathers."

"Messy" was an understatement, Arianne quickly learned as she began to clean and dress the birds.

Todd swam to the pool's edge. Laughing and adrip with water, he pulled himself out and ran to Arianne with open arms. She caught and swung him upward in a squeezing hug. After a quick kiss to his right cheek, she planted a loud smack on his left cheek. His face skunched in a childish expression of disdain.

Arianne kissed him again. After all, this was a dream, and in spite of a six-year-old's indignity of having his mother kiss him three times in public, in her own dream Todd would have to endure her display of affection.

So it was Arianne flowed in a half-awake, half-asleep state, afraid that some outside sound might bring her to full consciousness or that the need for rest would drag her down into deep sleep. Either way Todd would be lost to her. Although only a dream Todd, he was the only Todd she had, and after nearly two weeks away from her son, she discovered that she missed him far more than she ever thought possible.

Holding him balanced on her right hip, she hugged him close with one arm while she walked to a concession servo across a wide swath of manicured grass that edged the swimming pool.

"Look out, Mom! There's a spider climbing on you!" Playfully, his short fingers imitated the crawling legs of a spider that crept up the webbed front of her swimsuit.

Arianne laughed. "Cut that out, Todd. It tickles! If you're not careful, I'll . . ."

Consciousness flooded Arianne's mind. The feel of Todd's fingers was too real. Her eyes opened wide, and she stared down at her belly. A red multipede crawled up the Havenite blouse she wore. Ten centimeters of ugly languidly undulated from a round-eyed head to the tip of the creature's twin-stinger tail.

"Fax!" Her voice strained between whisper and scream. Her body remained motionless. "Fax, wake up. Wake up!"

A meter from her, Fax rolled over on the ground. His eyes blinked open sleepily. "Huh? What . . . what is . . ." His gaze focused on the oversized bug. "Don't move. I don't know what it is, but it looks nasty!"

Arianne had no intention of moving a muscle. Clearing her mind of fear, she conjured gentle, peaceful images, and wove a thread toward the creature.

The multipede halted. Whether her weaving actually effected the creature or it paused to puzzle the strange force that invaded its primitive awareness, she didn't know.

"Hold still." Fax rose and retrieved a portion of an unburned limb from the dying campfire. Smothering the embers in the ground, he lifted the stick. "I'll kill it."

"Stop!" Pau ordered from across the fire. Shoving to his feet, he eased to Arianne's side. "It's an *aultem*. Very deadly. We have no antidote for its poison."

"What can we do?" Fax asked, the limb in his hand lowering.

"Wait," Pau answered. "It might crawl away."

Arianne had no desire to wait and see if the bug's twin stingers buried themselves in her flesh. With the creature befuddled by the soothing tapestry she constructed upon its *dyami*, it was the time to act.

Her left hand held flat, she reached up. In one smooth stroke, she swatted the *aultem* from her belly. The creature hit the ground before its stingers could react. And in the batting of an eye, it died as Arianne found a stone and crushed the poisonous creature beneath it.

Angrily, she turned and glared at Pau. "Wait! Did you intend to just sit there and watch me die?"

The Havenite blinked, taken back by her unexpected outburst.

"If this was one of your damned tests, I've got another use for this rock." She shook the stone at him, leaving no doubt that she was capable of cracking his skull with the rock should it prove necessary.

The rest of the camp was awake now, but she didn't care. There was no purpose to this test. "Now, tell me what the hell is going on here?"

"The *aultem* was no test." Pau shook his head. "I don't even know how it got here. It lives in our rain forests to the south. The climate is too cold for it this far north."

She threatened him with the stone again. "So help me, if you're lying, I'll . . ."

"I'm not lying." The sincerity of Pau's words matched the sincerity that floated on his *dyami*. "I told you Havenfound was not an easy world. What I don't understand is how the *aultem* got this far north."

The rock dropped from her hand, and she nodded. Her eyes travelled over the faces that stared at her. "Go back to sleep. I'll be all right. I just need a few minutes to get over the *aultem*."

Questioning glances passed between the Havenites, but none spoke as they settled back to their sleeping blankets.

Arianne shoved to her feet and walked out onto the grassy plain beyond the glow of the campfire; it would be hours before she could even think of sleeping again. She stared at the star-sprinkled Havenfound heavens and shivered uncontrollably as the realization of how close she had come to death penetrated her initial anger.

"You were lucky. I thought . . ." Fax's words faded when he saw her shaking.

He opened his arms and drew her to him, holding her tightly. She made no attempt to slip from his embrace. Instead she rested her head against his chest, finding security in the warm touch of another human being.

"It's over," he whispered, his lips lightly kissing the top of her head. "You're all right. It's over. You're safe now."

"I know," she managed to nod as the quivering gradually lessened. "But one of them tried to kill me, Fax."

"Did you read them?" He lifted her chin with a fingertip, watching her shake her head in answer. "Then I wouldn't be so quick to label the Havenites would-be murderers. Remember MashuCo has an agent among us."

Arianne's gaze shifted back to the camp. Tawmer Cooke lay with his back to her. She touched his *dyami*; his dreams were undisturbed. She would have to await the morning before she could meticulously read the man's aura and those of the Havenites.

"Is there anything I can do for you?" Fax asked.

"Just stay with me for a while," she said, offering no protest when his arms tightened about her and his lips covered her mouth.

NINETEEN

Arianne awoke chilled and damp with dew. Slipping Fax's arm from around her waist, she eased from the warm hollow of his shoulder and quietly stood. He moaned softly, but didn't wake. Lost in dreams, he looked so much like Todd, so much like an innocent child.

A pleased smile touched her lips as she stared down at him. Last night had been good. Fax's tender caresses, the soothing touch of his hands had been a balm to her troubled mind. For a few hours she had found shelter in another human being. During those far too short minutes she had forgotten about her brother, her purpose in being on this alien world, the deadly *aultem*, and the very real possibility that someone had once more tried to murder her.

Her gaze moved from the predawn purples and grays on the eastern horizon back to Fax. She could not deny the love she felt for this man that she had sworn she had hated for so long. Nor did she refuse to accept the same feelings she had sensed in him. Did love ever die?'' Or was it merely misplaced?

She felt a rootless twinge of guilt. She had felt his need for her last night, but had not responded. Nor had he pressed her to make love. Instead he had held her until they had fallen asleep in each other's arms amid the high grasses of the Havenfound prairie.

With time, she thought. She still needed time to accept

this changed Fax, to let the scars of the past heal before they shared the same bed again.

Rubbing her arms to ward off a wave of gooseflesh, she glanced around. They had wandered a hundred meters from the Havenite caravan's camp, if the remaining travellers could be described as a caravan. As much as she had needed last night, separating themselves from the camp had been stupid. The Havenites still did not allow their offworld wards to carry weapons. She and Fax would have been easy prey for any prowling predator.

Leaning down, she reached out and nudged Fax's shoulder. He groaned and tried to roll away. It took a firm shake to open his eyes.

"It's almost dawn," she said. "If you'll get the wood, I'll see what I can scare up for breakfast."

"Couldn't we just go back to sleep?"

Arianne shook her head.

Sighing, Fax slowly pushed to his feet to stretch and yawn. He glanced at the camp. "The others aren't up yet!"

"Come on." She grabbed his arm and tugged him to the camp.

While Fax walked to the *netacs* to take an ax from one of the pack animals, she entered the dense stand of trees growing along the stream. The Havenite breakfast usually consisted of a hot, thin, mushlike cereal called *yelena*. The bland-tasting concoction was offset whenever possible by fruits, nuts, or berries. Yesterday evening during Pau's most recent test, she had noticed a bush laden with ripe *hastin* berries.

She halted ten meters from the bush and stared in surprise. She wasn't the only one who had made the discovery. The seven tikkas belonging to the Havenites sat in a circle about the bush plucking berries from the leafy branches and stuffing them into their mouths.

It wasn't the creatures' eating habits that interested Arianne; it was their warbling. What had appeared as meaningless chirping and chattering, now seemed to take on the distinct form of conversation. One of the red-furred animals would coo-sing and another would turn its head and answer. Was she imagining verbal patterns and physical gestures among the tikkas?

Lacking expertise in languages to confirm her suspicions, Arianne reached up and flicked the beak switch on her brooch transmitter that linked her to Halian Tonani aboard the *Sadr*. "Halian, make this top priority. Explore the possibility of Opat 4's tikkas being sentient beings. Begin with their warble songs. I am presently observing a group of the creatures and have the distinct feeling that they are communicating verbally."

She left the radio on for several minutes to record the tikkas' chattering chorus, before switching it off and approaching the animals to gather a share of the berries before they stripped the bush clean.

The bowl of berry-sprinkled *yelena* held little interest for Arianne. Although she spooned the cereal into her mouth, chewed, and swallowed, she didn't taste it. For the first time since her arrival on Havenfound, she watched, really watched, the Havenites and their tikkas.

The relationship between human and animal was not that of owner and pet. The Havenites treated the tikkas as though they were children. They groomed and fed them; the creatures were cherished and loved.

Why hadn't she seen it before? Worse, why hadn't she detected the subtle thread of surcease each tikka wove into the *dyami* of its adopted human?

Adopted human, she repeated. That was how Pau had originally described the human-tikka relationship. There might be more truth to his words than she had realized.

Finishing her breakfast, Arianne rose from the circle around the campfire and walked to where she had left her sleeping blankets on the ground the night before. As she knelt to roll them in a neat bundle, Fax approached and sat on his heels beside her.

"What's wrong?" he asked. "You had the strangest expression on your face while you were eating."

"It's the tikkas," she replied, explaining all she had discovered. "Think about it, Fax. What bonds have been unknowingly forged between human and tikka during the two centuries Man has been on this planet? For all we know, the Havenites might be addicted to the tikkas' subtle moodweaving. There's a possibility the animals have taken the place of mind-altering drugs here. Pau told me that it was rare to find a Havenite without a tikka as a pet."

"Tikka junkies?" There was no humor in Fax's voice. "And you think the creatures are sentient?"

She nodded. She wanted to tell him about the task she had dropped in Halian's lap, but couldn't without exposing the man as a Pillan Planets spy. And at the moment she had a use for Halian Tonani.

"The tranquilizing effects of the tikkas' low-grade moodweaving is the obvious human benefit from the relationship, if you want to categorize it as a benefit," Fax said. "The question *is*, what do the tikkas get out of the relationship?"

"Food, protection?" Arianne shook her head. "I don't know."

"The possibilities are interesting, especially if the tikkas are sentient." Fax stood as she rose. "There is another thing, which has nothing to do with the tikkas."

She looked at him, eyebrow cocked in question.

"Cooke," he explained. "Have you had the opportunity to read him?"

"I've read him, Lor, the Brodny, and all the Havenites," Arianne replied. "Nothing. If any of them are responsible for the *aultem*, I can't detect it."

"Which doesn't . . ." He fell silent as two Havenites approached. "We'll talk later."

Arianne nodded, walking to her *netac* to prepare for the day's ride.

*　　*　　*

The wild goats, a pair of young billys, charged down the steep-sided ravine. Head-on they hit the net, bleating loudly as they rebounded, their curved horns tangled in the mesh.

Immediately Arianne cut a single line that stretched the net tautly across the top of the gully. It fell, trapping the two animals in an inescapable rope web.

Spear in hand, Arianne leaped from the ravine's edge to the floor two meters below. Deftly she drove the long, steel spearhead into the sides of the struggling goats, cleanly piercing their hearts. Within seconds the bleating died, as did the animals.

"Goats!" His face streaming rivulets of sweat, Pau ran up the ravine. He stopped when he reached the animals and sucked down several deep breaths. "I hate their smell. But these two should be enough for the *nectacs* tonight."

Wiping the sweat from her own brow, Arianne walked to the side of the gully and leaned against the rock and dirt. Although Pau had chased the two goats—they *were* goats, the descendents of domestic animals that had escaped from early colonists and somehow managed to survive on Havenfound—she had strung the net. After a long day's ride astride a *nectac*, hunting the goats had left her physically exhausted.

"We'll rest here a moment, then drag these back to our mounts." Paul still panted when he collapsed beside her. "I hope the others have been as lucky as this. I feel like I could eat one of these by myself—stink or no stink."

Arianne did her best to smile, but felt too weary to expend the energy. The rumble of thunder rolled in the distance. She tilted her head back and studied the sky. Noon's misty overcast had transformed to dense gray clouds that blotted out Opat's light to leave the land shadowless and flat. Thunder clashed again, closer.

"Rain?" She looked at Pau.

He shook his head. "Not likely, at least not here. Maybe farther east tonight. But from here to the foot of

High Hold, the land is desert. Rains and water are very rare between the prairie and Kestkap.''

Great, Arianne thought, keeping her sarcasm to herself. She could imagine the tests in desert survival the Havenites might arrange. "It does rain here though." She waved an arm about her. "Wind didn't cut this ravine."

Pau nodded. "I said rains were rare, not nonexistent. When it does rain here, it's a deluge. This land is more rock than dirt. With no soil to absorb the water, it runs off."

"Flash flooding," Arianne added, recognizing the force needed to slice a gully this deep into the earth.

Pau's lips parted to comment when a large drop of water struck his nose. He laughed as a barrage of raindrops splattered his face. "So much for my weather predictions. Let's get the goats and the net out of here."

Arianne didn't protest. In the time it had taken him to speak, the few raindrops had transformed into a torrent of water falling from the sky. Ragged streaks of lightning leaped between the clouds. Thunder exploded on the heels of each glaring flash. A gentle breeze grew into a full-fledged wind.

Bending, she helped untangle the goats from the net, then bundled the web of rope, and tossed it over the top of the ravine. With Pau on one leg and her on the other, they dragged the first goat up the gully's now mud-slickened side. They slipped and slid back to the ravine's floor to retrieve the second goat.

Arianne cocked her head from side to side. Beneath the sound of the wind and storm, she heard—she wasn't certain what it was, except that it was deep, almost a vibration she felt in her bones.

"What is that?" she shouted over the wind. "Do you hear it?"

Pau paused as he reached for the goat's leg, then shook his head. "Help me get this to the top."

Taking the other hindleg, Arianne tugged the animal to the side of the gully. On hands and knees in the mud, gaining three centimeters only to lose two, they worked the dead weight upward.

The roaring increased. She heard it now; she was sure of that. She stared at Pau, blinking the steady stream of water cascading from her head away from her eyes. "Can't you hear that?"

He was too busy pushing the goat over the top of the ravine to answer. Cursing beneath her breath, Arianne followed him and the precious goat up. Reaching the top, she paused on her knees to regain her breath. Her eyes went wide when she looked up. The source of the roar was more than obvious!

"Down!" Pau shouted.

He threw himself at her, arms encircling her waist. Together they tumbled head over heels back into the gully— away from the three funnel-shaped clouds that tore across the Havenfound plain on a direct path toward the two hunters!

TWENTY

Disentangling arms and legs, Arianne and Pau staggered to their feet in the muddy swamp that now covered the bottom of the ravine. Rain, whipped by the increasing wind and feeling stone-hard, pelted their faces and bodies. Lightning sizzled its actinic light across the sky, but there was no thunder; the roar of the approaching tornados devoured all sound.

Pau grabbed Arianne's arm and pointed to the steep incline of the western wall. He tugged her forward, then threw himself flat in the mud and covered his head with his arms. Realizing what he wanted of her, she did the same.

The roar of the approaching funnels mounted. Arianne's ears popped as the air pressure about her dropped. From above an invisible hand reached out and snatched her by the collar. Arms and legs flailing at nothingness for support, she was lifted into the air and flung across the ravine. Her back slammed into the eastern wall. Pain flared in her skull like a blazing brand when her head snapped back and struck stone. Then there was darkness.

The rumble and the rain brought her from unconsciousness up a well of throbbing pain. Fighting through the ache that filled her head, she forced her eyelids open and blinked against the shower that washed her face.

She felt too miserable to appreciate the fact that she still lived, let alone to care that the force of the storm had diminished to a gentle shower. Gingerly, she probed the back of her head with fingertips. The painful throb radiated from a bump the size of her fist, but she could detect no damage beyond that.

As to the rumble that had awakened her, it came from her right to the north. Gritting her teeth, she managed to push through her initial dizziness and stand to peer up the gully. She saw nothing.

"Arianne?" The voice was weak, but it was Pau's. "Is that you?"

She turned. The Havenite lay against the eastern wall of the ravine. He stared directly at her, but his wide eyes and puzzled expression said that he didn't see. An angry red gash ran across his forehead; blood trickled down the side of his face to be washed away by the rain.

"Arianne?" He held out a groping hand. "Arianne, is that you? I can't see. Is that you?"

"I'm here, Pau." She moved to him, taking his hand. The cut on his head didn't appear to be as deep on second examination. "You've injured your head."

"I know. I can't see anything but fuzzy, distant light," he answered, then paused, his head tilting to the right. "Do you hear that?"

"Yes." She tore off a piece of her blouse, rinsed it in the rain, and began to bathe the mud from his wound.

He groped with a hand and gently edged her away. "Arianne, you've got to get out of this gully. That sound is water—a flood that will be on us in a few minutes. Start climbing. Get out of here!"

"And leave you?" She shook her head before realizing that he couldn't see. "You've still got your legs. I'll help you climb to the top. On your feet."

"I can't." His head moved from side to side. "My left ankle—I think I broke it."

Kneeling, Arianne hastily examined the swollen ankle. She found no broken bones. "It's sprained. It looks bad, but not bad enough to cost you your life. If you can't walk, roll over and start crawling. I'll be right behind you.''

''I don't think . . .''

''Don't think. Crawl!'' Her head twisted to the north; the faint rumble swelled to a roar. ''Crawl, dammit. Crawl!''

He did. With her pushing, pulling, shoving, cursing, and pleading, he made it to the ravine's rim and rolled to high ground.

Seconds behind him, Arianne clawed her way over the rim to his side. She managed one relieved breath before a wall of water boiled down the ravine. Still on her knees, she edged back to the gully's edge. They might have survived the sudden deluge, but she doubted it.

Standing, she peered about the rain-drenched rocky terrain. There was no sign of their *netacs*, or the stunted tree they had left them tied to before going after the goats. Frightened off by the storm or dead, she didn't know.

''Our mounts?'' Pau asked.

''Gone,'' she answered, while she squatted at his side. ''There are two boulders about ten meters from here. If you use me for support, think you could manage to walk that far?''

''Hop or hobble at best.'' He grinned up, his eyes failing to locate her position.

Looping one of his arms over her neck, she helped him to his one good leg, then bore most of his weight as he hopped the ten meters to the boulders. There she lowered him to the ground and propped him against one of the rocks.

''Pau, I have to leave you here.'' She stood and glanced to the south. ''I have to go for help. I can't carry you back to camp.''

''I understand.'' He nodded. ''I won't be going anywhere.''

''I'll hurry,'' she replied. ''I don't like leaving you here alone.''

''I'll be all right,'' he answered, managing a weak

smile. "But when you get to camp, just don't forget where you left me."

"I won't." She reached down and squeezed his shoulder before turning to begin her walk south.

She found three *netacs* at the campsite. Two dead, skulls crushed from debris hurled by the cyclonic winds that had raged through the camp. A third pack animal dined on the bodies of the first two.

Securing the shank attached to the *nectac*'s bridle to a weighty stone, she allowed the bird to continue its feast. Better a cannibalistic dinner than having a hungry *nectac* after her.

Other than the birds, there was no sign of anyone or anything else. She refused to let that bother her. Because of their ever-lessening numbers and the growing harshness of the semi-arid terrain, everyone in the caravan had split into pairs and gone in different directions to hunt earlier that afternoon.

She settled to the ground, wrapped her arms around her legs, and rested her head on her knees. The storm had struck without warning. If it had taken the others off guard as it had Pau and her, they were still gathering themselves together. All she had to do was sit and wait until they returned.

A tikka's warble brought Arianne from a half-sleep. She lifted her head from the pillow of her knees expecting to see Fax and the rest of the caravan riding into camp. What she saw was Rik limping in the full light of Gauri, the largest of Havenfound's two moons.

"Come here, Rik." She held out a hand and called to the creature. "Come here."

The tikka's voice rose an octave in excitement when its large, liquid eyes rose to her. She felt a familiar thread brush her *dyami* as Rik hastened his four-legged pace and scampered in her arms.

"Where is everyone else, boy?" The tikka warbled its

melodic song while she examined his right hindleg, the one he had shied from as he walked. The hair had been scrapped away, but she saw breaks in the pale skin. "Just bruised a bit. You'll be all right."

Rik settled on her shoulder. The pattern of color he wove was so much stronger than she had ever noticed before. Was it because he was frightened, or that he now directed his weave at her?

She blocked the tikka's thread. Now was not the time to worry about the animal's latent psi ability. She had enough trouble on her hands.

Glancing back at the stark white face of Gauri, she sucked in a deep breath. Like it or not, she had to face the fact that she was wasting time here. Half the night was gone, and still none of the others had come back to camp. Her had turned to the *netac*. Pau was out there alone; with the bird's strong back, she intended to bring him in.

"Here drink this." Arianne handed Pau the last mug of heated *vadr* sap as he sat up from his day-long sleep. "If your stomach can handle it, I've got *netac* steaks on the fire."

"*Nectac*?" Pau's eyes widened, and he almost dropped the mug.

"I couldn't see letting that bird gorge himself—," Arianne tilted her head toward the remaining live *netac*, "—on all that meat, when all our supplies are gone."

"Oh, the dead birds. I had forgotten about them." Pau glanced around what had once been their camp, his head cocking from one side to the other as his ears listened for what his eyes could no longer see.

Arianne studied him. She was certain that she had detected a touch of the mentor in his words. He had used the same tone that she had grown accustomed to during her numerous tests.

"No one's returned?" he asked, when his head turned back to her.

"We're still alone." She lifted a meat-laden skewer

from a small campfire and placed it in his hand. "Be careful. It's hot, but it's good."

"How did you know *netac* was safe to eat?" He used his fingertips to work up the wooden skewer to the meat, then nibbled tentatively.

"Rik told me. I prepared a strip of the meat, and he ate it without blinking."

"Rik? Is Rik here?" Pau's head snapped up.

"He slept by you most of the day." She glanced around, finding the tikka drinking from a puddle of water.

"Here, Rik. Come here." Pau called to the tikka and held out his arms. The animal forgot the water and trotted to the man. Pau's palms gently stroked Rik's silky fur. "I thought I had lost you."

Arianne watched the exchange of affection between man and tikka for a few minutes before taking her own skewer of meat from the fire. Rik's mood thread was barely discernable now as he once again directed it at the man he had bonded himself to.

Tearing a bite of the meat from the skewer, Arianne let it dance around on her tongue until it cooled. It was tough and stringy, and it tasted gamey, but she ate it anyway. It was the only food they had.

"Slept most of the day?" Pau's head lifted. "Did you say I slept most of the day?"

"It's almost sunset," she answered.

"Sunset," he repeated softly. He swallowed and closed his eyes. "And still none of the others have returned?"

"You're thinking the same thing that's been on my mind all day." Arianne licked the grease from her finger, and took another skewer from the fire. "That they're not coming back."

Pau's chin dipped toward his chest, and he nodded. "Or that they're lost."

"I've been telling myself the same thing." She had to, had to believe that Fax and Etenia were out there somewhere—alive. "Unless Etenia, Aziza, and the others are hurt, I think that they'll try to make it to Kestkap."

Again Pau nodded.

Arianne drew a steadying breath. She had decided what she had to do hours ago. Pau presented the only possible obstacle. "I think we should do the same thing."

The Havenite leader sat silent for several long, heavy minutes. "It won't be easy. It's three days across the desert. Having a blind man along won't make it any easier—especially a blind man who can't walk."

"You'll ride the *netac*," she answered, not mentioning her fear that the bird's hunger would eventually force her to kill the beast. "I found two empty *vadr* sap skins among the equipment the dead birds carried. Both are filled with water. If we ration ourselves, it should be enough to last three days. And I don't think that I'll lose my way. High Hold is an easy landmark to keep in sight, even at night."

"At night?" His head tilted in puzzlement.

"It's cooler at night. We'll travel then and rest during the day," she said, trying to sound as matter-of-fact as possible to conceal her own self-doubts. "We'll leave as soon as we've both eaten our fill."

Pau took a bite of the roasted *netac*. "This isn't half bad."

She smiled. His words said one thing, while his facial expression said the opposite. Tearing off another bite from her skewer, she looked westward to High Hold's distant pinnacle.

Three days, she told herself, *across desert*. She could make it—had to make it.

TWENTY-ONE

The berries were large—apple big—plump and juicy-looking. They clung to a bright, green-leafed plant with an exposed root system that spread out from the trunk in a diameter equal to the width of the foilage. Yet, Rik ignored the berries, walking instead to a thorny shrub with shriveled, wind-burned yellow leaves. The tikka carefully avoided the needle-long thorns and plucked the leaves to munch on them.

Following suit, Arianne picked one of the leaves and hesitantly placed it to her lips. She nibbed a small portion. The flavor was spicy as though the leaf contained a hint of white pepper. Yet, it was quite edible. Stuffing the rest of the leaf into her mouth, she chewed while she filled her pockets with leaves.

When she paused and looked up, she found Rik busily digging at what appeared to be an ant hill. A writhing den of white worms opened beneath his compact fingered paws. Eagerly the tikka dined on the squirming mass.

Arianne shook her head. She was hungry, but not that hungry. She called to the tikka and started back to where she had left Pau in the shade of a sand dune. Overhead the morning sun gathered heat. She had been correct in choosing to travel at night. Havenfound's sun promised to be as unmerciful as Sol had once been to portions of Earth.

Pau's head jerked to the right as she climbed the dune

and slid down the sand toward his position. "Did everything go all right?"

"Fine." She moved to the *netac* and unlashed a hunk of meat from the bird's pack. She had intended to wait until this evening before feeding the beast, but under this sun the final portion of dead *netac* would spoil. She tossed the meat to the bird. "Rik led me to a scrawny shrub with yellow leaves. They're a bit spicy, but they should go good with the last of our *netac*."

"A pepper-leaf plant from your description," Pau said while she unpacked the remaining two skewers of meat she had cooked last night. "We grind the leaves and use them for seasoning."

"Well, this morning, they're the main course with a side order of cold *netac*, and a mouthful or two of muddy water to wash it down." She placed the cooked meat in his right hand and piled half the leaves in his lap.

"How far do you estimate we travelled last night?" He asked between interspersed bites of meat and pepper leaf.

"About a third of the way, if I can judge by High Hold. It looks that much closer this morning."

"Forty *katers* behind us and eighty more ahead," he said. "How are you holding up? You sound tired."

"Sleepy mostly." She swallowed the last of the meat and washed the gamey flavor from her mouth with a swig of gritty water, uncertain which tasted worse. "I didn't rest much yesterday. Couldn't stop thinking about the others."

"Especially the one called Faxon Lorens?" Pau asked. "He is special to you, I have felt it."

"Was special," Arianne chewed at two of the pepper leaves. Their flavor did little to remove the taste of the water from her mouth. "Fax and I were married."

"He is the father of your son?"

"Yes, but we haven't been together for five years." She considered another drink of water, then passed on it. The water might be all they had later. It was best to conserve it.

"Yet, you spent the night with him two nights ago?"

Arianne laughed, sensing more than casual interest in Pau's questions. "We slept, that's all."

"That's good." A smile spread on his face. "He's not right for you."

Arianne let the remark slide by. Pau's *dyami* told her who he thought was right for her.

Glancing up at the sun, she silently cursed. They had no protection from its rays, not even a blanket to raise a makeshift tent. Anything would help, even something to throw over their heads.

"You should sleep now," Pau suggested.

"Exactly what I was thinking." Arianne stretched out on the sand and curled an arm beneath her head as a pillow. She was asleep within minutes.

Each step she took was its own private hell. Her sunburned arms and legs were on fire, while at the same time she shivered as the cool night air washed about her.

One step at a time, she told herself. *First the left foot, then the right, then the left again.*

She looked over a shoulder. Irrational hate flared as she watched Pau astride the *netac*, stroking Rik who sat on his shoulder. That he was injured and unable to walk didn't matter. She wanted to jerk him from the bird and force his feet to tread these damnable rocks that seemed to bite through the soles of her boots. *The son of a bitch can crawl for all . . .*

She caught herself. Pau could not help what had happened. However, if she could be certain that he would have done the same for her had their roles been reversed, it would have eased the burden. Somehow she felt that she would have died back in the flash flood if she had been the one blinded. After all, she was but an offworlder.

Left foot, then right, she forced her mind back to the rocky terrain. *Left, then right.*

She walked toward the coming dawn.

*   *   *

Had she not seen the blur of iridescent colors out of the corners of her eyes, she would have lost an arm. As it was, she reacted rather than thought. She threw herself out of the path of the oncoming smear of color, barely avoiding the traplike snap of the *netac*'s serrated beak.

Her hope that the beast could travel two days without food had been in vain. Only a day had passed since its last feeding, and she had been unable to find game large enough to sate the *netac*'s voracious appetite. Now the creature hunted for itself!

A frustrated squawk filled the air as the gargantuan bird's slender neck arched back an instant before the massive head savaged out again.

This time she was ready for the attack. A strong flick of her wrist sent the haft of the Havenite spear she carried flying up. Solidly, it smacked against the side of the *netac*'s head.

The creature's clear blue eyes blinked as it jerked away from an unexpected and painful defensive. Another bleating squawk ripped from the beast's throat.

Arianne's wrist flicked again, intent on bringing the steel head of the spear around and driving it into the *netac*'s exposed neck. She wasn't quick enough. The bird's long, violet-hued beak lashed out for a third time.

She ducked. The wickedly serrated beak snapped closed on empty air that had contained her head but a heartbeat before. Arianne lunged, driving the spearhead forward with all her might.

Not into the *netac*'s throat, but into the thick feathers of its stubby wings the spear skewered. The beast head lifted to the sky, and it screeched in pain.

Yanking the spear free, she lunged again. The cold steel plunged deeply into the bird's chest.

The *netac*'s yowl was a continuous scream now. The bird leaped back, jerking the haft from Arianne's grasp. For an instant she readied herself to leap away from the creature's charge. There was no need. The *netac* took one wobbly step forward before it collapsed to the ground, its massive body twitching spasmodically as life fled.

"Arianne!" Pau's panicked cry came from behind her. "Arianne, what's wrong?"

Grimly she turned to face the Havenite. "Good news. We'll have fresh meat for breakfast." She looked back at the bird's carcass. "The bad news is that you have to walk the rest of the way to Kestkap."

Although she had scraped every trace of meat from the *netac*'s shin bone and left it in the sun to dry throughout the day, it still carried the stench of rotting flesh. She glanced at Pau, who clung to her with one arm while his free hand used the bone as a short cane to help support his weight.

For the five hours since Opat had set, they had travelled thusly. For ten minutes they walked, then rested five to allow Pau to gather his strength. From the pained expression twisting his face, she realized it was time for another five-minute break.

"Time to rest again," she said while she helped him sink to the rocky ground.

"Can you judge High Hold's distance?" He turned his head toward the direction of her voice.

"We're making progress." She avoided a direct answer as her gaze lifted to the still distant night-shadowed mountain.

In spite of the strength provided by their unfortunate meal of roasted *netac*, Pau's inability to walk was hindering them. They were close to the mountain, but not close enough. And the question that ate at Arianne's mind was— were they capable of reaching High Hold before dawn?

"You could leave me here and continue to High Hold on your own," Pau said as though reading her thoughts. "When you reach Kestkap, you could send a search party back for me."

"Wrong," Arianne answered. She stood and half-dragged Pau to his feet. "This is a big desert and the only landmark I know is that damned mountain. We go into Kestkap together or . . .''

She swallowed the rest of her sentence, afraid that giving voice to the alternative might bring it to pass.

''Drink slowly, let it roll around in your mouth before you swallow.'' She placed the open waterskin to his lips. ''Slow and easy. Make it last.''

Pau did as she ordered. Then they rose and began to walk again, leaving an empty skin on the sand behind them—the last of their water.

''No sleep!'' Arianne nudged Pau's shoulder as his head nodded toward his chest. ''If we sleep here, we'll never wake. On your feet. We walk.''

Wearily they pushed from the sand and with Arianne half-carrying the Havenite leader, they pushed through the Havenfound day toward High Hold.

Arianne found the waterhole as Opat reached a fiery zenith—or Rik did. Baked by the heat until the ground was shattered by deep cracks, the small pond had shrunk to a puddle no larger than her foot.

She allowed the tikka two quick sips in reward for the find, then she knelt beside Pau and directed his lips to the muddy puddle. He drank his two sips slowly, leaving two for her. The remaining mud, she spread on their faces to shield their skin from the sun's harsh light as they once more walked-hobbled westward.

The tree was small with a dense stand of bushes growing to its right, but it's thick foliage provided shade from the afternoon sun. Lowering Pau against the trunk, she collapsed to the ground, staring at the mountain that towered above them.

''We've made it,'' she said, each syllable rasping her dry throat. She searched High Hold's slopes, but found nothing. Panic twisted into tight knots within her breast.

Had she somehow made a mistake and brought them to the foot of the wrong mountain? "Where is Kestkap? Where the hell is Kestkap?"

"You're sitting on it, Arianne Pillan. The entrance is up there hidden by those rocks—a cavern."

Her head snapped to the right. Ten Havenites stepped from behind the dense bushes. The men and women's gazes shifted between her and Pau.

Etenia stood at their head, smiling. "You have passed your final test, Arianne. You have been judged worthy to speak with our leaders."

"Test?" Arianne blinked, unable to comprehend her meaning.

"It was more than a test, Etenia," Pau spoke. "I feigned blindness as you had ordered, but my ankle was injured in the storm. We would have died had she not brought us here."

"Feigned blindness?" She stared at Pau, confusion dissipating in a rush of anger! The long desert trek had been but another of the Havenites' damnable tests! She wanted to get her hands around . . .

She caught herself, and drew a series of deep breaths to quell the mounting rage. Violence would gain her nothing, nor would an outburst of curses. She doubted that the Havenites would even understand her anger.

"We'll explain everything," Etenia said. "But first I have food and water for you. Eat and drink. Then we'll enter Kestkap."

TWENTY-TWO

They bathed her, washed and combed her hair, fed her again, medically examined her, and now two nurses—male and female—spread a cool ointment over her sunburned skin. Had she not been so weary, she would have enjoyed the soothing massage, perhaps even found it erotic. As it was, all she wanted to do was sleep, and the two pairs of hands were just insistent enough to prevent her from drifting off.

"There, that should help some." The female nurse announced while she screwed a lid on the ointment jar and handed it to Arianne. "Use this for three or four days and you'll be back to normal."

Arianne accepted the male nurse's hand as he helped her from the examination table. He handed her a small pile of neatly folded, clean, and fresh-smelling clothing. Although all she wanted to do was climb back onto the table and sleep, she managed to find the strength to dress.

"The others are waiting for you outside that door," the female nurse said when Arianne slipped the last button into its eye.

Before she could question who were the "others," the male nurse opened the door. In a larger room beyond the threshold stood Pau—arms draped over wooden crutches and ankle in a bandage—Etenia, and Aziza.

It was Aziza who stepped forward: "We've come to take you to the others."

Arianne shook her head. The Havenites had developed an irritating habit of using an indefinite "others." "What others?"

"Those who also passed their final test," Etenia answered as Arianne left the examination room. "Fax Lorens, and the white-furred Brodny Gariot."

A sense of relief flooded her upon hearing Fax's name. It was immediately replaced by flaring anger at the mention of "tests."

Arianne suppressed it; this was the Havenites' planet after all—their customs. No matter how deceptive Pau's blindness, or whatever injuries the other Havenites had feigned to force their wards into a survival situation, it seemed to her the tests were behind her, part of the past. It was time to concern herself with her purposes for being on this alien world. Simply nodding in acceptance, she followed the three from the room into Kestkap streets.

Unlike Earth's Deeprock, Havenfound's capital city lay in continual gloom. Only the perpetually burning streetlamps held back the man-made cavern's blackness. Nor did Kestcap have the arching domed ceiling that enclosed Deeprock. Flat and dark, Kestcap's rock ceiling was but an oppressive thirty meters overhead.

Like Havenfound's ten other major population centers— each claiming a quarter of a million residents—Kestkap was an extension of a natural cavern. In this case one that had sheltered the original colonists during their first years on a hostile world. The subterranean design remained as part of the Havenites' efforts to keep the surface of the world as unmarred and undisturbed as possible.

"There are farming communities built on the surface," Pau said. "But these are small and strictly regulated."

Arianne only half-listened as the three proudly described the layout of their city—a square grid—and the massive support columns required to keep the ceiling from collapsing on their heads. While only five meters of earth and rock separated Kestkap from the surface, the mass was enough to bury a quarter of a million people should the support system ever fail.

More than artificial sunlight and a spaciously arching ceiling, Arianne missed Deeprock's slidewalks. She estimated that she added another five kilometers atop her four-day desert walk before the Havenites halted outside a building they called *imamae*, which translated to "visitor's house." The block-shaped building stood three stories tall and had small windows that faced the Kestkap streets.

Inside was a cramped room that Arianne could only describe as a lobby area. A hallway lined with doors led from the back of the room and a stairway rose on the left to the second floor. Etenia and Aziza waited in the lobby while Pau did his crutch best to accompany her down the hall. They stopped before a door marked with the ancient Arabic symbol for "ten."

"These will be your quarters while you are in our city." Pau reached out and twisted a waist-level knob that opened the door to a small room that contained a bed, two chairs, a chest of drawers, and a desk. A narrow door on the right wall led to what appeared to be a toilet area. Noticeably missing was a ComNet console—or even a portable computing and logic unit.

Arianne's gaze hung on the bed. "Even a pile of straw would look good to me right now."

"I am supposed to tell you that Etenia will call on you early tomorrow morning," Pau said. "She will take you and the two others before our elders."

Arianne nodded and stepped over the threshold. She'd think about Etenia and the elders tomorrow. Now she needed sleep—a lot of it!

"Arianne," Pau called after her, waiting until she turned back to him. "I know that you judge us as a hard people—feel that I tricked you out on the desert."

She didn't answer; he said it all. She wasn't about to defend his actions for him.

"Remember this is our world. Be patient with us. Our reasons for what we had to do will become apparent to you after you have been here for a while," he continued.

She nodded. She had to accept what had happened; there was nothing else she could do.

"Such a waste." Pau drew a heavy breath and released it as a sigh. "Our ways part now. You must be about your offworlder matters, and I must attend my world."

He reached to close the door.

"Pau." There were no long hours of indecision, wrestling for an answer. She needed someone to help her, required contact with Havenfound. "I have something to ask of you."

He looked back at her, almost boyish expectation on his face. "I'll help if I can."

"I came here because of my brother, Pau," she began, explaining what had happened to Jon. "He searched for the Council of the Fully Realized. I must talk with that council."

Pau's head moved from side to side. "I've never heard of this council."

"Never?"

"But there is much I don't know about those who lead our people," he said. "My main task is that of a *orwid* . . ."

Arianne translated the word as "explorer," but it meant more—one who opened the unknown to others.

". . . However, I will find out what I can about this council for you," he said. "Now you must rest. Tomorrow will be here faster than you realize."

She didn't argue as he closed the door, leaving her alone in the small room. Stripping away her clothing, she stretched atop the bed and fell asleep in a matter of minutes.

TWENTY-THREE

"Damn," Fax cursed beneath his breath as they left the home of Gravas Contue, one of twelve elders they had visited in the past week. "We're getting nowhere. You know that, don't you?"

"They're shuffling us around," Arianne said, feeling the frustration contained in Fax's voice. "They've got us on a holding pattern. They know we're aware of it, and they don't care. Why? What are they up to?"

"Waiting to see who comes up with the best offer," Fax answered. "Trying to milk the most out of the situation."

If this planet had been any of the Tripartite Confederation worlds, she would have agreed. But it wasn't. The obvious was always more than it appeared with the Havenites. They were after something, but whatever it was they offered no hints.

"Sometimes I get the distinct feeling that these 'elders' we meet with are nothing more than an official greeting committee," she said. "We've been wined and dined. We've been treated to all the tourist attractions of Kestkap . . ."

"Which is saying little," Fax added with a grunt of disgust.

Arianne ignored him. ". . . We've been treated with the utmost respect and consideration. We've talked, but nothing has been said. It's as if this whole city is a puzzle that we're expected to solve without any clues."

"The only consolation we have is that neither the MashuCo nor Pillan Planets seem to be getting anywhere either," Fax said. "I can't tell about the Brodny. Bears are hard to read, but I don't think they're doing any better."

"They're not. I touched their *dyamni*," Arianne answered. "Dammit, Fax. It feels like we're in another Havenite test. Only this time I've no idea how we're being tested."

"I know what—" Fax stopped short as they approached their quarters. His eyes darted to Pau, who stood waiting outside the *imamae*. "There's nature boy again. He doesn't seem to be able to stay away from you."

"He's been a big help," Arianne couldn't ignore the bitterness in Fax's tone. "He's dug up several leads on Jon's activities while he was onplanet."

"All of which have dead-ended," Fax replied.

Arianne admitted that, but at least one of Pau's leads might shed some light on Jon's condition.

"You two off again this afternoon?"

"Pau found a farmer Jon visited," Arianne said with a nod.

"Then you'll excuse me if I don't take the time to say hello to your friend. I've more important things to do, like sit and stare at the walls of my room."

Before she could answer, he hastened into the *imamae*. Pau watched Fax disappear and shrugged when he turned to Arianne.

"I don't think he likes me." The Havenite grinned widely. "He doesn't like me spending so much time with you."

"He doesn't understand what we're doing," Arianne said, surprised that she made excuses for Fax's behavior. "Your elders are less than open with us."

"Maybe Taug Harkiner will be more helpful," Pau said. "We'd best be on our way. It's a two-hour ride to Widegreen from here."

"Ride?" Arianne glanced up at him.

"By *netac*," Pau answered.

Arianne shivered inwardly. After facing a hungry *netac* in the desert, she had hoped she would never see one of the birds again.

Neither Pau nor Arianne spoke as they reentered Kestkap that night. Dismounting the *netacs* at a stable, they walked through the city's streets, drawing a few glances and hushed whispers from bypassers who recognized her as an off-worlder.

Arianne's thoughts were on neither the bypassers nor their comments. The farmer Taug Harkiner had provided no more information about Jon than had the other six Havenites Pau had located. The man openly admitted that Jon had visited his farm, but his recounting made the visit sound as though Jon had been nothing more than a strange tourist who just happened by one day.

"I'm sorry about today," Pau broke the silence as they reached the *imamae*. "I had hoped Harkiner would know more."

Arianne shook her head. "It's all right, Pau. Something like this takes time. I'm just growing impatient. Everyone admits Jon was on Havenfound, but no one seems to know what he was doing."

"The same as the rest of the offworlders, I would imagine," Pau said, then glanced at the floor to hide his embarassment when they reached the door to Arianne's room.

Which includes me, she thought, but kept the comment to herself. "What about the Council of the Fully Realized? Have you been able to find out anything about them?"

Pau followed her into the room, closing the door behind him. "Nothing. No one has ever heard of such a council. Are you certain of its name?"

Arianne bit her lip and nodded. "That's what Jon called it." She sat on the edge of the bed. "Is there another Havenite council with a similar name?"

"No, nothing that I can find." Pau sat beside her. "I'd form one, if that would help."

Reaching out and taking his hand, she squeezed. "I know you would. You've been a good friend, Pau. I know it hasn't been easy for you. Offworlders aren't . . ."

"I feel more than just friendship, Arianne," he interrupted. His yellow-flecked brown eyes lifted, capturing and holding her gaze. "I think you also feel more."

"Pau," she started, only to be hushed by a finger he placed to her lips.

"You *do* feel more, don't you?"

She nodded hesitantly. She did; she had felt drawn to Pau since that first night aboard the ship. But like the mixed emotions she held for Fax, she pushed them aside, refusing to let personal matters interfere with her assignment.

"I sensed it." A smile uplifted the corners of his mouth. "It's called love. I'm not afraid to give it a name. I love you, Arianne. I think that I've loved you since I first saw you."

"Pau," she tried to speak again. This time he silenced her with a light, brushing kiss.

"I *do* love you." His lips returned, covering her mouth. His arms eased around her waist, drawing her tightly to him.

Had she wanted, she realized that she could have ended it with that kiss. She didn't want to stop it. Whether Pau or she confused love with lust, she didn't know or care. What mattered was that this felt right for here and now.

Together they sank back to the bed. While their mouths opened and their tongues met, their hands explored. Although she felt his need, Pau did not attempt to rush her at a frantic pace. Tenderly, gently, without the awkwardness of lovers sharing their bodies for the first time, he wooed her with kisses and caresses. Only when he sensed her own desire mounting, did his fingertips seek the buttons of her blouse. One after another he unfastened them to spread the released fabric widely so that his tongue and lips could possess her breasts and the erect nipples that stood atop those pliable mounds of summery flesh.

Shivery waves of excited gooseflesh transformed into delicious quakes of need within her core, as he gradually kissed his way down her stomach. His fingers slipped beneath the elastic band of her Havenite shorts and pulled them over her hips. She wiggled the cloth over her thighs and kicked the shorts away while he quickly stripped his own clothing and came to her.

In one quick thrust he entered her. In response she arched high, accepting him, clinging to him. At the same time she reached out, weaving a strand to touch and join their *dyamis* as intimately as their bodies.

Arianne went cold! Passion fled her body, leaving every muscle flaccid and unresponsive.

Pau's *dyami* was a blue—a flat, unshimmering sphere. He felt nothing—not even lust. There was no love, no desire, no hunger—nothing! He was a biological automaton performing a necessary function of life.

She closed her eyes and bit her lip to keep from screaming as his body pumped in a steady, unwavering, mechanical rhythm.

Pau left her room before Kestkap's chimes announced the coming of a new day in a city that dwelled in eternal gloom. Chilled by a horrible, icy cold, Arianne watched him hasten down the *imamae*'s hallway.

Tears welled in her eyes. What kind of man had shared her bed? The love and desire that had been missing from his *dyami* last night was there this morning. What had caused the unheard-of transformation? Although she knew that she still learned the Havenite mind, it did not erase the feeling that she had been used.

The question was—by what?

The thought that Pau was not a man, but some terrible homuncular entity conjured from her darkest nightmares would not leave her mind. No man, no human male, took a woman without some emotion—love, lust, anger, tenderness. In Pau there had only been biological need.

God, what have I gotten myself into? A shiver of unreasoning panic worked through her. She felt as though she had somehow entered a prison cell last night and now there was no escape. She needed someone to talk to, someone to tell about all that had happened. Unless she spread it out in the open, she sensed that she would never understand what had happened.

Arianne felt eyes on the back on her neck. She turned. Fax stood in the doorway of his room glaring at her.

"Bitch!" He spat the word as he strode to her. "Slut. Whore!"

She tried to shut the door, but he stepped across the threshold, blocking her.

"You're here on an assignment, which doesn't entail acting like a bitch in heat!" An angry violet tinged his cheeks. Veins stood out on his neck as his eyes narrowed to slits. "You couldn't restrain yourself, could you? You had to get him into your bed. You had to use him . . ."

"You bastard!" Arianne refused to listen any longer. "You've no right to talk to . . ."

"No, no. That wasn't it," he continued. "It wasn't him; it was me. You've been toying with me, leading me along. All the while, you've intended to sleep with Mister Nature. You did it to get back at me!"

"Out!" Arianne pointed to the open door. "What I do with my life is my business. You lost the right to say anything five years ago. Now get the hell out of here."

He glared at her, his hands balling to fists. "I'll go. But this is not the end, Arianne. Not even close to the end!"

He pivoted sharply and stormed from the room. Grabbing the knob, she slammed the door after him. A juvenile display, she realized, but she didn't care. What had occurred between Pau and her—and she still was uncertain what that was—had nothing to do with Fax!

She moved across the room and sat on the edge of the crumpled bed. "Damn!"

How had things become so knotted in the span of a few hours? She had made no promises to Fax. They weren't husband and wife, or even lovers.

And Pau? She did feel love for him. Or had felt it. Now she wasn't sure what the man evoked in her. The Pau who had entered her room last night and the one who had just left were not the same man who had shared her bed.

She drew three long breaths to help clear away the jumble in her head. As much as she wanted to turn and run from Pau, she knew she had to find him, to discover what forces were aplay in his mind, and if those same forces effected every Havenite mind.

As for Fax . . .

A knock came from the door.

She turned. Could that be Fax? Had he returned to spit forth more of his venom?

Another rap sounded on the wood. "Ms. Pillan?" A feminine voice called out.

Rising, Arianne opened the door and stood facing a petite, young blonde wearing a jumpsuit bearing a Pillan Planets emblem on its breast. She identified herself as Marrium Clanner.

"This is my second trip onplanet." She held out a folded piece of yellow paper. "Halian Tonani asked me to deliver this to you."

Arianne took the paper, thanked the woman, then closed the door. Sinking back to the bed, she unfolded the yellow sheet and read:

> *Return to the* Sadr *as soon as possible. Shuttles are arriving and departing from Base One on a daily basis. Please hurry! This is a matter of utmost urgency concerning the tikkas. The woman who delivered this can be trusted.*

Rescanning the message, she returned to the door to go after Marrium Clanner. The young blonde still stood outside as though anticipating Arianne's need of her.

"There was a Havenite here just a few moments ago? Did you happen to see him?" Arianne asked.

"Man or woman? There are several Havenites in the lobby."

Not bothering to answer or thank the woman, Arianne hastened down the hall. Pau stood talking to a Havenite woman she had never seen before. She waited until he looked up before signalling to him.

Before he could question her, she said, "I need to get to Base One as soon as possible. I've been temporarily called back to the *Sadr*. I need your help in arranging the journey."

"How soon do you wish to be there?" Pau asked.

"Like I said, as soon as possible," Arianne answered.

"Would this evening be soon enough?"

"This evening? How?"

"The easiest way would be the underground shuttle that runs to the coast, then a dirigible to your Base One." Pau said. "An airplane would be quicker, but I doubt if I could arrange for one until tomorrow. We could be at the base by then."

Arianne stared at the man. The arduous journey to Kestkap had scrambled her mind, ingraining an image of Havenfound as a backward world. Of course, these people had airplanes—even primitive spaceflight. They rode *netacs* by choice. She smiled. "Then you lied to us about the shuttle when we first landed."

Pau shrugged. "It was a necessary lie. You and your companions had to be tested."

"It doesn't matter." Arianne shook her head. "Right now we need to catch that shuttle."

"Follow me," Pau waved her to the *imamae*'s door.

An hour later they raced eastward on an underground monorail. Ten hours later, Arianne boarded a shuttle bound for the *Sadr*.

TWENTY-FOUR

"Sentient?" Arianne stared at the psiotic. Her first reaction was—*then I* was *right*! However, a healthy skepticism immediately interceded, and she said. "Prove it."

"I will. By the way, you were also right about their moodweaving ability. Low-grade to be certain, but it's there just the same. Probably the reason that the Havenite witch-doctor didn't detect you." Halian Tonani grinned and slipped a small silver box from the breast pocket of his jumpsuit. "The Net helped me design this little jewel. The programming is basically mine. I'll leave it at that, unless you want to know more. Then I'll gladly spend a day or five explaining the elegance of my techniques."

"An honest crystal hack," Arianne smiled. Programmers were all alike, they lived, ate, and dreamed programming. It was rare to find one who realized all anyone else really cared about from a program was that it worked. Unless, of course, another programmer was involved, then he wanted to know what secrets he could steal. "What is it?"

"Watch! I think it will speak for itself." Halian walked to a hatch on the right bulkhead of the laboratory in which they met and opened it. Five tikkas scampered into the room, warbling their melodic songs. Halian switched on the silver box and:

"She is new."

"She smells of home."

"One of ours?"

"Will she feed the Children of the Realized?"

"I will touch her."

Arianne stiffened as she felt a mood thread brush her *dyami*. She blocked herself, and stared at the box Halian held out. The voices came from the device—voices belonging to the tikkas!

"She does not feel me!"

"Touch the other."

"Why do they not feed the Children of the Realized?"

Halian's grin widened when he thumbed off the box. "To be certain they aren't the most intelligent creatures you've ever encountered, but don't underestimate them. They know their power, and they aren't afraid to use it to get what they want. Had to block them, didn't you?"

Arianne nodded, still numbed by Halian's revelation.

"So did I. If you're not careful, they can sneak up on you. They're subtle little devils, but they appear harmless enough." He switched the box back on, and the warbles once more streamed as words from its speaker. He flicked it off again and handed it to Arianne. "It's a miniaturized computer with a dedicated translation program. Keep it. I've one of my own."

Arianne found a slide switch on the box's side and pushed it up with her thumb.

"No color here. Children of the Realized like color."

"Food. We should be fed."

She depressed the switch. Looking back at Halian, she shook her head. "It's hard to believe. You did one hell of a job in a short time."

"I had Net helping." Halian answered, his chest swelling with obvious pride. "Net monitored their songs constantly. We had compiled a vocabulary of fifty words three days after I received your message. It's a simple language. Net wasn't really needed, a mere decoder would have broken it."

Arianne opened the switch once again:

"Floor hard."

"Children of the Realized are hungry. Why don't they feed us?"

"Cold here. Too cold."

The box clicked as she moved the switch down. She shook her head again.

Halian's wide grin spread from ear to ear. "Don't expect to learn too much from them. The tikkas are flighty. They have short attention spans, if any at all. First they'll chatter excitedly about one subject then leap to another without warning. If you try to follow them for too long, it'll drive you insane."

"What about translating my words into their tongue? Is this little item capable of that?" she asked, turning the compact computer over in her palm.

"Not yet. But I'm working on it. Having a little difficulty with recreating tones. It's quite a musical language," Halian answered with a shrug.

Arianne turned the translator on again, listening to the tikkas for several minutes. The psiotic was right; the creatures' attention span seemed to be non-existent. However, one phrase was repeated again and again. She flicked the computer off. "Children of the Realized?"

"That's what they call themselves," Halian replied.

"Close to Council of the Fully Realized, wouldn't you say?"

"Exactly. It's one of the reasons I asked you to return to the *Sadr*."

"It was the correct decision." She sensed that she held the pieces of a puzzle called Havenfound. All she had to do was place them into their correct positions. "Now, I need to put this to work. I have to arrange for a shuttle back to Opat 4."

"What about transmitting this information back to Alhim?" Halian asked.

Arianne froze for an instant. "I thought this system was jammed?"

"It is," Halian smiled. "But there are ways to get around that. I've been using the jamming shield itself.

Slight fluctuations in its energy level is all it takes. The shields itself becomes the signal.''

She hadn't expected this. If Halian could contact Pillan Planets, he had outlived his usefulness. She wasn't ready for anyone other than herself to know about the tikkas. ''Wait until you receive a message from me. There are a couple of things I want to check out on Havenfound before we contact Alhim.''

Halian nodded his acceptance.

''Good. Now I have to get back on planet.'' She opened the hatch to the lab and paused before exiting to glance over her shoulder. ''I'll see that you're appropriately rewarded for everything you've done.''

Halian grinned. So did Arianne as she hastened along a tunnel-corridor outside to find Captain Hamako Sarrantonio. It was time to put at least one of the spies aboard out of commission. It was the only way she could be certain that the psiotic didn't relay his discovery to Pillan Planets.

''Double agent?'' Arianne stared at the monitoring station's captain. ''Tonani is a double agent?''

''I think 'plant' is closer to his role,'' Sarrantonio replied with a touch of embarrassment in her voice. ''The Diplomatic Service ordered it. They wanted to be certain of your alignment.''

Alignment! Arianne silently cursed. Alignment was bureaucratese for ''loyalty.'' In simple terms, they didn't trust her. ''Damn!''

''The matter was beyond my command,'' Sarrantonio said. ''However, all the information he conveyed to you was correct. It came from your brother's real contact—a shuttle pilot.''

''Then the line you handed Fax and me when we arrived about the *Sadr*'s resources being totally ours was so much hot air?''

The captain shook her head. ''No. My orders specifically name you and Mr. Lorens as my superiors. You are in command of the *Sadr* if the situation should so warrant. Why?''

''I need a shuttle to take me onplanet,'' Arianne said.

''One's ready in the bay right now.''

Arianne shook her head. ''In five hours. I need some sleep before I return. It's been a long day.''

''What about the tikkas?'' Sarrantonio stared at her. ''Are they significant?''

''I believe they are, but just how they fit in still eludes me,'' Arianne said. ''I am certain Halian has given me enough to shake up the Havenites.''

Sarrantonio nodded. Her shoulders sagged as though they carried an invisible weight. ''I hope so. The situation has worsened during the time you've been on Opat 4. The Tripar is under extreme pressure from the Brodny, MashuCo, and Pillan Planets. All are threatening the use of military force to break our blockade of the Opat System. Unless the mining negotiations are completed and secured, Havenfound will become the first battleground of a war that will embroil every planet in the confederation.''

Arianne's stomach sank, then twisted into knots. ''How secure is the *Sadr*?''

''We can hold our own against a few ships,'' Sarrantonio replied with unrestrained pride. ''But if it comes to all out warfare, we're only a mining station.''

''Then I have to make certain it doesn't come to that.'' Her words contained all the bravado she could muster. Now she had to convince herself that she was capable of completing the job that brought her to the Opat System.

Arianne tossed to her back atop the bed. Her eyes opened wide, and she stared at the ceiling of the room. Sleep wouldn't come; Havenfound, Fax, Pau, and the tikkas crowded into her head, robbing her of rest.

Sitting up, she glanced about the room. The Net console drew her attention. ''Net, give me a visual on Opat 4.''

The console's monitor blinked on, filled with an image of the planet.

Arianne rose and crossed the room to drop into a chair in front of the console. She stared at the ringed planet. "If you could only talk and tell me what you're hiding."

"I have vocal capabilities," the Net responded in a female voice. "You have priority clearance. All my files are available to you."

Arianne smiled. "I was talking to myself, Net."

"Do you wish me to remain silent until I am given a direct command to respond?"

Arianne frowned and leaned closer to the monitor. Maybe the planet was trying to talk to her. "No. I want a closer scan of Opat 4."

Visual sensors homed on the planet and began to track across its surface.

"Stop right there." Arianne's eyes narrowed as they focused on a large almost circular yellow-tan patch of land on the continent of Paron. She was certain this was the desert from which Jon had last lifted offplanet. But it was changed! "Net give me a split-screen comparison with this and the recording of Jon Pillan's lander flight from Opat 4."

The screen winked to provide the images. Arianne sucked in a breath. She had been right! The desert area had changed; it had grown—rapidly! No longer was it irregular in shape, but had expanded in a circle that covered three times the area of the first image.

"Net, order Captain Sarrantonio and Halian Tonani to my quarters on the double!"

Both Sarrantonio and Tonani stared at the monitor screen. The captain glanced over her shoulder. "What is it? Have any idea?"

"Net, give the Captain the reading you gave me," Arianne said.

The Net replied, "Sensors indicated that area of concern is ringed by an unknown lifeform."

"What?" This from the psiotic. "Can't we get a closer scan?"

Net obliged, but the detail lacked resolution.

Arianne called to the console again. "Display the growth projection, Net."

The screen flickered to fill with an image of Opat 4. Arianne used a fingertip to point to the desert patch. "This was the way it appeared when Jon lifted." She paused while the Net switched images. "This is it today. Now for a projection based on the present growth rate."

The screen slowly flashed through a progression of six overlays. When the last image froze on the screen, the desert had expanded to totally cover Paron. Sarrantonio frowned in puzzlement, and Tonani's jaw sagged.

"That's one year from the original image," Arianne said. "If whatever is down there doesn't stop."

"What the hell is it?" Sarrantonio asked.

Arianne shrugged. "Net's sensors aren't close enough to Havenfound to even give us an educated guess. But I think you should take a look at this."

Ordering Net to project another series of images, Arianne explained. "These are recent images of Opat 4. Notice that the same desert patches are present on each of the five continents. And they're all growing. Whatever it is, it isn't limited to Paron."

Sarrantonio turned to her. "Have you formulated a course of action?"

"If you mean a detailed plan, no," Arianne replied as her gaze returned to the monitor. "But that desert is where my brother went, and that's where I intend to go."

"Then you might need this." Halian handed her a brooch identical to the one she wore.

Arianne frowned at him. "What's this?"

"A little improvement on this model," he answered as he unpinned the original brooch from her Havenite blouse. "This will provide us with both a visual image and audio. Oh, by the way, this one's permanently locked open, there's no way you can switch it off. So watch what you say and do."

BUNJINGI

TWENTY-FIVE

With no dirigible waiting at Base One to return her to Paron's coast, Arianne was required to once again board a Havenite ship for a two-day journey to the continent. While the others aboard slept or were too occupied with the vessel to notice her actions, she occasionally made use of Halian's translator. The tikkas flighty chatter provided little insight into the creatures.

However, Arianne became more convinced that the Children of the Realized were directly connected to the Council of the Fully Realized. It was the "how" that evaded her.

Reaching Eamint, she had no difficulty securing a seat on the underground shuttle, having already passed the Havenites' tests. Eight hours later she sat in Fax's room in Kestkap, explaining everything that had occurred.

"Sentient beings? Tikkas?" He stared in disbelief. "Are you certain?"

"Here's the translator Halian Tonani gave me." She withdrew the silver-cased computer and passed it to him. Fax made no mention of Pau, which was just as well. Arianne sensed she was close to something and needed Fax's help to get to the bottom of it.

"Then you were right about the Havenite-tikka link," he said while he examined the translator, then passed it back. "I think it's time we arranged a meeting with our Havenite friends and let them see just how much we know about their little pets."

"Exactly my thoughts," Arianne nodded. "I can contact Pau. What about Etenia or Aziza?"

"I'll get one of them to come," Fax replied. "We'll set the meeting just outside the entrance to Kestkap. That should avoid unwanted eyes and ears."

"Better here in the light. The Children of the Realized like the light. Dark is cold."

Arianne flicked off the computer that had translated Etenia's tikka's warble into words for the past three minutes. Rik was missing from Pau's shoulder. She looked at the two Havenites. "Which one of you cares to explain what is going on?"

Etenia glanced at Pau, then looked down at her feet. Pau drew a breath and stared at Arianne, then Fax. "What do you want from us?"

"Answers," Fax replied. "We're tired of the runaround. We'd like a few straight answers for a while."

"To begin with, I want to know what happened to my brother," Arianne said.

"We are not certain what happened to your brother." Etenia answered.

"Do you know *how* it happened?" Arianne pressed, sensing the hint of a lie in the *duman*'s words.

Neither Etenia or Pau replied, nor did their eyes rise to meet her's.

"Did it happen in the west, near the desert?" Fax questioned.

Pau nodded, and Arianne quickly added, "Will you take us there?"

"It is too soon," Etenia glanced at Pau.

"Too soon for what?" This from Fax.

"Too soon for either of you," Pau answered. "You haven't been on our world long enough. You have much to learn."

"We could ride west on our own," Arianne replied. "In fact we will, if you won't aid us."

"That would be unwise," Etenia's head snapped around.

"You must achieve understanding first, then Pau will lead you."

"You leave us no alternative," Fax replied. "We'll go on our own. Arianne, we can get *netacs* inside."

When Arianne and Fax rose and started toward Kestkap's entrance, Pau called out. "No, I will lead you to Haven Realized just as I took Jon Pillan there."

Arianne spun around. "You took my brother there?" She bombarded him a barrage of questions concerning Jon.

Pau held up his hands and shook his head. "All your questions will be answered when we arrive at Haven Realized. We can begin our journey as soon as our *netacs* are saddled. Haven Realized lies but a day to the west."

"Haven Realized." Pau waved an arm to the valley below them. "Here is where our ancestors first landed on Havenfound."

Arianne scanned the village at the foot of the gently sloping hill. She moved her whole body from left to right to make certain the visual sensor in her brooch captured the whole panorama for Sarrantonio and Tonani back on the *Sadr*.

"What is that?" Fax asked, not of the two hundred stone houses that formed Haven Realized, but a massive white stone spherical structure that rose a kilometer into the air just beyond the village.

"In part it is what I brought you, and Arianne's brother before you, to see." Pau nudged his *netac* forward. "Of all places on Havenfound, this is the most revered by my people and this monument most sacred."

"Monument?" Arianne asked.

"There will be no need for an explanation once we are inside," Pau said, leading them through Haven Realized's narrow dirt streets.

Here and there men and women hailed Pau, and, in turn, each was greeted by name. Arianne's brow knitted. The Havenite was far too familiar with the village's residents to be just an occasional visitor. "You seem to be well known here."

"I was born in Haven Realized," Pau answered as he reined the *netac* toward a broad stone ramp that led up to a wide opening in the spherical monument. "I bear the title of *ratinontitan* as did my father and his father before him. It is our duty to care for the monument so that all of Havenfound will remember."

Three villagers took their mounts when they reached the ramp. Swinging from their saddles, Pau led them upward—into the interior of a spaceship!

"What is this?" Fax stared in awe while they moved down a tunnel-corridor toward the vessel's interior levels.

Arianne's head turned from side to side, as did her body when she remembered the camera she carried. There was no hint of stone within the ship. It was all bright and shining metal!

"It's a replica of the ship that brought us here," Pau explained. "The hull is actually made from a portion of the original hull. In our early years the majority of the vessel's metal was cannibalized for other purposes. Most of what you see are recreations."

"This thing looks as if it could fly," Fax said, making no attempt to disguise the impression the monument made on him.

Pau laughed. "It is a working replica in every aspect—except the ability to fly. This ship was never designed to overcome a gravity well. The original was constructed and launched from space."

They entered a spacious level lined with walls of blinking lights. Pau spread his arms and turned a full circle. "This, too, remains from the original vessel that brought our ancestors to this planet—the ship's computer. Here is stored our total history."

"Your history?" Arianne asked. "You mean the history of the flight?"

"The flight from Earth and our time on this planet,"

Pau answered. "It is here that all our records have been stored."

He paused, turning to the two offworlders. "Now we must be leaving. The day grows late and the monument closes at sunset. Rest assured, I am not trying to hide anything from you. Feel free to explore our monument and village on your own tomorrow. Everything will be open to you; neither I nor my people wish to conceal anything from you. Now the time has come to provide the answers you desire."

Following Pau from the monument, they walked down the broad ramp to a campfire that burned ten meters beyond its bottom. Two large circular tents had been erected to each side of the ramp. Pau motioned to one then the other, noting one was for Arianne and the remaining one for Fax. Explaining he would spend the night within his own home in the village, he led them to the fire and the meal that was being prepared there.

"I will answer your questions while we eat." He seated himself cross-legged on the ground and accepted a portion of meat one of the men tending the fire passed to him.

"This is where you brought my brother?" Arianne asked while another man filled her mug with *vadr* sap. "We will meet with the Council of the Fully Realized here?"

Pau smiled. "There is no Council of the Fully Realized. Jon came to council with the Fully Realized."

"I think I sense word games," Fax said with no attempt to disguise his cynicism.

"I admit to them," Pau conceded, "until now. Their need has passed."

"Then who are these 'Fully Realized'?" Arianne pressed.

"I will begin at the beginning, when our ancestors first landed on Havenfound," Pau replied between bites of meat. "Both of you have been told the importance the tikkas played in the survival of the original colonists. But you were told only a portion of that story. Like you, the colonists discovered the tikka language. And from the tikkas came Realization."

Pau smiled like some benevolent mystic as his gaze shifted between his two guests. "The tikkas are the survivors of ancient sentient beings who once inhabited Havenfound, beings who were old and wise while Man still waded naked and knee-deep in swamp slime. They called themselves the *Yayndelaylah*—the Realized People. It is the *Yayndelaylah*'s racial memories the tikkas retain in their brains."

"The Children of the Realized," Arianne said the tikkas' name for themselves aloud. "The tikkas are what is left of the *Yayndelaylah*? How did they evolve into such simple creatures?"

"Genetic engineering is the closest humankind has come to their ability," Pau said. "They transformed their offspring, shaping them to withstand the violent flarings of a young sun."

"And were trapped in the minds and bodies of morons," Fax said.

"The *Yayndelaylah* were not fools. Although they knew that their time had passed, their children were shaped to carry their ideas and thoughts so that they might one day live again in the minds of other sentient beings," Pau explained. "Through union with the tikkas, the wisdom of *Yayndelaylah* is revealed."

"Union?" Arianne now understood. There was more than moodweaving in a tikka's mental thread. "A psi-bond between human and tikka?"

Pau shook his head and unbuttoned his shirt. He tugged the cloth down to expose his left shoulder. There his smooth skin was marred by a patch of fiery red fur. "A symbiotic union—mind and body—human and tikka are joined as one to become a Fully Realized."

"Rik!" Arianne barely swallowed the gasp that rose in her throat, although she could not escape the shiver that crept along her spine.

"Yes." Pau smiled as he closed his shirt. "Rik and I are one. The memories of his ancestors now are mine. It is this union that I now offer you—the opportunity to become a Fully Realized.''

"And it was this union that was offered my brother?" Arianne's mind stumbled, unable to accept that she had been so wrong about the tikkas and their role on Havenfound.

"It was this union he accepted,'' Pau replied, his voice growing solemn. "During his many visits to this world, he was found and adopted by a tikka. It was in this village that I placed a tikka on his shoulder so that the union of their bodies might begin. During the first minutes of the joining, Jon panicked. He rejected the tikka, throwing it from him. Like a man gone insane, he ran to his ship and lifted from our world.''

"You know that all of his memories were completely gone from his mind when he was discovered." Arianne was chilled by the description of what had occurred, what her brother had agreed to undergo. Yet she could not dwell on her own reactions, not while Pau was so open. "Why was that?"

"I have no explanation for what occurred to Jon,'' Pau replied with a shake of his head. "No man or woman had ever rejected the union before.''

"And Jon's tikka?'' Fax asked. "What happened to it?''

"It died as Jon lifted off,'' Pau said, his tone holding more sympathy for the tikka than it had for Jon. Abruptly the Havenite pushed from the ground and stood. "Now I and the others will leave you. I have offered the union, and you have much to consider. Take your time. I will leave you to your thoughts until tomorrow evening.''

Neither Fax nor Arianne spoke as Pau and the other Havenites quietly drifted into the night. Both sat, staring into the fire's flames, their minds attempting to assimilate all that had been revealed.

TWENTY-SIX

The Havenites—the few Arianne saw within the monument—
ignored her as she wandered through the replica of the ship
that had brought the colonists to Havenfound. As with
everything else Havenite, she couldn't shake the feeling
that Pau had brought Fax and her here for a reason that
went beyond the mere choice of joining the ranks of the
Fully Realized.

She shivered when she entered the ship's computer level.
Her skin crawled at the thought of a tikka melting its flesh
into hers, its mind uniting the memories of a long-dead
race of alien beings with her own.

That was on a simple emotional level. Intellectually, she
understood Jon and why he had agreed to the union. What
knowledge must be held in those memories! And all she
had to do was accept Pau's offer and that knowledge
would be hers.

And if I refuse the offer? She frowned as she seated
herself at one of the computer's stations. Pau had not
mentioned an alternative to union. Would it be wise to
ask?

She didn't know, yet somehow, she sensed there was no
alternative. The Havenites were far too secretive about the
symbiotic relationship they shared with the tikkas to allow
her to return to the *Sadr* carrying that knowledge—not if
she rejected the union.

Arianne sank into the chair and stared up at the massive

computer with its banked rows of flashing lights. There was no voice grille, only a keyboard for input. She whispered into the brooch on her chest, "Captain Sarrantonio, Halian, if either of you are watching, try to link Net with this computer. Might as well see what information it contains."

She expected to see a dancing array of blinking lights while Net electronically probed the computer and duplicated its memory banks. What she saw was nothing. Frowning, she reached out and typed in a command in Havenite. A monitor screen above the keyboard blinked and displayed the message:

Bad Command or File Mismatch

"English!" She smiled, recognizing the language of the computer's response. Her fingertips slowly tapped out "Catalog," only to receive the "Bad Command" answer again. She tried "Files" and was answered in same. Shrugging she tapped in "Help."

The computer answered:

For a list of the Operating System Commands type ? For an explanation of individual command type Help <command name>

Before Arianne could press the key bearing the question mark, a "?" appeared on the screen. Followed by the requested list. After that all she did was sit back and watch, realizing she had accidently given *Sadr*'s Net the clue it needed to unlock the computer and now those aboard the monitoring station had the situation well in hand.

Arianne's heart had tripled its beat by the time she walked from the monument's replica of the ship's engine level. She didn't know why she had doubted what Net had shown her on the screen, but she had. And she had gone to see for herself. Now there was no doubt.

The drive that existed on this level had never come from Earth. It had never even existed when humankind still inhabited its homeworld!

Hastening outward through the ship's levels, she slowed only when she reached the exit ramp. Glancing to each side, she saw no Havenites—except for Pau, who stood outside Fax's tent.

She looked westward. Opat drifted below the horizon. Evening was upon her—time to give Pau her decision about the union. The Havenite leader had to be avoided at all costs. She had to have time to think, to formulate a plan to gather the answers she needed, to delay giving her own answer on a union she would never accept.

The flap to the tent opened and Pau entered. Arianne waited and darted down the ramp into her own tent. Without pausing she moved to the back of the tent, dropped to her knees, and lifted the canvas. A hasty check to make certain that no one watched her, and she rolled outside.

Fifteen minutes later she crouched in the upper limbs of a nearby tree, watching and waiting.

The evening's grays deepened to night's black and still Arianne clung to her high perch. The massive manhunt she had expected never came. Instead, she had watched Pau exit Fax's tent and enter her own on three different occasions. Eventually he stopped several villagers to ask if they had seen her. When they shook their heads, Pau had begun to search Haven Realized's streets by himself.

Only then did she shimmy down the trunk and run to Fax's tent. Inside Fax sat cross-legged on a woven straw mat, reading what appeared to be an old printed book by the flickering flame of a single candle. His head jerked up at her entrance, and he grinned.

"Arianne! Pau's been looking for you all this evening. He was afraid you had wandered off and gotten lost or injured yourself." Fax closed the book. "Pau loaned me this old diary. It contains an account of one of the first human-tikka unions. It's quite remarkable. You should read it.''

Arianne pressed a finger to her lips to hush him, then glanced outside. Her movement had gone unnoticed. She looked back at Fax. ''Pau is the last person either one of us wants to see right now. We need to get some questions answered fast, then get out of here twice as fast!''

''What?'' Fax stood and frowned at her. ''What are you talking about?''

''To begin with, that monument out there isn't a monument! It's a spacecraft mere weeks from being a flight-worthy interstellar ship.'' She paused for a breath to calm her pounding pulse. ''I just discovered that it's equipped with a fully operational tachyon drive equal to anything we or the Brodny have. The questions we need answered are where did they get a drive that sophisticated, and what do they intend to do with it? Then, like I just said, we get the hell out of here.''

''Slow down,'' Fax said in a soothing tone. ''Unless *netacs* have suddenly developed the ability to fly in space, I believe we're stranded here.''

Arianne pointed to the bird-shaped brooch she wore. ''Optical and audio sensors. The *Sadr* has been monitoring my every movement since I returned from the ship. All we have to do is signal Captain Sarrantonio, and she'll send a shuttle to lift us out of here.''

Fax rubbed a hand over his shaven head, then moved past Arianne to glance outside. ''Then that changes the situation. The easiest course would be for us to abduct a Havenite, preferrably Pau, take him back to the *Sadr*, and let a psiotic have a go at him. The answers would come a lot easier with a mind merge.''

''I hadn't thought of that.'' Arianne started to turn.

Fax's hand shot over her shoulder. He ripped the brooch from her jumpsuit, threw it to the ground, and crushed it beneath a heel.

''Fax?'' She stared at him, her mind momentarily numbed.

''But of course, my love, I can't allow that,'' he smiled

and shrugged. "It would ruin all that I've worked for—destroy everything I had planned for you and Todd."

Arianne retreated, backstepping away from him. Something was wrong. There was a wildness in his eyes that she could discern even in the tent's dim light. "Fax, I don't understand. I . . ."

"You understand almost everything, but yet not quite enough," he said, still smiling. "Did you know it was your brother Jon who gave the Havenites that drive?"

"Jon?" Arianne stared at him. *What was he talking about*?

"Jon provided them the plans for a tachyon drive in exchange for a union with a tikka. Only he lacked the courage to complete the union. MashuCo sent me here for the same reason. Now I intend to take full advantage of Jon's mistakes."

"MashuCo?" She wasn't certain that she heard correctly. Fax was an agent for MashuCo? "Then you were the one who tried to kill me."

"*No*! I didn't know anything about that until the flash bomb back on Earth. That's when I began to realize that MashuCo was using me the same way the Service had for all these years. It was then that I knew what I had to do for us, for you, Todd and me." Panic twisted his face. "You have to believe me, Arianne. I never wanted to hurt you. I love you."

"I know," she forced herself to answer, watching that strange smile immediately return to his face. He had snapped, crossed the line into insanity.

"Then you'll understand why I had to do what I've done." He opened the neck of his jumpsuit and pulled the fabric over his left shoulder.

"Fax!" Arianne barely caught her shocked gasp, muting it. The head of a tikka protruded from his flesh, the rest of the creature's body was already joined to his. The tikka's unblinking eyes stared at her, wide and liquid.

"I accepted Pau's offer this morning after you entered the monument," he said. "The Tripartite Confederation is dead, has been for decades. The corporations now rule, Arianne . . .''

"Fax, how could you?'' Her eyes welled with tears, and her core flowed icy cold as she stared at the unblinking horror on his shoulder. "How could you do this to yourself?''

He continued speaking as though she didn't exist, ". . . When your union is complete, we will be an unstoppable team. All we have to do is secure the mining rights to Opat 6. Whether we sell them to MashuCo, Pillan Planets, or even the Brodny doesn't matter. We'll assure ourselves the position of royalty in the new order of the universe. And we can have those rights. Pau has placed them in our palms. All we have to do is snatch them up.''

"No.'' Arianne's head moved from side to side. The union had driven him insane.

"No?'' Fax frowned. "Don't you see it? The Havenites need us to control the *Sadr* so that they can launch their ship. We'll give that to them in exchange for the mining rights to Opat 6. Plus we'll have all the knowledge the tikkas carry in their memories. No one will be able to stop us, Arianne. *No one*!''

"Fax, listen to yourself. Listen to what you're asking me to do,'' she pleaded to the humanity that she prayed still existed within his breast. "Listen to what you're saying. What you're planning will cause war! I came here to stop that war. Listen to—''

"I know what I'm saying,'' he snapped. "I know what you're saying. I feared such stupidity. Arianne, there will be war no matter what happens on this planet. All we can do is chose to be on the side of the winner. MashuCo or Pillan Planets—it's of no concern to me. Either will pay our price. The choice is ours. With what we'll have to offer, we can make or break either. Make that choice, Arianne. Make it.''

The glittering fragments of the bird brooch sparkled amid the dirt. Her only hope for a clean escape shattered.

"Give me your choice, Arianne.''

"I've already chosen," she said.

Fax stiffened. "I had hoped what I planned would be for you, Todd, and me. But I think you can understand that I can not allow you to live, not when you know about the human-tikka union. I'm sorry, Arianne. I do love you."

Without the slightest hint of attack, he threw himself forward, hands outstretched for her neck.

Arianne reacted rather than thought. She ducked and shot by him. Immediately, Fax pivoted. His left hand, balled into a tight, white-knuckled fist, lashed out in a side-armed blow.

She jerked back, but not quickly enough. The strike grazed her chin. Pain exploded in her jaw, jarring through her skull. Blinking through the momentary daze, she saw Fax charge once again. This time she spun out of his path, twisting a full three hundred and sixty degrees. One after another her hands struck open-palmed blows to the left side of his lower back.

The internal vibration of the strikes penetrated to Fax's kidney. He howled in pain, but did not stop. Instead he swirled about, rage contorting his features.

Arianne didn't allow him another step. Her right leg snapped up, then lashed out to bury her foot in his groin.

This time he yowled and stopped, doubling over to clutch himself. Arianne stepped in, her left knee jerking up and slamming into his face.

Fax fell, tumbling back into a wooden cot that sat on the left side of the tent. An ugly crack sounded when his skull hit the unyielding wood. He collapsed to the ground, unmoving; a trickle of crimson flowed from his temple.

Kneeling beside him, Arianne placed three fingers to his neck. There was a pulse; Fax still lived. Her gaze fell on the tikka head that melted into his shoulder—if this still were Fax!

Arianne's neck jerked around. A terrible screeching filled the night outside the tent—the voice of screaming tikkas!

TWENTY-SEVEN

Arianne threw open the tent flap. Her eyes widened then narrowed.

Twenty-five meters beyond the tent, a hundred tikkas—two hundred of the animals—swarmed over the ground in the light of Havenfound's moons. Throwing back their feline-shaped, furred heads, they screeched a single word in unison, then in the next instant chorused each other, and in the next chanted in rhythm.

Nor was their frantic running random, but in a carefully defined pattern—a neat circle. No tikka overstepped either the inner or outer boundary as they leaped and bounded in an ever-increasing pace.

At the center of that living ring stood a shadow-cloaked man. He threw back his head, and his mouth wrenched wide. If a scream tore from his throat, it did not penetrate the barrier of sound created by the tikkas' screeching.

The man pressed hands to ears and stumbled; the ring of leaping tikkas instinctively flowed with his every movement. The perfection of their circle was never marred by so much as a ripple. Yet no tikka appeared to threaten the man. Instead they danced around him singing their one word chant.

Arianne's hand dug into a waist pocket of her jumpsuit, slipping out Halian's translator. Her thumb flicked the switch. Nothing—the computer's speaker was silent. Shaking the silver-cased device, she lifted it to an ear. It had not malfunctioned; its voice was but a whisper lost among the tikkas' cry.

"Devourer! Devourer!" the computer translated, changing rhythm to match the tikkas. "Devourer! Devourer! Devourer! Devourer!"

Devourer? Arianne's gaze shot back to the encircled man just as he swirled about, moonlight washing over his face. Horror, like a spike of ice, pierced her breast. She screamed, "*Pau*!"

For the span of a heartbeat, she thought that she saw a glimmer of recognition on his face. Then his neck jerked back, and he screamed at the moons again.

Arianne ran from the tent, the tikkas scattering as she pushed through their circling mass. "Pau! Pau!"

The Havenite's arms shot out, throwing her to the ground. A growl, more bestial than human, ripped from his throat. "No! Go away!"

"Pau, let me help you!" She tried to rise, and he shoved her back to the ground.

"Away! There is nothing that can be done. The time of full realization is upon me! My council is now with others like me!"

With that, he turned and ran westward into the night. But not before Arianne had seen his face in the full light of the two moons. More than agony twisted and knotted his features. The very muscles of his face seemed to have gained a life of their own. They shifted and rearranged themselves beneath his writhing flesh!

"Devourer! Devourer! Devourer!" The tikkas didn't follow the fleeing man. Instead they sat on their haunches, chanting as he disappeared into the darkness.

What did I see? Arianne picked herself up from the ground. Her mind refused to accept the grotesque contortions of Pau's face while she searched the night around her, certain of the Havenite eyes that watched. There were none; in spite of the tikkas' unholy howling, not one villager had come out of his home to investigate the screeching.

Her gaze shifted back to Pau. Whatever she had seen, she was certain that it had never been meant for her eyes. There was but one way to uncover the Havenites' secret—she ran after the man, following his screams into Havenfound's night.

The purples and grays of predawn were edged aside by golden light blushed with a hint of rose. Arianne stopped, collapsing atop a rounded boulder. She sucked the cool morning air into her burning lungs.

Throughout the night she had followed Pau, forcing her body to run until her muscles cramped, then moving ahead in a steady walk. While she often lost sight of him, she was never out of range of his anguished cries—screams that now held no trace of humanity in their wild strains.

It was such a cry, a rage-filled howl of a tortured animal, that twisted her head to the west. In the distance, she saw barren rocks and sand. She blinked and shook her head, finally recognizing the bleak terrain for what it was—desert! She was but kilometers from the edge of Paron's expanding desert!

The bestial scream rose again. A half a kilometer from her position Arianne found its source. Pau knelt on the ground with his arms clutching his stomach. Forcing her exhausted body to function, she rolled from the boulder and stumbled forward.

She had covered half the distance when he abruptly twisted about. His arms thrust outward, palms flat and fingers splayed wide as though signalling her to halt. His head moved from side to side. She ignored both and continued toward him.

A mere ten strides from where he knelt, she halted when his head lifted to her. A horrified scream pushed into her throat and froze there unreleased. She backed away. The face that stared at her held no resemblance to anything human.

Bloody empty sockets, eyeballs apparently torn out during the night, no longer sat at the center of his face. One had been twisted and pushed to what should have been Pau's left temple; the other opened a hole in his neck. Somewhere in between were two long slits, the stretched remnants of nostrils. The understructure of what had once been a nose no longer existed. Nor did his mouth, unless the swollen gash that ran across his forehead was elognated lips.

"No." Arianne's head shook from side to side in denial of what she saw.

Her refusal to accept the truth did not alter what Pau had become. While she stared on in horror, a thin red wound that oozed a single drop of crimson opened at his hairline. Like a fracture line running down a cracked egg, it split his face into two sections. These then separated!

There was no spewing fountain of red. Pau's flesh simply peeled back, curling like dry, brittle parchment then falling away. From his desiccated human husk emerged . . .

Arianne had no single word to describe the malformed thing that stood before her. But she had heard the tikkas' word and knew this creature to be a—*Devourer*!

A serrated mandible split the Devourer's sickly green, oval-shaped head from its forehead to chin. Jointed stalks topped by tiny pinchers, like miniature arms, lined each side of that snapping maw. Positioned an equal distance from that vertical mouth were two black bulbous eyes with multifaceted lenses that reflected a myriad of images of Arianne's face contorted by her frozen scream.

The Devourer took a shakey step forward on rail-thin segmented legs that ended in feet with long, yellow re-curved claws rather than toes. Its head bobbed hesitantly on a thick neck from which a webbed fan of spines bristled.

Insect! railed in Arianne's brain, but this was no insect! The creature stood on two legs and had but two arms that ended in hands with four fingers and an opposing thumb. Triple-jointed as they were, those digits resembled no human fingers. Recurved claws, as yellow as the taloned toes, tipped each finger. Hornlike protrusions pushed like spikes from each knuckle.

Nor was the Devourer's body armored in chitin. The same sickly green pallor as its disproportionly large head, the creature's chest, arms and legs were almost flaccid in appearance, and riddled with bulging blue veins.

The Devourer took another step toward Arianne, paused, its head weaving from side to side, then abruptly pivoted and ran westward in long bounding strides.

An overly held breath escaped Arianne's lungs in a loud gust of relief. She still lived—and she had no doubt that the Devourer had intended to attack her. Why had it turned away and fled? More importantly, exactly what was it?

"Take her!" A man's voice shouted from behind her.

Arms grasped Arianne before she could spin around. Rough fingers dug into her flesh. She twisted and kicked to escape, but the hands clamped tighter. A pair of arms encircled her waist, lifted her into the air, then threw her to ground. She groaned as knees pressed into her back, pinning her in the dirt.

"Tie her!" A voice she now recognized as Fax's ordered. "Tightly—hands and feet. We don't want her getting away a second time."

Thick, coarse rope looped about her wrists and ankles, biting into her flesh, threatening to cut off circulation. Taut knots were tugged closed, and the hands returned to roll her to her back. Fax leaned over her grinning while five villagers stood behind him.

"You bastard!" she spat, while she tried to kick out at him. The action only jerked the line that bound her arms and legs together; the rope painfully burned into her wrists.

"We had hoped that it wouldn't come to this." Fax stood up and glanced westward. "That you would not see the final transformation. Now that you have stared upon the face of a Fully Realized, there is no way we can allow you to live."

"You already said that." Arianne worked her wrists back and forth, trying to slip her hands free. She only managed to tighten the knots. "You were going to kill me because I witnessed a union with a tikka, remember?"

"The one you called Fax threatened that," he answered. "He is no more." He knelt beside her and pulled the translator from a jumpsuit pocket. "An interesting device, but no longer of any use to you."

Dropping the computer to the ground, he crushed it into the dirt beneath his booted foot. "In fact, you'll soon have no use for any material article—you'll be food for the Fully Realized, the Devourers."

He glanced to the desert again, then back to the villagers. "As for us, we'll be gone before the Realized turn on their children. With the knowledge your brother gave us and the memories the one called Fax has provided me, the stars will at last be ours. The ship we build and others like it under construction will free us from this imprisoning ball of clay. For that we thank you."

He turned and waved the others after him.

"Come back here!" Arianne shouted. "You son of a bitch, come back."

Neither Fax nor the villagers paused, but disappeared over a rolling rise to the east.

Arianne rolled to her side and bent her knees. She stretched her fingers toward her ankles, but could not reach the knots binding them. She rolled again, this time to her knees; her hands easily found the knots, but she could not wedge a finger into one to loosen it. Desperately, she began to claw at the rope with her fingers, jerking, tugging, tearing, anything that would open one knot. Nothing helped.

Remain calm, she ordered herself. She closed her eyes and sucked in several steadying breaths. If she approached the bindings coolly, in an orderly fashion, she knew that she could eventually work a knot free. And one knot would lead to opening the others.

Her eyelids reopened. In the west was the desert, and ringing that barren wasteland were—Devourers! *Unknown lifeforms*, she recalled the *Sadr*'s Net's classification. She shivered, wishing that she hadn't run into one of the monstrous creatures face-to-face.

They're eating! Arianne's eyes widened. Clawed hands and feet acting like scythes, the Devourers destroyed everything that lay in their path. Animal, insect, or plant, it didn't matter, the Devourers uprooted it or disemboweled it and then ate it—everything!

She now understood the secret to Havenfound's constantly increasing deserts. Worse, she understood Fax's meaning when he had said that she would soon be food for the Devourers! Before rising Opat sank to end this new day, the Devourers would have reached and passed her position by at least half of a kilometer!

TWENTY-EIGHT

Arianne closed her eyes and concentrated on wedging a fingernail between the strands of rope. She dug, widening the gap to admit her fingertip. For an instant the taut rope resisted, then shifted just enough for her to slip one finger, then two, and finally three between the strands. She tugged and the knot came free.

Two down, she congratulated herself, and then added, *two to go*.

She opened her eyes and glanced overhead. Opat steadily climbed toward the zenith. Most of the morning was gone, and she had managed to untie only two of the four knots that bound her ankles. Unless she worked through the remaining two at a quicker pace, the . . .

She shoved the thought aside and clamped her eyes shut again, refusing to glance westward. It didn't help. She imagined that she heard the crunching and tearing of the Devourers' mandibles.

Forget them, she ordered herself. *Work on the knots*!

Her fingers returned to the rope, probing for . . .

Thunder roared!

Arianne's eyes flew open; her head jerked from side to side. Only a few cottony clouds drifted across an otherwise blue sky. The thunder was not thunder at all, but the breaking rockets of a lander.

"Lander!" She shouted as realization penetrated her momentary daze. A lander with its thin, silver wings spread wide, banked in a tight turn, then glided toward the ground.

Forgetting her bonds, she tried to stand and wave her arms—and succeeded in tumbling herself to her side. She managed to roll to her knees in time to watch the needle-nosed craft gently touch the ground and ramble to a halt a hundred meters from her position.

"Halian!" She shouted when she recognized the psiotic who stood in the craft's opening hatch. "Here! Halian, I'm here!"

The psiotic glanced back into the craft, motioned two armed men out ahead of him, then leaped to the ground, running toward her.

"I didn't think that I'd ever see your face again," Arianne grinned when the man reached her side and knelt to attack the ropes holding her.

"I wasn't too certain about that either," he answered. "Captain Sarrantonio saw your sensors go dead last night, but wouldn't authorize a search until this morning. What happened?"

She quickly explained Fax's union and the insanity that had resulted. She paused for only the time needed to breathe a sigh of relief when he freed her legs and she stretched them before her. As she twisted around to let him at her wrists, she gave him a thumbnail sketch of her encounter with a member of the Fully Realized.

"You mean those things we saw to the west are the Fully Realized?" Halian whistled while he tugged the last knot binding her wrists free.

"The final metamorphosis of the tikkas after they're joined with a human," Arianne said. "At least, that's what I think is happening. I want a full sensor reading of the Devourers before we head back to the *Sadr*. I don't think that we'll get another chance at them. After it's learned that I've made it offplanet, no offworlder will be allowed back on Havenfound. I was supposed to be a Devourer's afternoon snack."

"No problem." Halian nodded as he helped her to her

feet. "We'll do a couple of flyovers and get everything we can."

Waving the two guards on ahead of them, he motioned for Arianne to lead the way to the landing craft.

"Five passes," the pilot turned to Halian. "Is that enough?"

In turn the psiotic glanced at Arianne, who nodded. "Time to head back to the *Sadr*."

Halian shook his head. "Not quite. You have the readings that you want. Now I'd like to go after a couple of things to do some readings on for myself. Like you said, I don't think we're going to be welcome here after today."

He turned back to the pilot. "Head us back toward the village. Keep low to the ground. I sighted what I wanted when we were coming in."

The pilot's frown was almost a reflection of Arianne's dubious expression, but neither of them questioned the psiotic. Five minutes later Halian grinned and jabbed a finger toward the ground. "There's the specimens I want to pick up."

Arianne smiled when she saw Fax and the five villagers still plodding their way back to Haven Realized. Before smashing her brooch last night, Fax had suggested that they abduct a Havenite and return him to the *Sadr* for a mind merge. Now he would fill the bill perfectly.

"You want me to send the boys out and get them all?" the pilot asked.

"Two or three would be nice," Halian answered. "But Fax Lorens by himself will do. Tell your men I want them *stunned* not dead!"

"Understood!" The pilot replied, then spoke into the control console to relay the command to the two guards who were stationed beside the lander's hatch.

Fifteen minutes later an unconscious Fax and two equally unconscious Havenites were stretched on the lander's deck as the pilot nosed the craft upward for the return flight to the *Sadr*.

TWENTY-NINE

"Net has compiled the first shuttle readings," Captain Hamako Sarrantonio called out. "You'd better take a look at this."

Arianne turned from the one-way mirror that windowed an adjacent room where Halian Tonani, assisted by six armed guards, had spent the last four hours merging with the minds of his three captives. Sarrantonio sat staring at an enhanced image of Havenfound that Net had compiled from the sensor readings of the three shuttles she had dispatched to orbit the planet upon learning of the Havenites' plans of launching interstellar vessels. Arianne sank into a contour-conforming couch beside her.

"There's the ship you discovered." The captain pointed to a pulsing point of red superimposed on the planet's image. "Look—another one."

Arianne recognized the location. The second ship was neatly tucked behind High Hold. She didn't doubt that an underground tunnel led from Kestkap to the ship.

One after another, twenty blinking red lights appeared on Opat 4 as Net slowly revolved the image. Sarrantonio sank into her chair and shook her head. "Your Havenite friends have been busy. And these are just the first readings. They could have another twenty ships tucked away down there."

"I don't think so," Arianne answered, re-counting the flashing red points to come up with the same total of twenty. "If you'll look, you'll see that the majority of the ships are built near Havenite cities. Each ship is capable of easily holding a quarter of a million people. The ten remaining ships are sprinkled throughout the continents. My guess is that they're centrally located and meant for Havenfound's rural population."

Sarrantonio stared at her. "You're implying that they intend to evacuate the entire planet?"

"It looks that way. They have the ships to do it. There's no other reason for building that many ships." The question that still puzzled Arianne was—why? Why had the Havenites schemed and worked so long and hard to construct ships to carry them from the world they loved so?

"She's right," Halian said from behind them. "The ships are meant for a planetwide evacuation—humans and tikkas. Only the Devourers were to be left onplanet."

Arianne and the captain glanced over their shoulders, watching the psiotic wearily walk across the room and drop into a chair. He sighed and shook his head. "It's hard to believe, but what we're basically dealing with is a matter of locusts."

"Locusts?" Sarrantonio frowned. "What are you talking about?"

"It's an ancient Earth insect that we managed to take to the stars with us via eggs in planting seed," Arianne explained. "You've probably seen them; they're usually called grasshoppers. A voracious insect by its own right, but periodically they swarm. That's when they earn the name 'locusts.' In massive clouds they move, stripping and destroying the vegetation in their path."

The frown faded from the captain's face and she uttered, "The Devourers."

Halian nodded. "Locusts to the nth power."

Sarrantonio turned to Arianne again. "But I thought the Havenite, this Pau, told you that the union with the tikka unlocked the memories of a long-dead, benign alien race?"

Arianne shrugged. "Apparently he lied."

"No," Halian corrected, "he only told half of the true

situation. There are memories of two alien races inside those men's heads—the tikkas and the *Yayndelaylah*.''

Opat 4 evolved two sentient lifeforms, Halian explained. The dominant was the *Yayndelaylah*, who like humankind developed and conquered its world. The tikkas isolated on the smallest of Havenfound's water-bound continents were trapped by their limited intelligence and their Devourer metamorphosis.

"The tikkas can bind themselves to any animal," Halian said. "By keeping their numbers small, they survived the once-every-thousand-year cycle of the Devourers' transformation."

"The metamorphis occurs but once a millennium?" Sarrantonio asked.

"A thousand-year cycle," Halian repeated. "The culmination of that cycle is the Devourers. Their lifespan is relatively short, months by our standards, but their effect is devastating."

He continued to recount the memories that he had shared during the merges with the Havenites by explaining that the tikkas' continent was the last discovered and explored by the *Yayndelaylah*. Recognizing the strength of these newcomers, the tikkas immediately linked themselves to the *Yayndelaylah*.

"The *Yayndelaylah* offered an escape from their continent and the Devourers," Halian said. "Between cycles the tikkas were spread to all of Opat 4's continents. In that same period the *Yayndelaylah* entered its industrial revolution, conquered the sky, and began to reach for space."

"Then the Devourers reappeared," Arianne said, realizing where the psiotic was leading.

Halian drew a deep breath and nodded. "The metamorphis almost destroyed the *Yayndelaylah*, sending them back to the most primitive of existences. They never achieved their former glory. Each Devourer period diminished the *Yayndelaylah*'s numbers until they were no more. The tikkas destroyed them—and their own hope of escaping the planet that now entrapped them."

The psiotic paused and glanced at the monitor screen. "I believe the Devourers would have eventually destroyed their own world and the tikkas during this metamorphosis. Their numbers will be too great for anything to survive."

"But the colonists arrival on Opat 4 once again gave them a route of escape," Sarrantonio said, her own eyes returning to the red points on Havenfound's image. "The ships—that's why they're building the ships!"

Arianne caught her breath. Pau had brought her and Fax to Haven Realized for more than offering them a union with the tikkas. Was it his love for her, or the last vestiges of humanity reaching out to save what he had once been? She didn't know, but she didn't doubt that he had wanted to reveal the truth of the human-tikka union to her.

"And intend to launch them in a week," Halian said. "They now possess the means to spread themselves across the galaxy and infect all of humankind's worlds— thanks to us."

"But we have the *Sadr*." Arianne pushed to the edge of her chair. "We can stop them."

"Not with the *Sadr*," Sarrantonio said. "This is a mining ship, not a war vessel. We can defend ourselves if necessary, but we haven't the maneuvering capability to deal with twenty ships equipped with tachyon drives. We could probably take a few, but the rest would slip into tachyon space before we could train energy beams on them."

Arianne refused to accept defeat. "You have three weapon-laden cruisers sitting outside. Why not put them into action?"

The captain stood and paced for a few moments before she again shook her head. "If we had a month—even two weeks—we could. But I don't have the crews needed to handle ships like that. All I have in my command are shuttle and tug pilots. You can't just turn them loose with cruisers. You have to train them."

She paused and looked at Arianne. "Next you're going to suggest that we use the cruisers' own crew. Do you really think you can trust them to comprehend the situation? Given the chance, they'd turn their guns on us!''

Arianne didn't press the captain; she sensed the pressure pushed Sarrantonio toward panic.

"Even if I had the capabilities to take such action, it would be madness! The Brodny would see it as an act of aggression, and the corporations would use such a move on Opat 4 as an excuse for open warfare against the Tripar. And that's the very thing we're here to avoid," Sarrantonio concluded.

"That's what we *were* here for." Arianne shoved to her feet and moved to the room's hatch. "As of this moment, I assume command and responsibility for the *Sadr*." She palmed the hatch open.

"Where are you going?" Halian asked.

"To my quarters to think," she answered and left the two staring after her. She didn't have time to waste arguing; she had to find a way to destroy those ships and Havenfound with them, if at all possible.

She walked among her miniature forest, watering each of the bonsai with a long-necked, copper, watering pail. Tonani had done an excellent job of caring for the plants during her long absence. She reminded herself to tell him so when there was time.

Placing the pail beside the backdoor to her temporary home, she smiled and entered the house. The few brief minutes spent with the trees equalled hours that others spent in meditation. Her mind was clear and felt refreshed. Now she was ready to tackle the problem before her.

Inside her bedroom, she switched on the Net monitor. Weeks away from Earth had not erased the habit of requiring the security of an ever-present monitor screen. She frowned when she saw Net display the image of Havenfound.

"Net, give me a view of the outside. Anything but Opat 4. Just scan space if you want," she ordered.

The image flickered, replaced by a gently shifting image of the void that surrounded the *Sadr*. Arianne glimpsed the cruisers that hung above the monitoring station. There was her solution—if she had the crews to man the ships.

Which I don't, she told herself. *What I do have is a mining ship as big as a small planet that I have to . . .*

Her gaze drifted back to the screen; her heart doubled its pace. It was so obvious; the very thing that Earth feared would serve her here. Why hadn't she thought of it before now? "Net hold that image."

She moved to the monitor and leaned down to stare at the field of rocky debris that stretched endlessly away from the *Sadr.* Her attention focused on a massive chunk of flotsam floating near the edge of the asteroid belt.

Placing her finger atop the touch-sensitive screen, she asked, "Net, what are the dimensions on this?"

"Twelve kilometers in diameter," Net responded.

"Give me some figures on what would happen if this rock fell to Opat 4."

"At what speed?"

"Various speeds." She settled into the chair before the console. Sarrantonio had said all that she had in her command were shuttle and tug pilots. Arianne bit her lower lip; those pilots might not be trained in warfare, but they did know how to pluck an asteroid from its orbit and maneuver it through space.

A second later, the screen blinked and filled with several columns of figures. She found what she wanted when she reached an entry velocity of twenty-nine kilometers per hour. In spite of the asteroid's iron and nickel content, approximately two-thirds of its mass would burn up in Havenfound's atmosphere.

However, a small mountain of rock three point nine kilometers would impact the planet. And that impact would produce the results of a seven megaton explosion. A crater eighty kilometers in diameter would be ripped into the surface of the planet.

Arianne's pulse raced, her temples pounding. "Net, what is the largest chunk of rock within Opat's asteroid belt?"

"Two hundred and fifty-three point seven six kilometers in diameter."

"Beginning with asteroids twenty kilometers in diameter and stepping ten kilometers at a time all the way to two hundred and fifty, give me a projection on the damage an asteroid at each step moving at a speed of twenty-nine kilometers an hour would do if it struck Opat." A cold sweat prickled over her body when she read the list Net produced. Her mouth gone cotton, she swallowed and ordered. "Tell Captain Sarrantonio to meet me in her shell-level office immediately."

An unnatural chill suffused every cell of her body as she rose and walked from the house to join the captain. She had the weapons she needed, but could she use them?

THIRTY

An unexpected serenity settled over Arianne Pillan's mind as she watched the first of thirty ninety-kilometers-in-diameter missiles enter Havenfound's atmosphere. The images of screaming men, women, and children devoured in a planet-shattering holocaust that had haunted her for five days were gone. The time to back out had passed; it remained for history to judge her decision as that of a savior or madwoman.

The asteroid's underbelly glowed cherry red warmed by the friction of its meeting with Havenfound's atmosphere, then white-hot an instant before flames engulfed its mass. Like a piece of hell, it fell toward the planet, two-thirds of its mass seared away.

"My god!" Halian Tonani gasped when he entered the office and stared at the monitor screen as the asteroid struck the planet. "I saw Net's figures, but I never imagined anything like this!"

Arianne had; like a loop of spetape the horror of this moment had repeated itself in her mind day and night. Reduced to a mere thirty kilometers in diameter, the asteroid impacted Havenfound, exploding with a force equalling three thousand six hundred megatons. It ripped a five-hundred-kilometer-wide crater from the face of the planet, while sending chunks of earth soaring into space. In that instant a two-thousand-two-hundred-forty-kilometer-per-hour wind, heated to four-thousand four-hundred twenty-six degrees centigrade, lashed out from ground zero, vaporizing any living thing in its path.

Those were the visible effects, Arianne realized. Worse was the shock wave that shuddered through Havenfound. It would circle the entire planet three times before subsiding. In spite of the massive columns that supported their ceilings, none of the Havenites' ten underground cities would survive.

And if they did—twenty-nine more asteroids would strike the ringed world at one-hour intervals.

"The planet won't hold together," Halian said, as though just realizing what she had unleashed.

"It will, but it won't be the same world. Nothing will be alive on or beneath its surface," Arianne answered. "Net predicts that we'll send it into a new, highly elliptical orbit."

"It had to be done." This from Captain Sarrantonio, who leaned against the office's wall, half-hidden by the shadows. "They could never be allowed to leave Opat 4."

"I feel silly," the psiotic said, embarrassment in his tone. "All I came to tell you was that all the tikkas aboard have been destroyed."

"Good." Arianne turned from the screen. "But that doesn't eliminate the possibility that some of the tikkas have already joined with human hosts here on the *Sadr*. Or the Brodny."

"The time of the metamorphosis is upon them," Sarrantonio answered. "They'll reveal themselves soon enough, and we can dispose of them. Until then, we make damn certain no one leaves this ship."

Arianne looked out the office's bubble blister at the three cruisers. The ships presented a risk until they were certain all the Devourers had been eliminated. The simplest thing to do would be to destroy the vessels, but she couldn't. They and their ordnance just might be needed before all was said and done.

She glanced back to the monitor. For a moment Jon pushed into her head. In spite of what he had done, she harbored no anger or hatred for her brother. Instead she felt relief that he was spared from witnessing the result of his trade with the Havenites.

"How many from the *Sadr* were still onplanet?" Halian asked.

"With the representatives of MashuCo, Pillan Planets, and the Brodny," Sarrantonio said, "they totalled a hundred and thirty-five. Fifty were stranded on Base One."

Arianne tried not to think about the tidal wave that would engulf the island. In all likelihood the base's personnel had been killed by the Havenites after they learned of her escape offplanet. Communications from Base One had ended four days ago.

"There'll be war," Halian said softly. "Even if the Brodny can ignore their deaths, MashuCo and Pillan Planets won't."

"It's a possibility that has to be faced." Arianne had resolved herself to that very real threat. "However, we still hold the means to divert it—Opat 6. Captain Sarrantonio has orders to move the *Sadr* outward toward the planet. This ship does have the power to destroy that world. With the exotic elements as a bargaining lever we might, just might, avert open confrontation and keep the Tripar from hanging us. A few dead bodies mean nothing to governments and corporations when such wealth is to be had."

"A bit cynical, aren't you?" The psiotic arched an eyebrow.

"No," she answered, "realistic."

Her chest contracted as Todd's image pushed into her mind. God, how she ached to hold him in her arms, to see his smile, hear his voice. The same realism that told her it was in her grasp to divert war, also told her that her father would never release Todd. Her son was too strong a lever to use against her, especially while she held Opat 6's treasure. Today she died along with those still on Havenfound.

She closed her eyes. Earth, Retrieve, Fax, Pau, and Todd—they were all lost to her now. In the matter of a few weeks she had unraveled every seam to her life. The only bright light amid the shambled ruins was Kate Dunbar. How she hoped that the Net mode had managed to implant itself in that vulptuous young body! With so much death, she had to believe that she had helped create one new life.

If Ishi Mallas did eventually climb from her accelerator tank, and if the *Sadr* and she somehow survived what she had done this day, she would like for Kate Dunbar-Ishi Mallas to be brought abroad. Not only would she enjoy meeting Kate in the flesh, but Arianne could think of no one better-suited to rebuilding the memories needed to fill Jon's blank mind.

A dream, she admitted to herself as the weight of the moment returned. She opened her eyes and looked at Halian. "And if we fail, then we can find some comfort in history. Humankind has survived countless wars in its past. It will survive another one. That is something the tikkas would have denied us."

Having nothing else to say, nor wishing to watch another asteroid slam death into Havenfound, she walked from the office and took a dropshaft down five levels. She needed the peace that only her bonsai trees could provide.

NETSURANARI

"Bonsai" or "The Potted Tree"—a play written by Ishi Mallas. Recent archeological discoveries on the planet Lanatia, dating back to the last days of the Tripartite Confederation, present evidence to the probable existence of a person or persons represented by the fictional character Arianne Pillan whose timely diplomatic efforts diverted open warfare between the major powers of the Confederation at that time.

If this is indeed true, these actions eventually led to the peaceful formation of the Klausterhol and our present Sharhol system of government, which stemmed from those ancient corporations. One can only lament the harsh decades (centuries?) of the Quirin Rebellion, a dark time that robbed us of so much of our rich history. Humankind has just begun to see a glimmering of its past greatness.

Yet, one should not allow history to weigh too heavily on this classical play. To do so would destroy the elements of fantasy—such as men capable of reading the thoughts of others, machines capable of producing human bodies to house them, and alien creatures cloaked in white fur—Ishi Mallas has so expertly woven into the fabric of her plot. Nor should one neglect that these elements achieve a certain realism by her inclusion of a Moodweaver, of whose talents all are well aware on every world of humankind.

—Notes on the Play "Bonsai," Tahoman Mashu
during his first year as Charhol of MashuCo.

Stories
✠ of ✠
Swords and Sorcery

⚜⚜⚜⚜⚜⚜⚜⚜⚜⚜⚜⚜⚜⚜⚜⚜⚜

✿✿✿✿✿✿✿✿✿✿✿✿✿✿✿✿✿

Please send the titles I've checked above. Mail orders to:

BERKLEY PUBLISHING GROUP
390 Murray Hill Pkwy., Dept. B
East Rutherford, NJ 07073

NAME _____

ADDRESS _____

CITY _____

STATE _____ ZIP _____

Please allow 6 weeks for delivery.
Prices are subject to change without notice.

POSTAGE & HANDLING:
$1.00 for one book, $.25 for each
additional. Do not exceed $3.50.

BOOK TOTAL	$_____
SHIPPING & HANDLING	$_____
APPLICABLE SALES TAX (CA, NJ, NY, PA)	$_____
TOTAL AMOUNT DUE PAYABLE IN US FUNDS. (No cash orders accepted.)	$_____